TESS THORNTON

A CHRISTMAS WISH

FOR THE
Cowboy

RIDEGEVIEW RANCH

BOOK 3

EAGLE CREEK
PRESS

Contents

The Ridgeview Ranch Brothers Series

One

Lauren

"**Y**OU'VE GOT TO BE kidding me," I muttered, staring at my phone as it buzzed again with another message from Stacy.

This one read, *So, are you going to change your mind about the 'job offer'?* My phone lit up with a flood of laughing emojis underneath.

I groaned, rubbing my temples. *Some 'job offer'* I texted back. *I'm never going out with a stranger again.*

Stacy had been the one to push me into the whole online dating mess in the first place. "You need to loosen up, meet people," she'd said. As if one disaster date hadn't been enough, she had to push me into a second that ended up even worse. And now she was making jokes about the creepy guy's follow-up message.

I had responded sarcastically, of course. It wasn't like I took him seriously. If I never heard from that guy again, it would still be too soon.

The morning had started off so well. I'd finally finished planning out a marketing campaign that had been in the works for weeks—a big one, the kind that would put me in front of the right people at the company. Maybe even open the door to that promotion I'd been working toward. The whole team was buzzing about it. Clients were already responding positively to the rollout. For the first time in months, I felt like I was exactly where I needed to be. I even had my calendar organized—every task, every meeting scheduled perfectly.

I leaned back in my chair, savoring that small moment of control. I thrived in this environment—the deadlines, the fast pace, the constant movement. People said social media was all about short attention spans, but to me, it was the opposite. It was about capturing attention, steering it where it needed to go. And I was good at it.

"Hey, you ready for the meeting?" Alyssa, my colleague from the next cubicle, popped her head around the corner, her arms full of reports.

"Yeah, just about," I replied, tapping my fingers on the edge of my keyboard. "I'm putting the final touches on this proposal. It's going to be a big one."

She grinned. "You think this is *the* one? The one that gets you in front of Rebecca?"

"If all goes well," I said, unable to hide my own smile. "I've been waiting for a shot at this for months. It's finally falling into place."

Alyssa nodded approvingly, then lowered her voice. "And how's your love life, Lauren? Any more bad dates? I'm still laughing about the one last month—Carl, the used car salesman?"

"Don't even get me started," I groaned, half-laughing and half-cringing. "Stacy set me up with another complete disaster last night. You can do a lot of things online, but finding love is definitely not one of them."

"Oh, come on. It's just a way to meet people! That's how my brother met his wife, and I've never seen anyone more compatible. Give it another try. It can't hurt, can it?"

Of course, it had hurt. The guy—what was his name again? Brian?—had spent the entire evening bragging about his "investments and assets" and hinting at... other things. By the end of the date, I'd been dying to leave, but he'd messaged me after, making it clear he was looking for more. An indecent proposition from a sleazy crypto money launderer who wanted me to "come on" as his "underling." Emphasis on the "under"... he'd typed that part in all caps.

I'd replied to Stacy afterward with pure sarcasm, venting my frustration and telling her to delete my profile, and she *still* kept teasing me about it. Like, she didn't know when to give it a rest! But right now? I didn't want to think about it. Today was about work, about nailing this campaign.

"No updates on that front," I said, grabbing my coffee and taking a sip. "Let's just say he was more interested in 'dessert' than dinner. If you know what I mean."

"Aw, man. I thought Stacy said he was cute! Too bad he was a dud." Alyssa laughed as she waved and headed back to her cubicle. "Good luck in the meeting!"

I smiled, shaking my head. No distractions today. The presentation was in an hour, and I had a few more things to tighten up before I could fully focus.

Just as I turned back to my screen, my phone buzzed again. This time, a notification from Stacy popped up at the top of the screen.

Did you mean to post that?

My stomach clenched, but I ignored it, focusing on the task at hand. She just wouldn't quit ribbing me about that stupid dating app. She'd probably sent some silly meme or comment I didn't have time to deal with right now. Work came first. I pushed the phone aside, determined to get this report finished before my meeting.

Five minutes later, another buzz. This time, my phone rattled against my desk, with multiple notifications lighting up the screen. I sighed, reaching for it, more annoyed than concerned.

Then I saw it.

Lauren! What in the world were you thinking?

My heart skipped as I opened the message from Stacy. Beneath it was a screenshot. My stomach dropped. There, clear as day, was the message I had sarcastically texted her about the guy after the date, but it wasn't in our private chat.

It was posted. On my company's account.

Oh no. *No, no, no.*

I stared at the screen, the message taunting me. *Sure, because that's the kind of job offer I was hoping for. A romp with the boss and all his money.*

Beneath it was the company's logo. It was public.

I dropped the phone, scrambling to log into the company's social media dashboard from my computer. My fingers flew over the keyboard, sweat breaking out along my hairline. I found the post, saw it sitting there like a ticking time bomb, already gaining traction. Likes. Comments. Shares. And Heaven only knew how many screen shots.

I clicked delete. *Please let that be enough.* But I knew better.

The damage was done.

My phone buzzed again, followed by another. And another. I picked it up, my hand trembling. Screenshots were spreading. The company profile was too big. People were sharing it everywhere—on Twitter, Instagram, even LinkedIn. The comments were brutal.

This is how she gets her clients?

Real professional.

Yikes.

I heard the chair behind me scrape across the floor. Alyssa had stood up, her eyes wide as she looked over at me. "Lauren, what's going on?"

I couldn't speak. My pulse was thundering in my ears. This wasn't happening. It *couldn't* be happening! I had built my entire career on managing other people's online presence, protecting their brands from exactly this kind of disaster.

But now? It was my name, my face, tied to something that looked horribly unprofessional, suggestive even.

And I'd posted it.

Me.

The phone rang. Rebecca... my boss's boss's boss.

I didn't want to answer. But I had to.

"Lauren?" Her voice was calm but clipped, like she was trying to hold something back. "I assume you've seen it?"

"I—yeah, I'm trying to fix it. I deleted it, but people already—"

"Screenshotted it," she finished for me. "Yes, we've seen. It's spreading fast."

"I didn't mean to post it, Rebecca. It was a mistake. I thought I was texting Stacy McCallum, and—"

"I understand that, but this looks bad. Really bad. This kind of screw-up isn't like you, Lauren."

I stared at the computer screen in front of me, unable to form the right words. Everything I'd worked for, all the trust I'd built, was slipping through my fingers. My vision blurred as Rebecca's voice droned on, her tone even but stern.

"Lauren, I think it's best if you take some time off. Let this die down."

"What? Wait, I—"

"We can't afford bad press like this right now. It's almost the holidays anyway."

"No, I can fix this," I said quickly, my voice shaking. "Please, just give me some time. I can handle the fallout. We can put out a statement or something."

There was a long pause on the other end of the line. Rebecca sighed. "*I* will handle it. Take a break, Lauren. We'll talk in January."

The line went dead.

I set the phone down slowly, my hands limp in my lap. The sounds of the office buzzed faintly around me, but I felt completely removed, like I was watching my life unravel from behind glass.

A ping from my phone jolted me back. Stacy again: *Good grief, it's everywhere. Did you mean to post that publicly? I mean, I knew you were upset with me, but I was just teasing, and...*

I turned the phone face down on my desk. I didn't want to look at it anymore. *Couldn't* look at it anymore.

It wasn't even noon, and my career was potentially over. All because of a stupid sarcastic message about a date that had gone horribly wrong.

I blinked at the screen in front of me, unable to focus. My eyes darted to the clock. I couldn't be here. I couldn't sit in this office while the entire internet was laughing at me.

"Take a break," Rebecca had ordered. *Where* exactly was I supposed to do that? My apartment was sort of a gathering place for *all* the same people who were turning me into a meme at this very moment! I sure didn't need that! They'd all come find me. Probably snap selfies with me looking miserable in my pajamas.

No, if my boss wouldn't let me handle this from the top, I needed to get out of town completely.

My first thought was to go to my dad's place, but even as it crossed my mind, I dismissed it. He wouldn't be much help, and his girlfriend—some chick he'd met a year ago who was barely older than me—probably wouldn't even care. They'd likely just tell me I was being dramatic, like always.

Big River Valley. The words came unbidden, a memory of home creeping into my mind. Emily wouldn't judge me. At least, I hoped she wouldn't. And I could probably vanish forever in the clutter of Mom's second-hand store. Nobody'd ever see me again.

I could catch a plane for Thanksgiving instead of waiting until Christmas.

I pulled out my phone again, opening the airline app. Time to go home.

Trent

"Y OU'VE GOT TO BE kidding me."

I yanked the wrench again, harder this time. The bolt didn't move. It was stuck like everything else on this blasted ranch. The tractor sat there, a cold hunk of metal, refusing to do the one thing it was supposed to—work. I'd been at it for two hours, fighting with it while the temperature dropped and my temper frayed. Days like this made me wonder what in blazes I was doing. Everything was always breaking, and there was never enough time or money to get it all done.

I wiped the sweat off my forehead, though it wasn't sweat—it was just the cold air condensing on me and turning me into a frost sculpture. I should've been inside by now, working on something else, but no. The tractor had to be fixed. Winter was barreling down on us fast, and the next storm would hit soon. This thing needed to be running, and I wasn't about to let another job pile up on top of all the others.

I yanked the wrench again. Nothing. And it was buried too deep for me to get my blow torch out and break it loose with heat.

I stood there for a second, breathing hard, willing myself to keep my cool. But it was one of those days where nothing seemed to go right. It had been like that all week—something always going wrong, one more thing to fix, and never enough hands to do it. I kicked the tractor tire, hard enough to make a sound, not hard enough to dent anything. Of course, the tire didn't care. None of this cared.

I'd ask Gage for help, but he was over in Twin Falls today at a stock sale with his buddy Luke Walker. Not that we could afford to buy any more head just now, but... well, we were sorta beholden to the Walkers at the moment, and when Luke called asking if Gage wanted to go with him, Gage didn't feel like he could say no. Nor did he *want* to say no... it got him out of here for the day.

I pulled my phone out of my pocket, stared at it, and thought about calling Chase. He was probably at White Pines with Kate, helping her with something over there, while I was here, dealing with all this by myself. He'd been over there more and more lately, and I didn't begrudge him that, not really. He had his life, his future, and yesterday, I caught him tucking a little square ring box into the pocket of his coat. Well, good for him.

But I couldn't help the way my gut twisted when I thought about how I was always the one left holding the bag over here.

I scrolled through my contacts, stopped at his name, and sighed. What would be the point? I knew what he'd say: "I'll be there soon," but soon was never soon enough. Not with everything piling up. He'd be here for a few hours, and then he'd be off again. I didn't need someone to half-fix things. I needed someone who could be here for the long haul, but apart from Gage—who was pretty useless whenever his team-roping pal Luke called—everyone had their own life now.

Chase had Kate. Cole had Emily. Even the boys we'd taken in, Ethan and Liam, had their own baggage, and they weren't exactly jumping in to help unless you cornered them into it.

I let the phone fall back into my pocket. It wasn't worth calling. What was Chase going to do—fix the tractor over the phone? No. This was on me, like it always was. Just me, my two hands, and a long list of chores that never seemed to get shorter.

I crouched back down, grabbing the wrench. My gloves weren't thick enough to keep the cold out anymore. I could feel the metal seeping through, biting at my fingers. One more pull. Just one more.

I twisted the wrench, gritting my teeth. The bleeding thing still wouldn't move. I threw the wrench down, harder this time, letting the clatter echo through the quiet.

What I wouldn't give for something—*anything*—to go right today.

I stood up, breathing hard, staring at the tractor like it was the enemy. Maybe it was. Lately, it felt like everything was working against me. And the worst part? I couldn't even say why it bothered me so much. I'd done this work my whole life. Fixing things, getting things back in order—that was what I did. But lately, every broken fence or busted engine felt like a personal insult. Like no matter how hard I tried, things wouldn't stay fixed.

I pulled my phone out again, just out of habit this time, like maybe someone would magically call me with a solution. Not likely.

Another thought crept in, the kind I tried to push away, but it always came back. *Christmas.* It was coming, whether I wanted it to or not. I hadn't even thought about what that meant this year. Last Christmas was different. My brothers had all been around, but this year, two of them would probably be AWOL. Spending the day with their other halves.

I'd tried that idea. Even thought I had a head start on something big, though after the first month, I knew my thing with Cassie wouldn't last. Wasn't for lack of trying on my part. That was just another thing I'd let drag on longer than it should have.

Cassie. She'd always had a way of pulling me back just when I was ready to walk away. It wasn't love, not really. It was guilt. Every time I thought about breaking it off, she'd start crying and talking about how hard life was, how no one understood her. I didn't either, but I'd stuck around longer than I should've, thinking maybe I was the one being unreasonable.

But six months in, it was clear as day. We were oil and water. She didn't understand ranch life, didn't get why I had to work so stinking much. Heck, even *I* didn't want to work this much, but the ranch didn't care. It needed what it needed. She'd told me I was too cold, too distant. The truth was, I didn't have the energy for all the crazy, so I'd just sucked in my head like a turtle in his shell. I barely had enough to keep the ranch from falling apart, and she was one more thing I couldn't fix.

When she finally sent me that text to break it off, I was furious. But after a few days, I realized that I was more mad that *she* got to be the one to break up with *me*, when I should've had the right to call it quits first. Wasn't like I hadn't been wanting to. And I sure as heck would've been decent enough to do it in person, not over a text message.

I should've felt more, but mostly, I'd been relieved. One quick text message, and she was gone. No big conversation, no tearful goodbye. Just a message on my phone, saying she couldn't do it anymore, and then she blocked my number.

It was almost a joke how little I'd cared. I'd finished mucking out the barn and moved on. Now, it was just me, the ranch, and the tractor that refused to work.

I kicked the tire again, harder this time. Still, nothing. Maybe it was me. Maybe I was the one that couldn't stay fixed.

I stood there for a while, my hands tucked in my pockets, looking out over the fields. They'd be buried in the snow again soon. No matter how much I worked, no matter how many hours I put in, there was always something else. And no one else was around to help.

I glanced at the house, at the faint glow of light in the window. Mom was inside, probably going over the books again, trying to stretch out the finances like she did every year. She was tough, no question about it. But even she couldn't make the numbers look good. I knew the truth. The ranch wasn't doing as well as we needed it to. If we didn't figure something out soon, we'd be looking at another rough winter.

I pulled out my phone again, this time scrolling to Cole's number. He was spending all his time at Walker Ranch, or White Pines, with Emily. Maybe they were out training horses together, or maybe they were sitting at home just enjoying the peace and quiet that came with not having to deal with ranch work. I couldn't blame him. He'd settled into something real with Emily, and he had a day job that paid the bills for him. He didn't have to worry about this stuff anymore.

I stared at the screen, thumb hovering over the call button, but I didn't press it. What was the point? Cole had moved on, just like Chase had. Just like everyone did. I'd end up standing here in the cold no matter what.

I shoved the phone back into my pocket. This was my mess to fix. Always was.

The sky was getting darker now, the kind of gray that promised more snow. I couldn't afford to lose any more daylight, but there was a part of me that didn't care anymore. The ranch, the tractor, the endless list of things to do—it was all starting to feel like I was chasing something that wouldn't catch.

I grabbed the wrench one more time, my fingers numb from the cold, and gave the bolt another turn. Nothing. Just like before.

I let the wrench fall to the ground. If the storm rolled in before I got the tractor running, we'd be in trouble. But I'd need some sort of specialized tool to get in there and break that thing loose. Maybe Bobby Eckhart or even Jess Walker would have something.

I bent down, gathering my tools into the bag, feeling the cold seep into my bones and all my ambition just... drain out. And for a second, I thought about Christmas. About how it used to mean something. Family. Warmth. Dad and Mom and all my brothers with all our silly traditions.

But now? It was just another deadline, another thing to get through.

Maybe, just once, I wished something would change. But I didn't make wishes. That wasn't how life worked.

I slung the tool bag over my shoulder and started back toward the barn, the tractor still sitting there, as dead as before.

Two

Lauren

"**M**A'AM, I'M REALLY SORRY, but we're out of SUVs."

I blinked at the rental agent, trying to process her words. "What do you mean, out of SUVs? I reserved one yesterday."

She gave me a polite smile, the kind that felt like a slap in the face. "Yes, I see that, but we've had a lot of people extend their rentals because of the weather. So, unfortunately, we're out."

My mouth went dry. The weather? Did she not *hear* herself? "Okay, so what am I supposed to drive? I have to go all the way to Custer County. They barely bother paving some of those roads, let alone keeping them plowed." My voice was tight, on the edge of something that felt suspiciously like panic. I *needed* an SUV. That was why I'd reserved one!

"We do have a compact available." She typed something on her keyboard as if that would make the situation better. "It's all-wheel drive, though! So that should help a bit."

A bit? I stared at her, unable to stop the words before they slipped out. "A compact?" I couldn't help the way my voice pitched. "I'm driving up into the mountains. In a snowstorm!"

She gave me that smile again. "It'll be fine. The all-wheel drive is great for light snow, and we're expecting the roads to be clear for most of the trip."

Light snow? The forecast had called for at least six inches, but sure. Let's pretend that wasn't happening. "Look, I know all you're used to around here is open roads and freeways, but I have to get *off* the freeway eventually. There's no way you can get me something bigger? Anything?"

Another quick glance at her screen, followed by that irritating smile. "I'm sorry. This is all we have right now."

"Well... can you try another company? I paid for the upgrade. Can't you make some calls?"

She gave me another patronizing smile, and her eyes flicked over my shoulder to the growing line behind me. "I'm sorry, ma'am, but all the other companies are having the same problem. Returns are being delayed, and the airport is even talking about canceling flights, so cars will start going fast. Would you like me to transfer your reservation to the compact?"

I could feel my pulse ticking in my throat, the familiar burn of frustration rising fast. This was not how the day was supposed to go. It was bad enough that I was coming back to Big River Valley earlier than planned—by like a whole *month*— because of the whole social media disaster. Now, I couldn't even get the right rental car. This was just... perfect.

"Fine," I said, my voice sharper than I intended. "I'll take it."

She nodded, as if I hadn't just panicked and snapped in front of her, and handed me the key fob. "It's in slot 42. Just outside. Have a safe trip."

Safe trip. Sure. In a compact car with no snow tires, on the way to the one place I never thought I'd come back to without a natural disaster or—heaven forbid—a death in the family to force me. I grabbed my bag and headed out to the lot, and almost immediately, my boots slipped on the pavement. Sure, there was de-icer sprinkled everywhere, but apparently, I found the *one* patch they'd missed. Great. Just what I needed—freezing temperatures to match my mood.

The car was tiny. I stared at it for a second, wondering how in the world I was going to make this drive. It looked like the kind of car you'd use for zipping around a city, not for winding through snow-covered mountain roads. But I didn't have a choice. This was what I got.

After loading my suitcase into the trunk—it barely closed—and sliding into the driver's seat, I took a deep breath. I could do this. I'd driven in snow before—after all, I'd taken Driver's Ed in Big River Valley in January. I knew what I was doing. I just needed to be careful, stay focused, and keep my mind off the disaster waiting for me back in San Diego. Or worse, the disaster following me online.

I pulled up the directions on my phone, plugged it into the media center so I could see my map, and started the car. "Okay, let's do this."

The first two hours weren't too bad. Boise was clear, the roads only dusted with a bit of snow. But as I headed further north, the weather shifted. The snow came down heavier, and the little car felt less steady by the minute. I gripped the wheel tighter, focusing on the road ahead. The mountain range loomed in the distance, reminding me that I was heading straight into winter's worst.

My phone buzzed on the seat beside me, and I glanced at it briefly. An email notification from my boss. Probably something about how I needed to "lay low" for a while longer, until the situation with the viral post died down. That *stupid* post! I couldn't even think about it without feeling the burn of humiliation needling my scalp. One moment of sarcasm, one accidental post on a client's account, and now my entire career was hanging by a thread.

And it was all because of that *stupid* guy.

I gritted my teeth and forced my eyes back on the road. It was done. The post had gone viral, people were laughing at me, and there wasn't a thing I could do to change it now. "An early holiday break," Rebecca had said, though we both knew what that really meant. They wanted me out of sight while they cleaned up the mess. Maybe, if things calmed down by January, I'd still have my job.

Maybe.

But what if I didn't? The thought hit me hard, like a punch to the gut. What if I lost my job over this? My career, everything I'd worked for? What would I even do then? Move back to Big River Valley? Start over? I laughed bitterly at the thought. As if moving back home was even an option. No. I had to figure this out. I had to get my life back on track, no matter what it took.

I glanced out the window, watching the snow pile up along the sides of the road. It was coming down harder now, the little wipers struggling to keep up. The roads weren't as bad as they could've been, but the car didn't handle well in this kind of weather. The tires slipped now and then, just enough to remind me that I wasn't driving an SUV.

Four hours—five, actually, with the snow. That was all I had to get through. Just make it to Big River Valley, and then I could crash at Mom's place, curl up in a warm bed, and figure out the rest of my life. One step at a time.

The mountains loomed closer, and I my shoulders were burning and hardening like hot lava. I was almost there. Another hour or so, and I'd be pulling into town. I'd called ahead to let Mom know I was coming early, but she must have been busy with the store—shocker— and Emily was usually terrible about checking her messages during the day. She always had ranch work or whatever else she had going on with Cole.

Our little family seemed so far removed from what I was dealing with. I couldn't exactly call home for advice on how to salvage my career after a PR disaster. That wasn't the kind of help they were good at giving.

I swallowed the lump in my throat and kept driving.

The closer I got to Big River Valley, the worse the roads became. The snow was thick now, covering the blacktop in a layer of white. I knew these roads well enough—I'd grown up driving on them in worse conditions—but that was when I had a reliable car, not this glorified tin can.

I slowed down as I neared the turnoff to the side road that would take me to Mom's place. Almost there. Just a little further.

That was when the car slid.

One second, everything was fine, and the next, the wheels lost traction. The back end of the car fishtailed, and my heart shot into my throat. I gripped the wheel tighter, trying to correct it, but the car wasn't listening. The tires skidded, and the car slid off the road, straight into a snowbank.

"Are you kidding me?" My voice cracked as the car came to a halt, nose-first in the snow.

I sat there for a second, my breath coming in short bursts. This could *not* be happening! I didn't even care about the stupid car anymore. All I wanted was to get home, to get out of the cold, and now I was stuck. Of course, I was stuck.

I reached for my phone, hands shaking, and pulled up Mom's number. No service. Beautiful. I dropped the phone in my lap, staring out at the snow-covered road. It wasn't far now. Maybe a mile, two at the most. I could walk it. But in this weather?

I shoved the door open and climbed out to walk around the car, stare at the wheels half-buried in the snow. There was no way I was getting it out of there on my own. Great. Just great.

The panic was creeping in now, and my fingers were starting to tremble as I checked again for cell service. Still nothing. I needed a plan. I needed to figure out what to do, and fast. Sitting here wasn't going to help. I stumbled alongside the road for about fifty yards, though what I thought I would see up ahead, I couldn't say. Still no phone service, and I'd have to hike farther than fifty yards to find it. The road was twisty, with all kinds of blind corners and snow piled high on the shoulders. It was deeper than I thought, already up to my calves. This wasn't going to be easy.

Maybe I would have to walk. The road didn't look like it had been plowed since the last snowfall, and there were only a handful of tire tracks stamped in it. And it was getting later. I took a few steps, just to test it. The snow was soft, almost powdery, and I could feel my feet sinking with every step. I wasn't dressed for this—city boots, not snow boots—and I knew it. But what choice did I have? I had to get home. I had to get out of here.

I fumbled with my phone again, scrolling through my contacts. A text might be able to get out. At least let someone know to come looking for me—Maybe Emily. Maybe her husband—he had a truck, right? Heck, I'd take *anyone* at this point, if I could just get something to go through.

Just as I was about to hit send, I heard the sound of a truck engine coming up the road. My heart leaped. I turned around, squinting against the snow, and saw the headlights approaching. A truck. Big, with a heavy-duty front grill and snow tires. Exactly what *I* should've been driving.

Relief washed over me as the truck slowed down, and dipped to the shoulder of the road to pull in behind me. At least I wasn't stranded alone out here, hoping this stupid car didn't just leave me for dead.

Trent

I SHOULD'VE KNOWN BETTER than to think this storm wouldn't hit early. I shifted gears, hearing the rattle of the parts I'd just picked up from the farm store. Tractor still wasn't running right, but with the new fuel line, I figured I'd have it going before morning. If the snow didn't get too deep, that is. If the weather kept up like this, I'd have other stuff to worry about back at home before tinkering with that tractor.

When I came around the bend on Knobby Hill, I saw the tail-lights. Someone was stuck, no doubt. Sure enough, as I got closer, there it was—a compact car, wheels buried in a snowbank. And it had that telltale rental bar code in the window. Great. Another city slicker thinking they could take on mountain roads without a clue. No snow tires, no chains, just driving along like they were still in some California suburb.

I grumbled under my breath, slowing down. Folks like that had no business driving out here this time of year. Should've known better. I'd probably have to dig 'em out, too, which would be another twenty minutes of my day I didn't have.

As I pulled up, I spotted the driver walking around the car. Or trying to. A woman, of course. High-heeled boots with fur around the tops. The kind they sell in stores that have no clue what real snow looks like. She stepped into the drift like she was walking into a shallow puddle, and I almost laughed.

"Heaven help us," I muttered, killing the engine.

I opened my door and stepped down, tucking my gloves into my jacket as I walked toward her. "You all right there?"

She turned, and I got a good look at her face. Late twenties, maybe. Long, dark blonde hair that curled in thick waves down her back. Looked like she'd stepped off a magazine cover, which didn't match the scene of her sinking into a snowbank in city boots. Her cheeks were flushed from the cold, but she tried to hide it behind an irritated look.

"I'm fine," she snapped, trying to tug her coat tighter around herself. "Just need to get my car out."

I let my eyes drift to the little compact that was buried nose-first in the drift. "You don't say."

She bristled at that, straightening up like she was about to tell me off. Probably used to handling things herself, or at least acting like she did. But I didn't have time for a back-and-forth.

"I'll get it out," I said, brushing past her and heading toward the car. "You got a shovel?"

"A shovel?" she echoed like it was the strangest question I could've asked.

"Right." Of course she didn't. "Step back, unless you want snow all over those fancy boots."

I half expected her to argue, but she huffed and took a few steps back. I grabbed the shovel from the back of my truck and started digging the snow out from around her tires. The snow was powdery and fresh, but deep enough to give her little car trouble. I worked quickly, not bothering to make small talk. She was still standing there, arms crossed, probably freezing. But I'd be done soon enough.

After a few minutes of shoveling, I leaned against the car and gave it another once-over. Something didn't look right. "Hold up," I said, crouching down to check the tires. Sure enough, the front right one was sitting lower than it should've been. I gave it a push, and it caved under my hand.

"You've blown a tire," I muttered, standing back up.

She looked over at me from where she was brushing snow off her coat. "What?"

"Your tire," I said again, pointing to the flat. "It's blown."

Her shoulders slumped as she stepped closer, peering down at the tire like it had personally offended her. "Can you fix it?"

I shook my head. "No spare on board. You've got run-flat tires. Most rental places don't bother with spares when these are installed."

She blinked, her brows furrowing in confusion. "Run-flat tires?"

"Yeah," I said, standing up straight. "They're made to keep going for a bit after they're damaged, but this is more than damaged. The whole thing's shot to pieces. You'll need a tow."

Her face tightened with frustration, her breath coming out in short puffs of cold air. "A tow? That's just great." She muttered something under her breath and glanced toward the road, then back at the snowbank. "And of course, I can't get a signal out here."

"Service is spotty in these parts." I reached into my jacket for my gloves, more out of habit than anything. "We'll have to call once we get back into town."

She ran a hand through her hair—a cascade of loose, "old-money blonde" waves that looked like they'd been styled in some fancy California salon. It was the kind of hair that screamed class and attention to detail. Definitely not practical for around here.

She sighed and rubbed her forehead. "Well, what do I do now?"

I looked over at my truck, the idea already forming in my head, though I wasn't thrilled about it. I didn't exactly feel like playing chauffeur. "I can give you a ride into town. Call for a tow when we get service."

Her eyes flicked toward my truck, then back to me. "You don't have to do that."

"You don't have many options," I said, not in the mood to sugar-coat it. "You're not gonna get that car out of here on your own, and walking in this snow? Not a good idea."

She hesitated, chewing her lip like she didn't want to admit I was right, but after a few seconds, she let out a resigned sigh. "Fine. I'll take the ride."

I nodded and turned toward the truck, tossing the shovel in the back. She grabbed her bag from the car. Now, Mom would have been after my hide if she'd seen me letting a woman drag her own bag to my truck like that, but I kind of enjoyed watching her huff a little as she slogged through the snow in those ridiculous boots. Like that fur around the tops would somehow make them practical for winter. They were about as useful as a screen door on a submarine in this weather.

She climbed into the passenger seat and buckled in, pulling her coat tighter around her. I started the engine and glanced over at her as I pulled onto the road. "You got family in town?"

"Yeah," she said, still fidgeting with her seatbelt. "My mom lives above the secondhand shop in town. I've been trying to call her, but no luck."

I nodded. "Service gets better the closer we get to town."

She blew out a breath and stuck her hands up to the heater. "Thanks for the ride. I didn't catch your name, by the way."

"Trent," I said, keeping my eyes on the road.

"Well, thanks, Trent. I'm Lauren. Lauren Carson."

Wait... I squinted. "You said your mom lives above the second-hand shop?"

"Owns it, actually."

"Any chance you got a sister named Emily?"

She turned to stare at me. "Yeah. Why?"

This gal did *not* look like Cole's wife. Emily was breezy and wind-blown—classy without even trying, same as this Lauren girl, but Emily had the look of a girl who'd cut her teeth on bailing twine and who didn't even know what a blow dryer was. Lauren was... not that.

I swallowed and shrugged. "Small town. Name rang a bell."

"Oh. Well, sorry, I can't say the same."

I nodded again and focused on the drive, my mind turning over the fact that this was Emily's sister. How old was she? We *had* to have gone to school together, but school was a long time ago, and I'd barely gone to class enough to squeak out a passing grade. Cole would know more. He hadn't heard much about Emily's sister, except that she'd left for California years ago to chase some kind of career. Looked like she'd left everything ranch-related behind, judging by the way she was dressed and the attitude she carried. City slicker through and through.

We drove in silence for a while, the snow continuing to fall lightly against the windshield, the road ahead winding toward town. I couldn't help but wonder how she had ended up back here—because, from the looks of it, she didn't seem too thrilled to be in Big River Valley again. It wasn't a long drive into town, just a few miles. When we got to her mom's place, she popped the door and slid out of my truck, stomping her feet a bit, as if that would knock off the snow.

"Thanks for the help," she said, clearly trying to sound grateful, though the irritation hadn't left her voice. "Do you know if there's a tow truck I can call? They should probably get the car before morning, right?"

I couldn't help but chuckle. She blinked, frowning at me. "What?"

"You're not in California anymore," I said, leaning against the truck door. "Tow truck won't be up there until tomorrow at the earliest. Maybe later, depending on how busy they are."

Her face fell, confusion flashing in her eyes. "But... don't they work twenty-four hours a day?"

I laughed again, though not unkindly. "Around here, people work when they work, and the crisis jobs take priority. Especially in a storm."

She stood there, staring at me like I'd just told her the moon was made of cheese. "How'd you guess I came up from California?"

"It's written all over you."

She stared at me for a second, probably deciding if I was making fun of her or not. I shrugged. "Go on inside. I'll give Danny a call, make sure someone picks up the car tomorrow. Or the next day."

She opened her mouth to say something, but then stopped herself, nodding instead. She gave me a quick thanks before turning toward the secondhand shop, heading for the door.

I watched her disappear inside, then climbed back into the truck. I pulled out, shaking my head. Another city girl in the country for the holidays.

Three

Lauren

I WASN'T EVEN HALFWAY through thanking my "chauffer" before I started toward the door of my mom's store, grateful to be rid of him. Out of his truck, and out of that tiny car. The lights in the store were still on, glowing warm and inviting against the cold. It was the day before Thanksgiving, and, of course, Mom was working late. She always did. Black Friday was her big moneymaker of the year. She'd probably been tagging things all day, getting everything ready for the sale.

The bell above the door jingled as I walked in. The smell of old books, lavender, and whatever candle Mom had burning in the back filled the air, and for a second, I just stood there, taking it in. It was a little surreal. I hadn't been here in years, but everything looked almost exactly the same.

Except for the woman behind the counter.

Mom looked up from her tagging gun, her eyes wide. She froze for a second, like she couldn't believe what she was seeing. And then, just like that, she dropped everything and ran toward me.

"Lauren? Lauren!" Her arms were around me before I could even say a word, squeezing me so tight it hurt, but I didn't care. Tears sprang to my eyes, and I hugged her back, burying my face in her shoulder like I hadn't done since I was a kid.

"I didn't know you were coming early!" she cried, stepping back but still holding onto me, her eyes brimming with tears. "Look at you! My goodness, you look... you look wonderful!"

I forced a smile, though the sting of the past few days was still too fresh. "Surprise," I managed, brushing away my own tears. "I figured I'd just... come home for Thanksgiving, too."

She wiped at her cheeks with the back of her hand and looked me up and down like she couldn't believe I was standing in front of her. "I'm so glad you did. It's been too long." She glanced at the clock, then at the few scattered items left to tag. "You know, I've been at it all day, and I don't care what's left of this mess. I'm closing up the store. C'mon, let's go upstairs. We need to catch up!"

Before I could protest, she was already heading back to lock the front door and flip the sign. I stood there, looking around the store. It felt smaller than I remembered. Or maybe I was just bigger. The shelves were still packed with knickknacks and furniture, clothes on racks, books stacked high. The store had always been full, almost overflowing, just like Mom's life.

She hurried back to me, grabbed one of my bags, and led me toward the back staircase. "Come on, let's get you settled in."

We climbed the stairs, and I couldn't help but feel that strange mix of nostalgia and dread as we got closer to the apartment. Emily had warned me. Mom's place had always been a bit... cluttered. "She's trying," Emily had said on the phone. "But you know how she is."

I braced myself, expecting the usual chaos of mismatched furniture, piles of things she couldn't sell and meant to donate but never got around to, stacks of papers, and receipts in random corners. But when she opened the door, I blinked. The apartment was... neat. Still a bit crowded, sure, but nothing like the mess I'd remembered. The couch wasn't buried in laundry, the kitchen counter was actually visible, and the floors were clear.

"You cleaned," I blurted out, and immediately regretted it.

Mom laughed. "I've been trying to keep things a little more organized. Emily's been on me about it." She set my bag down near the couch. "Come on, let me show you to Emily's old room. I'm glad I got an early start on it—got it all ready for you last weekend when I was on a cleaning blitz."

I followed her down the hall, my surprise still lingering. I'd only been here a couple of times after Mom moved in... after the divorce. Emily's room looked just as I remembered it—simple, with a twin bed against the wall and a bookshelf full of horse magazines and trophies from her competitions. I dropped my bags on the floor, glancing around.

"Seems weird that Emily's married and moved out," I mused. "I still think of her as my kid sister."

Mom waved a hand. "We'll go see her as soon as we can. She's all settled in with Cole in their cute little mobile home at White Pines."

I nodded, trying to shake off the weird feeling that came with being back in my little sister's room, surrounded by all her things. It felt like I was intruding, even though Emily was living a whole new life now.

Mom sat down on the edge of the bed, patting the spot next to her. "So, tell me, why are you here early? You didn't mention anything about coming home for Thanksgiving when we talked."

I hesitated. The truth burned on the tip of my tongue, but I couldn't bring myself to say it. The mess with work, the embarrassing viral post, the fact that my boss had basically kicked me out until things blew over. I couldn't. Not yet.

I forced a smile, sitting down beside her. "I just... decided to take a long vacation. I've been working hard, and I had the time off banked, so why not?"

Her face lit up. "You're staying through Christmas? The whole month?"

I nodded, feeling that twinge of guilt in my chest. "Yeah, I figured it was time to use some of that vacation time. I've been at the company long enough. I earned it, right?"

Her eyes sparkled. "Right! Oh, Lauren, I'm so glad you're here. I've missed you."

I smiled, but it felt tight. "I've missed you too, Mom."

She gave my hand a squeeze, and for a moment, the worry in her eyes flickered back. "You're sure everything's all right? At work, I mean?"

I swallowed hard. "Yeah, of course. Everything's fine."

She didn't look convinced, but she let it go again, and I exhaled in relief.

"So, what's the plan for Thanksgiving tomorrow?" I asked, trying to change the subject. "I assume Emily and Cole are coming over? Just the four of us?"

Mom's face brightened again. "Oh, no! We've all been invited to Cole's family's house for a big Thanksgiving. It'll be wonderful—everyone's going to be there."

I tried not to let my expression slip, but I felt my stomach drop. "E...Everyone?"

Mom nodded. "Yes! All of Cole's brothers—such a nice family—and some other folks from around town. It's going to be a real feast."

I forced a smile, though my head was already spinning. A big family Thanksgiving? With people I didn't know? I'd barely been able to deal with that surly cowboy who gave me a ride, and now I had to sit through an entire meal with strangers?

"That sounds... great," I said, my voice coming out strained.

Mom didn't seem to notice. She stood up, already talking about how excited she was to see everyone. But all I could think about was how I'd gone from escaping one nightmare back in San Diego to walking straight into another here.

Trent

I OPENED THE DOOR to the house and was hit with the thick, warm smell of baking pies and roasting meat. It wasn't just one pie—no, it smelled like an entire bakery had exploded in the kitchen.

I walked into the chaos, every burner on the stove occupied, the oven crammed full, and the countertops crammed with what seemed like a mountain of food. Pies. So many pies. There had to be a dozen of them, maybe more, stacked up like she was planning to feed the whole town.

Mom stood at the kitchen table, elbow-deep in stuffing, mixing it with her hands while something bubbled away in a big pot on the stove behind her. She didn't even look up as I stood there, trying to make sense of it all.

"Mom?" I called out over the noise of the boiling pots.

She glanced up, her hair a little wild, flour dusted across her apron. "Oh, Trent! You're back. Perfect timing." She said it like I'd walked in at the exact moment she needed me to stir a pot or set a timer.

I glanced around the kitchen, overwhelmed just looking at it. She had *three* turkeys brining in coolers. "What's all this for? There aren't that many of us."

She waved me off like I was asking the silliest question in the world. "Oh, I invited a few friends over. Nothing special."

I raised an eyebrow. Friends? Mom didn't exactly throw dinner parties. "Who?"

She shrugged, keeping her hands busy with the stuffing. "The boys, of course."

"Uh-huh." I set my hat on the hook by the door, turned around, and gave her a look. "And who else?"

"Oh, you know. Cole and Emily, naturally," she said, still not meeting my eye, like this was all casual and normal.

I folded my arms across my chest, waiting. "And?"

She paused, then got that sheepish grin she always wore when she knew she was caught. "Well, Kate's parents are coming, of course. It's just so much easier for her mom if she doesn't have to cook a big meal. And besides, I have a sneaky feeling about those two! I'm going to have a new daughter soon," she crooned in a grinning, sing-song voice.

I nodded slowly. "Right, Kate and her family. And who else?"

Mom pulled her hands out of the stuffing, brushing them off on a damp towel over the sink—because she couldn't get to the faucet. "Well, Kate asked if Walter—one of her therapy clients—could come. He doesn't have any family in town anymore, poor thing. And maybe a couple of the other White Pines clients who live alone."

I blinked at her. "A couple."

She gave me a quick nod, the grin never leaving her face. "Yes, you know, just a few more people. It's Thanksgiving, Trent. No one should be alone."

I rubbed my forehead, trying to hold back the groan rising in my chest. "So, how many are we expecting?"

She turned back to her work, waving a hand like it was nothing. "Oh, maybe thirty."

I stared at her. "Thirty?"

She smiled as if this was the most normal thing in the world. "It's not a big deal. We've got plenty of food, and we can always make more if we need to."

I threw my hands up. "How are we supposed to feed thirty people?"

"Oh, come on. Everyone's bringing a dish or drinks or rolls or something. Less for me to do, really."

"Like fun, it is. And where are we gonna put them all? This house isn't big enough."

Mom just shrugged. "We've got the living room, and we can set up some folding tables and chairs. We'll make it work."

"Thirty people," I repeated, still stuck on the number. I glanced around the kitchen again, the amount of food now making a lot more sense. "And where do you expect them all to sit? On the roof?"

She laughed, a sound that made the whole situation seem more absurd than frustrating. "Oh, don't be dramatic. I've got all my big, strong boys to help set everything up."

I shot her a dirty look, but it softened almost immediately. Typical Mom, springing something like this last minute and expecting me to just roll with it. And typical me, doing exactly that.

"Fine," I muttered, shaking my head. "Just point me to where the work is."

She gestured vaguely toward the barn. "Gage and Liam are out there screwing some sawhorse legs to plywood to make more tables. They'll need your help bringing everything inside. And I need you to move some of the furniture out to the shop, just to make room."

I sighed, already feeling the ache in my shoulders. "Sure."

Mom gave me an innocent smile, then turned back to her stuffing. "You're a gem, Trent."

"Yeah, yeah." I grabbed my jacket again, pulling it on as I headed out the door. The wind carried little flurries of snow as I made my way toward the barn. I didn't relish the idea of stumping through this with the rocking chair on my back to get it out of the way.

Inside the shop, Gage and Liam were hunched over a makeshift table, drilling legs onto plywood sheets. The setup looked about as sturdy as a house of cards, but I wasn't about to be the one to tell them.

"More tables?" I asked, stepping in and grabbing a pair of gloves.

Gage looked up and grinned. "Thirty people coming over, can you believe that?"

I shot him a look. "Yeah. I heard."

Liam snorted. "Good luck finding enough chairs."

I grabbed one of the plywood sheets, hefting it up. "You two finish with these. I'll get started on moving the furniture out. Where's Ethan? I can use his help."

Gage looked up and blinked, like I'd just asked him to do calculus in his head. "Uh... Haven't seen him for a while."

I rolled my eyes. "Whatever. I'll do it myself."

They nodded, and I headed back toward the house, wondering how in the world we were going to fit thirty people inside without the place turning into a circus. But then again, this was Ridgeview. If there was one thing we knew how to do, it was pulling off the impossible.

Lauren

T HANKSGIVING MORNING STARTED WITH a sigh.

I was still trying to thaw my toes from the night before when I got the call from "Danny" at the tow company. "Sorry, ma'am, we won't be able to dig your car out today. It's a busy holiday, you know, and it's just me on duty."

A busy holiday? The guy just wanted to take the day off. Who was calling a tow company on Thanksgiving, anyway? Just me, I was willing to bet.

Mom bustled around the kitchen, getting ready to head out to Ridgeview Ranch, where we'd spend the day. Apparently, Cole's mom was handling almost everything herself, but my mom was bringing cinnamon twists and her special cranberry slushie drink, and she was testing it in the freezer to make sure it had set up. "Still no luck with the tow company? Don't worry, we'll take my car, sweetie," she said, pouring me another cup of coffee. "You're not missing Thanksgiving over a stuck rental car."

Too bad. I sighed and nodded. Great. First, I got stuck in the snow, and now I had to be driven to a family holiday where I barely knew half the people. Just the kind of day I'd been hoping for.

By the time we got to Ridgeview Ranch, the snow had started falling again, swirling in light flurries around the big house. I stepped out of Mom's mini-SUV, scanning the landscape. The ranch was impressive—a rambling old ranch house with live-edge plank siding, wide, sprawling fields dusted with snow, and a driveway already filled with cars. The place looked like it had seen its fair share of big family gatherings. It made me feel smaller, and somehow even more out of place.

Before I could gather myself, I heard a voice shout my name.

"Lauren!"

I turned just in time to see Emily running toward me, her arms wide. A smile spread across my face as she practically tackled me in a hug. "Emily!" I hugged her back tightly, laughing at how much energy she had, like nothing had changed. It *had* been too long.

She pulled back, her cheeks flushed. "You look great! I'm so glad you're here. This is going to be fun!"

I wasn't so sure about that, but I nodded anyway. "It's good to see you."

"Come on, you have to meet Cole," Emily said, dragging me toward the house.

"It's not like I don't know who he is," I protested. "We video chatted—"

Emily wasn't slowing down to listen. I barely had time to catch my breath before a tall, broad-shouldered guy with sandy-blond hair appeared in the doorway. He smiled warmly as Emily pulled me over. "This is Cole," she said, grinning like she'd just won the lottery. "My husband."

He extended his hand, and I shook it, trying not to be overwhelmed by how natural he seemed in this whole ranch setting. "Nice to meet you, Cole," I said.

"Likewise. Emily's been talking about you non-stop." He gave her a teasing look, and she blushed a little.

"Can you believe we're actually *married?*" Emily giggled. "It's like a dizzy dream! I still can't believe I did it before you."

"Uh, yeah. Congratulations," I said, though the word felt hollow. The thought of how my life back in San Diego had unraveled recently, and my baby sister was all settled and focused on her future, was something I'd rather not dwell on, especially today.

Before I could say much else, more people started arriving. Emily wasted no time dragging me through the house, introducing me to what felt like half the town. The names blurred together—Cole's brothers, family friends, some of the therapy clients from White Pines. I even thought I heard something about foster kids, but I couldn't keep it all straight. The house was packed with people, all of them friendly, but it didn't help me feel any less like an outsider.

The kitchen was buzzing with activity. Nora, Cole's mom, barely had time to say hello before she was pulled back into some whirlwind of pies and casseroles. My own mom was in there too, elbow-deep in whatever they were cooking, along with Kate—at least she was one familiar face—and Kate's mom in her wheelchair. They seemed to have things under control, so I decided that the best way I could help was to stay out of the way.

I hovered near the living room, trying to blend into the wallpaper. There were folding tables and chairs set up everywhere, people bustling around, setting out food, and rearranging furniture to make room for the massive crowd. I didn't see how they were going to fit thirty people in this house, but they seemed determined to make it work.

Just as I was starting to think I might escape to a corner with a drink and stay hidden for the rest of the day, the front door opened, letting in a blast of cold air.

A man stepped in, shaking snow off his coat, dusting it from his shoulders and hat before hanging it on the hook by the door. His work boots were caked with mud and snow, and his clothes were worn from a day out on the ranch. This must have been the brother who got the short straw—I thought I remembered Cole saying something about his other brother still feeding cows. He hadn't even bothered to change, and his cowboy scarf was still tied tight around his neck and ears, so I couldn't see much of his profile.

And then he turned around.

My heart sank as soon as I saw his face.

It was *him*. Trent—the grumpy cowboy who had rescued me yesterday when my car was buried in the snowbank. The one who had made me feel like an idiot without actually saying anything rude—just with those looks he'd given me. His eyes flickered with something—surprise, maybe recognition—but he didn't say a word.

His gaze shifted, glancing past me toward the dining room, where Emily was busy setting the table. It didn't take long for him to piece it together. The look on his face changed, like a switch had flipped, and he gave me a nod, a barely-there acknowledgment that said he remembered everything. Then, without a word, he walked off into the kitchen, where he disappeared into the crowd of people, blending in as if nothing had happened.

Great.

I took a breath, trying to regain my composure, and turned back toward the dining room, where more people were bustling in and out. Just stay out of the way, I reminded myself. Maybe I could survive the day without too many more surprises.

Four

Trent

THE HOUSE WAS BURSTING at the seams, and I could barely move without bumping into someone. Mom had invited practically half the town for Thanksgiving, and I wasn't sure how she thought we'd fit thirty people in here, let alone make sure everyone had room to put a plate on a table. Every room was packed, folding tables crammed into every available space, chairs squeezed in so tight you had to hold your breath to get through.

I carried a tray of dishes toward the kitchen, navigating through the crowd. A couple of kids—I didn't know whose—were wrestling with chairs in the dining room, trying to make room for more plates. I sidestepped them, muttering a quick "excuse me," but it was no use. The house was just too small for this kind of gathering.

Somehow, I ended up near the doorway between the kitchen and the living room. I turned the corner, dodging more kids running by with plates of rolls, when I bumped into someone. I barely had time to register it before my arm jerked, and the tray of dishes I was holding tipped.

"Watch it!" a sharp voice called, and I looked down to see the cranberry sauce sliding right off the dish and landing square in Lauren Carson's lap.

Her eyes went wide as she looked down at the mess, a bright red stain spreading across her light-colored jeans. "Are you serious?" she cried.

I froze for a second, my brain catching up to what had just happened. I'd bumped into plenty of people today—no way to avoid it in this crowd—but of course, it had to be *her* who caught the big red stain. "Sorry," I muttered, reaching for a napkin and offering it to her, even though I knew it wouldn't do much.

She took the napkin, clearly unimpressed, and dabbed at the mess with a tight, forced smile that didn't reach her eyes. "It's fine," she said, though her tone made it clear that it definitely *wasn't* fine. "Just great."

I watched her for a second, then cleared my throat, feeling awkward. "I didn't mean to—there's just no room in here."

Lauren shook her head, the napkin now useless. "Yeah, I noticed."

I didn't know what else to say, so I just turned and went back toward the kitchen, hoping to avoid any more accidents. The cranberry sauce was a goner, but there was still plenty of food, and Mom was determined to make sure everyone had their fill. By the time I got back to the dining room, the plywood table we'd set up in the living room had been covered with a sheet, and chairs were being lined up around it. I sighed, knowing exactly where this was headed.

Sure enough, Mom appeared, handing me a stack of plates. "Trent, can you take these to the living room? We're running out of space in here."

I nodded and carried the plates into the living room, where a few people were already sitting around the makeshift table. There was barely any room to walk, let alone carry dishes without knocking into someone. I set the plates down and glanced around, already dreading the seating arrangements.

"Why don't you sit here?" Mom said, coming up behind me and patting the chair next to Lauren. "Be social!"

I bit back a sigh. Of course, she'd stuck me at the plywood table with the one person who probably wished I'd disappear into thin air. Lauren didn't look up as I sat down, still brushing at the cranberry stain on her jeans with a napkin that wasn't helping at all.

"Sorry again," I said, trying to keep the conversation going. "I really didn't mean to—"

"It's fine," she interrupted, her voice clipped.

I shifted in my chair, which wobbled a bit on the uneven floor. The plywood table wasn't exactly the most stable, and every time someone put their elbows on it, the whole thing shook. "At least it's not too cold today," I tried again. Small talk. Always a safe bet.

She glanced at me, clearly unimpressed with my attempt at conversation. "Not cold? It's freezing."

I rubbed the back of my neck, realizing I had no idea what to say to this woman. She might as well have come from another planet, the way she looked at me like I was speaking a different language. "Well, not for here, I guess."

She just stared at me as if trying to figure out how anyone could think this wasn't cold. I felt the silence stretching out between us, and it made my skin itch.

I tried again. "So... how's your mom?"

She blinked, finally breaking her stare. "She's right over there. I assume you can see for yourself."

I cleared my throat. "Yeah, she and my mom have been running around the kitchen all day."

Laurel gave a tight smile. "Looks like it."

I sighed, giving up on trying to make this conversation work. The truth was, I didn't know what to say to her. She clearly didn't want to be here, and I couldn't blame her for that. Thirty people crammed into a ranch house wasn't exactly the most comfortable setting, especially for someone who wasn't used to this kind of crowd.

Dinner was served shortly after, and everyone squeezed in, passing plates and bowls down the table. I tried to focus on eating, but with the makeshift setup and the constant shifting of people, it was hard to concentrate. Laurel barely spoke to anyone, her eyes darting around like she was searching for an exit.

At one point, she dropped her fork, and I bent down to grab it for her, only for my chair to tilt dangerously to one side. I caught myself just in time, setting the fork back on the table with a muttered, "Here."

"Thanks," she said, her tone flat.

I tried to tune out the noise of everyone talking, but it was impossible. People were shouting across the room, clinking glasses, laughing—it was the kind of chaos that Mom thrived in, but for me, it was just exhausting. I caught bits of conversation from lots of different corners—talk about ranch work and upcoming projects. Kate was talking to someone about the therapy clients, mentioning how much progress they'd made. Every now and then, I'd glance at Lauren, but she just looked like she was trying to survive the meal without losing her mind.

Eventually, dessert came around, and I could've sworn there were at least ten different pies to choose from. Mom had outdone herself, as usual. I grabbed a slice of pecan pie and settled back in my chair, trying to enjoy at least that much of the meal.

Lauren picked at a piece of apple pie, not really eating it, just pushing it around with her fork. I wanted to say something, to ask her what was wrong, but I already knew. She wasn't like the rest of us. She didn't fit in here, didn't want to fit in.

The thought lingered in my mind as I watched her glance at the door, probably counting the minutes until she could leave.

I wasn't sure why it bothered me, but it did.

Lauren

B Y THE TIME WE made it back to Emily and Cole's place at White Pines, I felt like I could finally breathe. I wasn't used to feeling so out of place, but today? Today had been rough. I leaned against the doorframe for a second, letting the cool air from the outside seep in before closing the door behind me. I'd borrowed a pair of clean jeans from Emily, but the smell of turkey and pie still clung to the rest of my clothes, and my stomach churned at the thought of eating even one more bite.

Emily bustled around, already pulling out cups and a pot of decaf coffee. "Here, let me make us something warm," she said, setting the pot on the counter. Her energy hadn't faded a bit, even after the chaos of Thanksgiving at Ridgeview. I wished I could say the same for myself. I usually loved big groups, thrived on the buzz of people talking, moving, the energy flowing through a room. But today, I felt like I'd been hit by a truck.

"You okay?" Mom asked as she took a seat at the little table by the window. It was a cozy spot, and Emily's place had a calmness that Ridgeview had definitely lacked. I sank into the chair beside her, feeling every bit of the exhaustion that had been building all day.

"I'm fine," I muttered, rubbing my stomach. "Just... if I never see another bite of turkey, it'll be too soon."

Emily laughed as she brought over the coffee. "You didn't take any of the leftovers Cole's mom sent home, did you? We've got enough to last a week."

I groaned and shook my head. "I couldn't. I'm stuffed."

"Same here," Mom said, though I could see she was still eyeing the container Emily had set on the counter, as if one more slice of pie might be tempting after all. "But it was a good meal. I've never had a deep-fried turkey before. The smoked one and the oven-baked ones were good, too, but I think the deep-fried one is my new favorite."

I couldn't argue with that, even though I'd spent half the time trying to dodge people and the other half trying not to spill more food on myself. The food had been good, sure, but everything else? It was like being in a completely different world. The noise, the sheer number of people, the constant introductions... I'd never felt so disconnected in my life. Usually, big crowds made me feel energized. But today, I felt like I was sinking deeper into myself with every conversation.

Cole leaned over, giving Emily a quick kiss on the cheek before heading to the door. "I'm gonna go feed the horses. Morgan's family had a big gathering today, too, so I figured I'd help out."

Emily smiled up at him. "Thanks, hon. I'll be out in a bit to check on things."

I watched him leave, feeling a little twinge of envy. He seemed so at home here, like everything about this life just fit him perfectly. He and Emily had found something good here, and I couldn't help but wonder how they managed it.

Once the door closed behind Cole, Emily sat down with us, handing out the coffee cups and settling into her chair. The warmth from the cup seeped into my hands, but it didn't quite reach the unease still churning inside me.

"So," Emily started, giving me a careful look. "How are things going at work, Lauren? You've been busy, right?"

My stomach tightened again, but this time, it wasn't from the turkey. Work. The last thing I wanted to talk about. I forced a smile, swirling the coffee in my cup. "Yeah, it's been... busy."

"Busy's good, right?" Mom chimed in, her eyes searching mine. "I mean, you've been working hard for a long time. You deserve a break."

I nodded, trying to keep my face neutral. "Yeah, that's why I'm here. Just taking some time off, you know. Figured I'd get away for a bit."

Emily tilted her head, squinting strangely at me. But instead of asking, she smiled and switched the topic. "Well, you've got some time to relax here. Things are pretty calm here at White Pines most of the time, and Cole and I are giving the show horses a break for a few days. I'm not too busy right now."

I took a sip of coffee, grateful for the change in conversation. "What exactly do you do here? I mean, I know you're training horses, but it sounds like more than that."

Emily's face lit up, the same way it always did when she talked about her work. "It's a mix. Cole and I don't actually work here at White Pines, but you know Kate does. Cole and I just rent the mobile home, but as part of our rent, we're chore backup or night help or whatever extra pair of hands Morgan needs. You should head up to the therapy barn sometime and watch a session—it's super fascinating."

"Right. Horses and kids, that sort of thing. I got it," I said. "What else?"

Her bright expression dimmed somewhat. "Well, there's our work at Walker Ranch, but you knew about that. Cole and I are helping Cody get some horses ready for the spring show season, so right now it's all pretty methodical, back to basics kind of work for a month or so, so we can make sure the horses peak at..." She stopped with a frown. "But that probably isn't all that interesting to you."

I sighed and shook my head with a smile. "Sorry, Em. No, to be honest, it doesn't make much sense to me. But it sounds great."

Emily's features shone again. "I'll take you out there and show you. You'd get it once you saw."

I leaned back in my chair, watching her. She'd always had that spark, ever since we were kids. Horses were her life, and she'd made a real career out of it. Meanwhile, here I was, dodging questions about my job and hoping no one would find out about the mess I'd made.

"So you're at two ranches?" I asked, trying to keep the conversation going. "You don't spend any time at Ridgview too, do you?"

She laughed. "No, not really. I mean, yeah, Cole still helps out a lot at the family ranch, but right now, they're kind of struggling. It's not enough income for all the brothers, so Cole can't afford to be there full-time. Hopefully, they'll get back on their feet again in a year or two. Great family, aren't they?"

I raised an eyebrow. "They're... not what I expected."

Emily laughed, leaning back in her chair. "Yeah, they're a little rough around the edges."

"That's one way to put it," I muttered, thinking back to the chaotic dinner and the cowboy who had spilled cranberry sauce on me. Grumpy, quiet, and intense. Not my favorite combination.

"They're good people, though," Emily added quickly. "You just caught them at a busy time. The holidays always bring out the stress."

I nodded, not entirely convinced. "They seemed kind of grumpy."

She laughed again. "Oh, that's just Trent. And maybe Gage. But honestly, they're amazing. Cole's family has been through a lot this past year. It's been one financial hit after another, and they're doing everything they can just to hang on."

"Wow, that's the second time you've said that in that many minutes. Is it really bad?"

Emily's smile faded a little. "It's been tough. They lost a lot of business last year when the market dropped, and then there were some equipment failures, vet bills... you name it. They almost lost the whole thing when their grazing rights were threatened. Ridgeview is a big operation, but big means expensive. They're trying to hold on, but it feels like they just need *one* big thing to change, you know?"

I set my cup down, frowning. I hadn't realized things were that bad over there. Ridgeview had looked big, sturdy... but appearances could be deceiving.

"What could change?" I asked, curious but hesitant to pry too much. I'd only just met these people, after all.

Emily shrugged. "I don't know. Gage and Trent have been doing everything they can to find new ways to bring in income. Kate's been trying to help with some ideas from White Pines. But they're not sure what'll stick. It's like they're just waiting for the right break, but none of us know what that is."

I nodded, a strange sense of empathy settling in. I knew what it was like to feel like everything was on the brink of falling apart, to be holding your breath, waiting for something to change. "That sounds... rough."

"It is," Emily said softly. "But they're strong. They'll figure it out."

Five

Lauren

T HE KNOCK ON THE apartment door startled me out of my thoughts. I'd been staring at my laptop, trying to scroll through job postings—hey, you never knew, right?—when really, I was doing my best to avoid thinking about Thanksgiving. My stomach still churned from too much pie and cranberry sauce—some of which had, unfortunately, permanently stained my jeans, courtesy of Trent Langton. Not exactly the highlight of my trip so far.

Mom was already halfway across the room, wiping her hands on her apron as she called over her shoulder, "It's probably Emily!"

Sure enough, Emily burst through the door with her usual whirlwind energy. Her jeans and boots were still dusted with barn dirt, her golden curls bouncing as she moved.

"Morning!" she chirped, letting the door swing shut behind her. She spotted me on the couch and grinned. "How're you feeling after last night? Ridgeview can be a lot for the uninitiated."

I arched an eyebrow at her. "Uninitiated? Is that what we're calling it now?"

Emily laughed and plopped down on the couch beside me, grabbing a throw pillow and hugging it to her chest. "Okay, fair. It was chaos, even for us. But it's fun, right? Being part of a big family gathering like that?"

"Fun might be a stretch," I muttered, though her enthusiasm was contagious.

"Well, you survived, and that's what counts," Emily said, her grin widening. "Speaking of survival, I was thinking... you should come out to Ridgeview again today."

I blinked. "What? Why?"

"Look, I know yesterday was overwhelming, but you didn't really get to see the ranch. I mean, really see it. You were stuck inside, dodging folding chairs and cranberry sauce. But the ranch itself? It's incredible, Lauren. And... I was thinking, maybe you could help."

"Help?" I repeated, my tone skeptical. "Help how?"

Emily hesitated for a moment, then shrugged. "I don't know—ideas, maybe. You're good at that kind of thing. Marketing, business, all the stuff we don't think about out here."

I opened my mouth to protest, but Emily held up a hand.

"Just come with me. No pressure. Cole's helping his brothers with some stuff so I'm going to go anyway. You can see the place, maybe toss out a suggestion or two, and if nothing else, you'll get some fresh air." She glanced pointedly at the laptop still balanced on my knees. "Better than sitting here, staring at that glowing screen all day. I don't know how you do that. I'd go nuts."

I bristled, but she wasn't wrong. The truth was, I didn't want to spend another day cooped up, thinking about how uncertain everything felt. A part of me was curious about Ridgeview, even if it meant running into Trent again.

"Fine," I said, snapping the laptop shut. "But if Trent dumps any more food on me, I'm holding you personally responsible."

Emily laughed, grabbing my arm to tug me off the couch. "Deal. Let's go."

Trent

T HE WRENCH SLIPPED, CLANGING hard against the engine block. I bit back a curse and straightened, flexing my stiff fingers as I glared at the tractor. The stupid thing had been coughing smoke and making me cuss a blue streak for weeks, but of course, it chose now—when we had a half-dozen other crises to deal with—to finally give up the ghost.

I yanked off my gloves and wiped my hands on a rag, squinting at the mess of hoses and belts. The new water pump wasn't lining up right, and I was two steps away from kicking the whole machine.

"Trent!"

Gage's voice carried across the yard, drawing my attention to where he was jogging over from the barn. He was carrying a bucket of tools, his face flushed from the cold.

"Where's the fire?" I asked, tossing the rag onto the tractor's wheel well.

"No fire," he said, catching his breath. "Just letting you know Cole and Emily are here. Brought her sister with her."

I stared at him. "Lauren?"

He nodded, smirking. "Yeah, the one with the fancy boots. Thought you'd want a heads-up before you head in."

"Head in, what do you mean?"

"Mom's looking for you. Not sure why. I think it had something to do with Emily's sister."

I grunted. "Great. Just what I need—another city girl telling me how to do my job."

Gage shrugged. "Hey, maybe she's got some big ideas for fixing that hunk of junk you're wrestling with."

I shot him a look, but he was already heading back toward the barn, his laughter trailing behind him.

By the time I made it up to the house, Emily and Lauren were standing with Mom by the kitchen table, chatting like they'd known each other for years. Lauren was dressed in another one of those polished outfits—jeans that looked brand new and a jacket that probably cost more than the tractor I was trying to fix. Her hair was loose, and like always, it looked... well, kind of amazing, actually.

"It doesn't matter how many years I've been doing this," Mom was saying, her face lighting up with pride as she flashed her phone in front of Emily. "I just love the calves. Look at this little guy. Isn't he just the cutest?"

Emily grinned. "He's adorable. I always like a black baldy."

I glanced at Lauren, who was giving the picture on the phone a doubtful look.

"Uh.... Yeah," she said. "Looks like an awkward, hairy teenager to me. And is that snot hanging off his nose?"

Mom gasped, clutching her phone dramatically to her chest. "It is not! That's just... moisture."

"Sure," Lauren said with a small smile. "Moisture."

I sighed. I didn't have all day to watch them trying to gross out the city girl with pictures of calf snot. Why did they want me to come up here, anyway, if they were just going to ignore me and stare at Mom's phone? Finally, I cleared my throat. "What's going on in here?"

Lauren turned toward me, her blue eyes narrowing slightly. "Oh, great," she muttered under her breath. "The cranberry cowboy."

I leaned against the doorframe, crossing my arms. "Morning to you, too."

Mom threw me a quick "don't start" look, then turned back to Emily and Lauren. "You know, Lauren," she said brightly, "you should let Trent give you a proper tour of the ranch. He could show you the pastures, the barns... all the places the magic happens."

"I don't think magic involves that much manure," Lauren said, glancing at me from the corner of her eye.

"You'd be surprised. Ever wonder why our pastures are the greenest in the county?"

"Uh..." Lauren cleared her throat. "I never spent much time thinking about that."

"See? The more you know, as they say."

"You might as well give up," Emily laughed. "Nora loves telling people all about ranching, and you won't get out of here until you've had a complete crash course in everything from range management to herd health to tractor maintenance."

"I just think it's important for people to know where their food comes from," Mom shrugged. "You don't think they manufacture it at the store, do you?"

"I did grow up in Big River Valley until I was a teenager," Lauren reminded her.

"Perfect! This will be like a homecoming. Smelling the fresh air, getting out a little—"

"You know, I really shouldn't." Lauren tried to back up. "You guys are busy, and I don't want to monopolize your time. I don't even have... uh..." She looked down and kicked up one of those fancy boots to show Mom her footwear.

Mom waved her hand dismissively as she went to the kitchen counter to grab the insulated coffee mug I'd left there this morning. "Nonsense. Trent can take you on the four-wheeler when he does his morning herd checks. It'll keep you from slipping, and you can buzz around easier. Anyway, he'd really be the best tour guide—better than me, you know. He knows every inch of this place."

"Pass," I said immediately, pushing off the doorframe.

Mom ignored me, smiling sweetly at Lauren. "He's just being modest."

Lauren tilted her head, her lips twitching as if she was holding back a laugh. "Modest, huh?"

"Don't worry," Mom said, patting her arm. "I'm sure we can find some mud boots around here if he makes you walk."

I stared at Mom, feeling the beginnings of a headache coming on. "I don't have time to babysit."

"Fine," Lauren said, stepping closer to the table. "I wouldn't want to waste your precious time, anyway."

That was when Mom cleared her throat and gave me *the look*.

I groaned inwardly. No point in arguing—she'd made up her mind, and though I was a grown man, never once had I pulled one over on my mom. Thought I had a few times, but she'd always been a few steps ahead, and never took no for an answer.

But the weird part was that somehow, that look brought Lauren to heel, too. She tugged at her sweater uncomfortably, glancing at her sister. Emily was practically standing at attention, her eyes roving from her sister to my mom. Yeah, she knew the drill—couldn't be married to Cole without learning the ropes around the ranch, I guess—and she was nudging Lauren in a way that looked almost pleading.

"Uh…" Lauren coughed slightly. "On second thought, I… I guess it's been a while since I saw a working ranch. Up close, I mean. Might be cool to see what's different about yours."

Something about the way she said it caught my attention. Different? This was a ranch, like a thousand others. What could possibly make us stand out?

But I didn't ask. Instead, I grabbed the coffee mug Mom was handing me—dang it, my coffee was cold now—and muttered, "Well, bundle up, I guess. I'll be heading out for the upper fields in a few."

L AUREN

The four-wheeler rumbled beneath me as I gripped the cargo bars for dear life. It wasn't much help—leaning back and grabbing the rusty rails behind the seat and hoping they wouldn't snap off—but it was better than wrapping my arms around a cowboy I didn't know or like.

Trent hadn't even glanced back at me since we'd pulled away from the barn, his focus fixed straight ahead. I could barely hear myself think over the growl of the engine and the freezing wind whipping at my face.

"This is definitely not what I signed up for!" I called over the noise.

He gave a single nod, his hat tilted low. "Nobody asked you to."

My teeth clenched, but I let it slide. The last thing I wanted was to lose my grip and land face-first in the snow.

We crested a hill, and Trent eased off the gas, slowing the four-wheeler to a stop. He turned to look at me, and for some reason, when he did that, I caught a view of his cheek bristling with that five o'clock shadow look that I usually couldn't resist. No trouble resisting it now, though.

"First stop," he said, gesturing toward the pasture below. "We call them.... cows."

My lips twitched despite myself. "Thanks for clearing that up. I wasn't sure."

He smirked, just faintly, before sliding off the four-wheeler. I followed, trying not to slip and fall on my rear on the glazed surface of the snow. The field below stretched out in uneven patches of white, dotted with cattle moving in slow, deliberate motions. Their breath fogged the air as they nosed at the ground.

"They're eating... what, exactly?" I asked, careful to keep my voice neutral. "It looks like they're digging for something."

"Stockpiled forage," Trent said, gesturing toward the snowy patches. "Grass we let grow during the summer and leave standing for winter grazing."

"You don't feed them hay?"

"Only when we have to." He crouched, brushing a hand over the frost-dusted grass. "Stockpiling saves us money on hay and fuel. Plus, it's better for the land."

"Better how?"

He looked up, his brow furrowing slightly, like he wasn't sure if I was pulling his leg. "The roots stay intact. Keeps the grass stronger for spring. Cuts down on erosion, too."

I nodded, filing that away. "And you came up with that idea?"

He straightened, brushing his hands off on his jeans. "Not just me. It's something a lot of ranchers are doing now. Makes sense if you want to stay in business without going broke."

I watched the cows for another moment, noting the way they moved, slow but purposeful. They didn't look as dumb as I'd always imagined. "So, they dig through the snow to eat the grass underneath?"

He nodded. "They're good at it. Doesn't take them long to figure out where to find the best patches."

"That's actually kind of impressive," I admitted.

He glanced at me, like he was trying to decide if I was being serious again. "They're not as clueless as they look."

I almost laughed at that, but something about the way he was watching me—quiet, steady—made me feel unsteady on my feet. I crossed my arms, looking away toward the horizon.

"Well," I said briskly, "what's next on this magical mystery tour?"

He gave me a funny side-eye. "Look, I ain't out here to entertain you. I'm checking the stock."

"Fine," I sighed. "Guess you don't have a sense of humor. Where to now?"

He didn't answer me for a few seconds. His eyes had gone unfocused, drifting over the herd, dancing down the fence line, and skimming over a water trough in the distance. Finally, he seemed to come back to the present, and it was like he'd just heard my question. "Yearlings. Let's go."

We climbed back onto the four-wheeler, and the engine rumbled back to life. The ride was bumpy, and I had to grip the sidebars tightly as Trent took a winding path toward a fenced-off area at the edge of the pasture.

What in the world was I doing out here? I should be hanging out with my mom and sister, since I had hardly seen them in the last couple of years. I should be on my laptop, trying to figure out how to salvage my career. Not bouncing around on the back of a four-wheeler, looking at something I was never interested in.

But... well, this wasn't all bad. Something about the open space—acres of snow-covered fields stretching to the horizon—made the quiet feel less awkward. But where in the world were we going? It felt like we were putting along forever. I could see old tracks in the snow stretching out before us, so obviously, this was a usual route, but it felt like the middle of nowhere. Until we stopped at a gate.

I rolled my eyes. *Here we go...* Passenger always gets to hop off and get the gate. That was one rule I remembered from when I was a kid growing up here. We didn't have a ranch, but we had an old gate across the driveway, and Dad always made me hop out and get it.

But Trent didn't say anything to me. He just eased the throttle a little, and I realized he was rolling onto some little pressure plate. Sure enough, it triggered a mechanical rocker system of some kind, and the gate lifted up in the air like magic as we drove under it.

I spun to look back at it as we drove away, my jaw open. Another trip plate went off, and the gate slowly lowered back into its original position. "That thing wasn't electric. How did it work?"

Trent's profile turned to me a little. "The gate? Oh, that was one of Chase's contraptions. He found the schematics online somewhere and built it for us. It was always a pain to get that stupid gate, 'specially if we're out here by ourselves, but electric gates are expensive, and we couldn't justify it. Even with a solar panel. This was easier, and he had the parts lying around, so..." He shrugged as he kept driving like it was no big deal.

Sure seemed like a big deal to me. Kind of ingenious, really, how they'd figured out how to make something that worked for practically free.

We putted along a little farther, and pretty soon, we were in kind of a protected valley. There was hardly any snow here, but most of the grass was crunchy with frost because there wasn't a lot of sun, either. Trent stopped near a series of narrow paddocks divided by temporary fencing.

"What's with all that?" I asked, pointing. "Looks kinda... haphazard."

"Well, it isn't supposed to last until Kingdom Come. It gets moved a lot. We rotate grazing," he said, climbing off the four-wheeler again.

I followed, brushing snow off my sleeves as I stared at the fences. "What does that mean?"

"Cows only graze one section at a time," he explained, pointing to the paddock where a group of cattle was gathered. "We move them every few days, so the grass has time to recover before they come back to it. It's harder work, but it keeps the land healthy."

I tilted my head, studying the setup. "So it's like... giving the grass a break?"

"Exactly," he said, his tone warming slightly. "Even in the winter, when the grass is dormant, it matters. We change the cycles this time of year, but it still makes a difference. If you let them eat wherever they want all the time, they'll overgraze—rip out roots, kill off the plants' energy reserves. That's bad for the grass, bad for the soil, and bad for the herd. Rotation keeps our parasites down, cuts our health problems, and makes the land more productive in the long run."

I nodded slowly, genuinely impressed. "That's... smart."

He glanced at me, his eyes narrowing slightly like he was trying to figure out if I was mocking him.

"I mean it," I added.

"Thanks," he said, but his tone was clipped, like he didn't quite believe me. "I mean... it's just what we do, working with what we've got."

"Do other ranches do that?"

"Sure. Everyone's got their own program, I guess, but yeah, they all rotate somehow. We sorta had to really double down on our program these last couple of years because..." He stopped and shook his head. "Well, anyway, these guys are good. Let me go check the water."

We drove about a thousand yards down to the end of the separated field. It looked to me like all the rotational fences had been set up to intersect at a water trough with a solar-powered pump, like spokes on a wheel.

"This one's been a game-changer," Trent said, crouching by the trough. "It uses motion sensors to release water when the cows come up to drink."

I leaned closer, brushing a snowflake off my cheek. "How does that work?"

He tapped the edge of the trough, his gloves leaving faint smudges in the frost that crusted the outside. "See this upper basin? It fills when the sensor detects movement nearby. Once the cows are done and wander off, the water drains into the lower part here." He pointed toward an insulated compartment beneath the trough.

"So it's always fresh?" I asked, tilting my head.

"And warm enough that they'll drink more," he said, straightening. "In the winter, cattle don't always drink as much as they need. If the water's too cold or stagnant, they avoid it. That messes with their feed intake and overall health."

"Warm water makes them drink more," I said, processing the logic.

He nodded. "Keeps them hydrated, keeps their digestion working right, and ultimately keeps them gaining weight through the winter."

I crouched beside the trough, running my fingers over the edge of the upper basin. "I don't get it. There's no heater on that thing and according to the thermostat on my mom's car last night, it was four degrees outside. How does it stay warm?"

"The insulated portion is deep," he replied. "The top, where they drink, is shallow enough that it would freeze solid if we left it there all night. But this system keeps it moving, and it stays in the lower part most of the time."

"That's... genius," I said before I could stop myself.

He glanced at me, his expression unreadable, but there was a flicker of something in his eyes—maybe surprise or just quiet pride. "It's efficient," he said simply. "Saves water and energy."

"And it saves you time," I added, standing and brushing snow off my knees. "You don't have to haul buckets or break ice."

His lips twitched, the faintest hint of a smile. "Exactly."

The trough wasn't the only clever touch. The next stop was a line of trees—young but growing steadily—that stretched along the edge of a pasture.

"Windbreaks," Trent said, gesturing toward them.

I squinted at the bare branches. "You planted these?"

"Years ago," he said. "They block the worst of the wind in the winter and provide shade in the summer. Cattle handle cold better than heat, but the wind can make things miserable, especially for calves."

I could picture it—the icy gusts cutting across the open fields, the snow swirling. Even bundled in my thickest coat, I felt the chill. For the first time, I realized how much the cattle relied on these small interventions to survive the harsh seasons.

"And it helps the land, too," he continued, brushing snow off his gloves. "Windbreaks reduce erosion, hold moisture in the soil, and even create better grazing conditions."

"That's a lot of return on investment," I said, genuinely impressed.

He shrugged, his shoulders lifting in that understated way I was starting to recognize. "You do what you can with what you've got."

"I guess."

I followed him back to the four-wheeler, watching as he brushed snow off the seat for me with a quick, practiced motion. That was... well, okay, that was kind of sweet. But then he turned around and didn't look at me again as he started the engine and waited for me.

I climbed up behind him a little more slowly this time. Mostly, I was looking around at everything I saw with new eyes. What struck me most wasn't just how much Trent knew, but how deliberate it all was. Every choice they'd made—whether it was planting trees, adjusting their grazing patterns, or installing mechanical gates or state-of-the-art watering systems—came back to the same thing: staying in business without cutting corners.

Maybe he didn't say much, but he didn't have to. The land itself was proof of his work, his stubborn determination to make Ridgeview something more than just another ranch.

By the time we headed back toward the barn, I found myself looking at the ranch differently. I still wasn't thrilled about being roped into this tour, but I had to admit, it wasn't what I expected. The Langtons weren't just running a ranch—they were running an ecosystem, one they'd built and rebuilt to survive.

As Trent parked the four-wheeler, cutting the engine, I glanced at him. His hat was dusted with snow, and his jaw was set in that same stoic line I'd seen since Thanksgiving.

"You're doing some interesting things out here," I said, sliding off the seat.

He raised an eyebrow. "We're just trying to keep the lights on."

Something about the way he said it stuck with me.

Six

Trent

I WAS JUST ABOUT to hitch the hay trailer to the tractor when I heard the barn door creak open. A second later, Liam and Ethan stepped inside, both bundled up in oversized coats that made them look like a couple of walking marshmallows.

"You're late," I said without looking up, sliding the pin into place.

Ethan scoffed, shoving his hands deeper into his pockets. "It's Saturday."

"And?" I shot back, dusting snow off my gloves as I straightened.

"And normal people sleep in on Saturdays," he muttered, slouching against a post.

"Normal people don't eat unless they work for it. Grab the bucket over there and help Liam feed the chickens. Wait—actually, grab the pitchfork and clean up some of this loose hay."

Ethan rolled his eyes but didn't argue. Liam, on the other hand, darted toward the feed bags, his boots clomping across the concrete. He was always quicker to follow orders, though I wasn't sure if it was out of respect or just to avoid an argument.

As they worked, I leaned against the wall, watching them out of the corner of my eye. Liam measured the grain with careful precision, his tongue poking out of the corner of his mouth as he concentrated. Ethan, meanwhile, tossed the hay like it had personally insulted him, his movements jerky and a little too forceful.

"You're gonna break the pitchfork if you keep that up," I said.

Ethan glared at me, his dark eyes flashing. "Maybe it deserves to be broken."

I bit back a sigh. "It's a tool, not a punching bag."

He muttered something under his breath but eased up on the shoveling. Progress, I supposed. I got back to what I was doing, but I kept one eye on Ethan. He wasn't working, really. Just pretending to scrape the tines of the fork over the ground whenever I wasn't looking directly at him. Finally, I'd had enough, and I stopped to stare at him.

He just stared back, his face blank.

"So?" I demanded.

"So," he said, a sly grin spreading across his face as he deliberately dropped the pitchfork. "Who's the blonde?"

I frowned. "What?"

"You know. The one you were riding around with yesterday. Liam saw you on the four-wheeler with her. Said she's some city girl."

Liam turned bright red and immediately moved behind the hay stack, where I couldn't see him.

"Lauren," I said flatly, grabbing the pitchfork off the ground. "She's Emily's sister. She's here visiting for the holidays."

Ethan's grin widened. "She's hot."

I narrowed my eyes at him. "Watch your mouth, kid. And get back to work."

"Come on, man, really? You gonna say you didn't notice? You're just gonna work here in the barn when you could head to town and hit—"

"Get your mind out of the gutter. She's just here for a few weeks."

"So, you're saying you don't like her?"

I stopped what I was doing, fixing him with a look that usually shut him up. "I'm saying it's none of your business. Now get back to work."

Ethan snickered but picked up the pitchfork again. Liam came around the corner of the hay stack just then with his arms full of alfalfa. He glanced at Ethan, then shot me a sheepish glance, mumbling something about needing to check on Hickory before darting out of the barn.

After the boys had finished their chores and taken off, I lingered in the barn, re-stacking the feed bags on the pallet after Liam had shuffled through to dig out Hickory's special Senior Horse supplement from the bottom of the stack. The weight of each bag tugged at my shoulders, a familiar ache I'd stopped noticing years ago. The barn was quiet now, save for the occasional shuffle of hooves or a soft whicker from one of the horses.

I grabbed another bag, hefting it onto the growing stack, and paused to brush the dust off my gloves. My mind wandered back to the day before, unbidden. Lauren perched on the back of the four-wheeler, her hair catching the sunlight as she rattled off one question after another.

She'd started out with that snarky edge, looking and acting like she'd rather be anywhere else but on the back of a cold four-wheeler running through frozen pastures. I couldn't blame her, really. Why did Mom think Lauren needed a tour of the ranch, and why make *me*...?

Okay, I knew *why*. Mom never missed a chance to set one of us up with a nice girl, but I thought she'd be over that by now. She used to complain that she'd never have any grandkids, but with Cole and Emily married, and Chase packing a ring around in his pocket, waiting for the right time to propose to Kate, I guess I figured she'd have let up a bit.

Guess not.

I still didn't get why she sent me off with Lauren, though. Lauren wasn't... well, she was a city girl. Wouldn't know a Hereford from a Holstein, and didn't care, anyway. She'd all but begged not to go out.

But somewhere between the windbreaks and the water troughs, things *had* shifted, no denying it. Her questions had come faster, her tone softening, her gaze sharpening like she was actually seeing the ranch for what it was.

"Great," I muttered, setting the last bag in place. "Now I'm thinking about her."

I kicked a stray piece of hay across the barn floor, watching it skitter into the corner. People like Lauren didn't stick around in places like this. She wasn't going to trade her polished city life for snow-covered boots and the endless grind of ranch work.

I grabbed a broom, sweeping the scattered grain back into the feed bin. The rhythmic scrape of bristles on concrete was grounding, pulling me back into the present.

But even as I worked, her face kept flashing in my mind—the way her brow furrowed when I explained the solar trough, or the way her lips curved into a small, genuine smile when she called it "genius." I shook my head, gripping the broom handle tighter.

The barn door creaked open, and Gage poked his head in. "Thought you'd be done in here by now."

"Almost," I said, leaning the broom against the wall. "What's up?"

He stepped inside, the cold air following him. "Liam wanted to know if you'd check Hickory's stall later. Said something about the latch sticking again. And Marty got out again this morning. Better check his latch, too."

"I'll take a look," I said, tugging my gloves back on.

Gage grinned, his eyes narrowing slightly. "Oh, and Ethan said to tell you not to get too distracted thinking about the 'blonde on the four-wheeler.'"

My jaw clenched, and I turned back to the feed bin. "Tell Ethan to worry about his own chores."

"He's just messing with you," Gage said, his grin widening.

"I know," I muttered, brushing past him toward Hickory's stall. "Doesn't mean he's not annoying."

I walked over to the Old Pensioner's stalls, as I called them. Hickory and Marty—two retired rope geldings past their prime and now living fat as kings. Hickory was Liam's special buddy, thanks to Mom's little idea.

But Marty used to be my dad's horse. Now, he was nobody's, really—nobody dared try to fill Dad's shoes. Not that Marty would let 'em, anyway. He only ever loved Dad. The rest of us were just here to be his valets and housekeepers.

And sure enough, the old coot had broken his stall latch again. "What have you been up to, you old pain in the neck?" I grumbled as I fetched my screw gun. "By golly, if you haven't broken the darn thing." I sighed and rummaged around in a spare parts bucket for another catch. Marty was *always* getting out, but this ought to hold him in for a few days. Until he figured out how to defeat this one.

Next came Hickory's stall. I slid the door open, inspecting the latch. Sure enough, it was sticking, the cold making the metal stiff. I fished a can of lubricant from my back pocket and gave the hinge a few sprays, working it loose.

Hickory turned his head toward me, his ears flicking forward. He let out a soft, low nicker, his breath puffing into the chilly air.

"You've got it easy," I said, patting his neck. "No questions. No attitude. Just food and a warm stall."

Hickory huffed, nudging my shoulder like he thought I'd forgotten something.

"All right, all right," I muttered, grabbing a brush from the wall. As I worked the knots out of his mane, my thoughts wandered back to Lauren again.

She'd been snarky, sure—that crack about "Cranberry Cowboy" still sort of rankled with me. But by the end of the tour, there'd been something else. Genuine curiosity. Like she actually cared about what we were doing out here—not in a condescending, let-me-fix-this-for-you kind of way, but in a way that made me wonder if she could really see the work, the effort, the heart that went into this place.

I shook my head, brushing Hickory's coat a little harder. She wasn't staying. She had even less interest in the ranch than Cassie did. People like her didn't stick around—not for the long haul, anyway.

But that didn't explain why I kept seeing her face every time I closed my eyes.

Lauren

I WOKE UP ON Saturday to the faint sound of the secondhand store's bell jingling downstairs. For a moment, I lay there, staring at the ceiling, disoriented by the muffled voices and faint clatter of hangers on racks. Then I remembered where I was: Mom's apartment, above the cluttered little shop that had always smelled faintly of mothballs and cinnamon candles.

It was late—later than I'd intended—and the sunlight pouring through the window didn't let me pretend otherwise. With a groan, I sat up and swung my legs over the side of the bed, running a hand through my hair.

My reflection in the mirror made me wince. The curls had won the overnight battle, springing out in tight spirals that would've made Emily proud. I grabbed my flat iron from the dresser and plugged it in, waiting impatiently as it heated up.

Fifteen minutes later, my hair was sleek, smooth, and sophisticated again—the way I liked it. I glanced at my reflection, satisfied. No one had to know I was just as curly-headed as my sister.

I pulled on a pair of jeans and a sweater and wandered into the kitchen, grabbing my phone off the counter. The lock screen lit up, showing two missed calls and a voicemail.

The tow truck.

Heart sinking, I tapped the voicemail and held the phone to my ear.

"Hey, this is Danny, calling about your tow. Got your car back. It's sitting out front, keys are under the mat. Tire's fixed. You're good to go. Just gimme a call when you're ready to square up."

I froze, the phone still pressed to my ear. Sitting out front? With the keys in it? Anyone could just—

I hurried to the window, pulling the curtain aside. Sure enough, the little rental compact was parked at the curb, looking none the worse for wear. I let out a breath but didn't feel much calmer.

The cost. I hadn't even thought about that. Small town, busy holiday weekend. They could gouge me if they wanted, and I'd have no say in it because they'd already just gone and picked the car up without giving me a quote first.

Fumbling with the phone, I called the number back. Danny picked up on the second ring.

"Danny's Towing," he said in a gruff, cheerful voice.

"Hi, this is Lauren Carson—you fixed my rental car this morning?"

"Sure did."

"How much do I owe you?"

"Oh, I hadn't worked up an invoice yet," he said breezily. "Let's say a hundred."

A... a *hundred*? That was less than a local tow should've cost, and he'd had to dig it out of the snow, fix a tire... of course, he'd taken three days to do it, but still... It was probably stupid to argue at this point.

"Can I pay online or something?" I asked, hoping to get this over with quickly.

Danny chuckled. "Don't have that. I'll swing by later and pick up a check."

I stared at the phone. "I don't have checks."

"Well, cash works fine."

"Cash?" My voice cracked. "I didn't bring... is there an ATM around somewhere? The banks are all closed."

"Don't worry about it," he said. "I'll swing by on Monday or so."

Before I could argue, he hung up.

I sank onto the couch, staring at the phone. Who didn't have an app for payment? Or at least take cards? He was really going to just... "swing by" on Monday? That was so weird, I didn't even have words for it.

I was still stewing over the call when my phone buzzed again. Emily's name flashed on the screen.

"Hey," I said, trying to sound normal.

"Get dressed," she said, her tone bright. "I'm picking you up in ten minutes."

"What? Why?"

"Because you need to see Walker Ranch," she said, like it was the most obvious thing in the world. "Cole and I are working some horses today, and I want to show you what I do."

I didn't have a chance to argue before she hung up.

Ten minutes later, Emily's truck pulled up outside, and I climbed in, my annoyance melting slightly when she grinned at me.

"I can't wait for you to see this," she said, practically bouncing in her seat as we drove toward Walker Ranch.

The ranch was sprawling, with neatly fenced pastures and barns that looked freshly painted even in the middle of winter. Cole was already in the arena when we arrived, riding a stocky sorrel horse that moved like his feet were on fire, all sharp and crisp and still smooth as glass. I'd never seen an animal move like that.

"Isn't he gorgeous?" Emily said as we walked over.

"Which one?" I asked dryly, eyeing Cole.

Emily elbowed me, laughing. "The horse, obviously."

She waved to Cole, who tipped his hat to us before turning his attention back to the horse beneath him.

"Cole's working on cow cutting," Emily explained as we leaned against the fence.

"Cow what?"

"Cutting," she said, her eyes sparkling. "It's a competition event. The horse has to separate a cow from the herd and keep it away long enough to show control. It's all about precision and quick reflexes. Watch."

I tried to follow what she was saying, but it was hard to keep up. Cole moved the horse with what seemed like invisible cues, guiding it to block a calf's every move. Emily cheered him on, throwing out terms like "cow sense" and "getting underneath himself" that made no sense to me.

"Impressive," I said, though I wasn't sure if I meant Cole or the horse.

Emily laughed again. "Come on, let me show you the training barn."

As we walked through the ranch, I started to notice the differences between Walker and Ridgeview. The cattle here were in feedlots, chewing on grain and silage instead of grazing like Ridgeview's herd.

"Why do you feed them like that?" I asked Cole when he joined us later.

"It's more efficient for fattening them up," he said, tightening some loudly-colored silk scarf up around his ears. "Grain and silage give them the nutrients they need without relying on pasture."

"But Ridgeview doesn't do that," I said, glancing at Emily.

"Nope," Cole said, leaning against the fence. "Ridgeview's all grass-fed—or haylage, when the grass runs out."

"Haylage? I've heard of silage..."

"Same idea, except it's fermented hay instead of corn stalks. See that stack of car-sized marshmallow-looking things over there?"

I followed his hand and nodded. "Yeah."

"We have a big machine that basically shrink wraps the bales. Fun to watch, really. It saves the hay for later use, and the fermentation makes it more nutritious by the time we actually feed it. But it's still hay. We don't feed grain or corn at Ridgeview."

"And..." I had to jog to keep up because Cole had slung a halter over his shoulder and was marching toward a pasture. "... and Walker Ranch does feed corn. Why?"

"They have about four thousand head to our eight hundred. It was a management call. Both methods work, but it's just a different approach. At the end of the day, we're all selling to the same buyers."

I frowned, his words sticking in my head. "So, Ridgeview doesn't... market that?"

Cole shrugged. "It's not something we think about much. As long as the buyers are happy, we're happy."

I nodded absently, my mind already spinning with ideas. There was something here—something Ridgeview wasn't taking advantage of.

But before I could figure out what it was, Emily tugged me back toward the barn, already launching into another explanation about the horses she was training. As we walked back toward the arena, her phone buzzed. She glanced at the screen and smiled. "Mom says she's working late tonight—you know how she gets for the Christmas sales."

"Em, it's a second-hand shop in a tiny town. How can she possibly be that busy?"

Emily shoved her phone back in her pocket. "It's not the shop. She says it is, but the real truth is that she has that little tea nook in the back where she and all her friends sit and wrap presents together after they shop for the day. They'll be at it for hours."

"Ah. Of course," I said, rolling my eyes.

"You should come up to the house for dinner. Cole's already got his special chili in the crock pot, and Chase and Kate are planning to stop by."

I slowed my steps, eyeing her suspiciously. "Chase and Kate?"

"Yeah," Emily said, her expression cheerful and oblivious. "It'll be fun. We'll have dinner, hang out for a while…"

"And what about any… other cowboys?" I asked, narrowing my eyes.

Emily stopped walking, giving me a genuinely baffled look. "What?"

"You know." I gestured vaguely. "Any other cowboys I might know?"

Her frown deepened for a second before realization dawned. "You mean Trent?"

I didn't answer, but my face must've said enough.

Emily burst out laughing. "Oh my gosh, Lauren, no. Trent's not coming. He doesn't even like socializing, let alone driving all the way over here for dinner. Why would you think that?"

"I don't know," I muttered, crossing my arms. "You just seem very eager to have me meet people lately."

Emily shook her head, still laughing as she nudged me toward the truck. "Relax, drama queen. No one's setting you up with anyone. It's just dinner with family. Promise."

"Fine. Okay," I said, sighing as I climbed into the passenger seat. "I'll come."

"Great," Emily said, her grin as bright as ever. "You'll love it. Cole's chili is amazing, and Kate will probably bring pie. That girl *knows* how to make pie."

"Fantastic," I said, though my voice lacked her enthusiasm.

As we drove away from Walker Ranch, I stared out the window, watching the snowy fields blur past. I wasn't sure why I felt so jittery—whether it was the idea of dinner with more ranch folks, or the fact that Trent had come to mind way too easily.

Whatever it was, I pushed it aside. Tonight was just dinner. Nothing more.

Seven

Lauren

E MILY'S MOBILE HOME WAS warm and smelled like chili and cornbread when we stepped inside. I tugged off my boots, trying not to track snow across the floor, and glanced around. It was cozy, with simple furniture and a mix of photos on the walls—some of Emily and Cole, others of horses, and one or two of his family and their friends.

Cole was in the kitchen, ladling chili into bowls and garnishing each bowl with shredded cheese and cilantro. He grinned when he saw us. "Just in time. Hope you brought an appetite."

"Starving," Emily said, bouncing over to kiss him on the cheek before grabbing a bowl.

I followed more slowly, glancing around. I'd been here a couple of days ago, sure, so it wasn't my first time seeing it, but it was maybe the first time I'd really paid attention to the vibe. The space felt homey, but in a way that made me acutely aware of how temporary my visit was

.

Before I could dwell on it, there was a knock at the door, and Emily rushed to open it. Chase and Kate stepped inside, both bundled up against the cold.

"Hey!" Emily said, hugging them both. "Good grief, come in before you freeze!"

Kate smiled bashfully, pulling off her gloves. But when she held them in her hand, everyone saw the ring.

For a second, there was only silence. Then Emily gasped. "Is that—? Oh my gosh!"

Kate's cheeks turned pink as she nodded. "He proposed on Thursday night."

"Finally!" Cole said, walking over to slap Chase on the back. "Took you long enough, man."

Chase grinned, looking uncharacteristically bashful himself. "And here I thought I was rushing things."

"Hey," Cole laughed, "when you know, you know."

Emily grabbed Kate's hand, examining the ring. It wasn't big, but it was beautiful—a ruby solitaire flanked by two small diamonds, set in a bezel that looked both sturdy and elegant.

"It's perfect," Emily said.

Kate smiled softly. "I love it. It won't catch on anything while I'm working, and... well, rubies have always been my favorite. Chase must've been keeping notes."

"I pay attention sometimes," Chase said with a shrug, but the warmth in his eyes as he looked at Kate said more than words.

"Congratulations!" I said, stepping forward. "Do you have wedding plans yet?"

Kate laughed, tucking her thick, frizzy hair behind her ear. "Not really. Morgan offered White Pines for the ceremony, which would be amazing."

My mind immediately started spinning. "You could decorate it with garlands, maybe some fairy lights in the rafters. And you could set up a rustic arch for the vows—"

Chase held up his hands, chuckling. "Not to throw cold water on the planning, but Kate and I talked about keeping it small. We'd rather save for a honeymoon."

Kate nodded. "Somewhere warm. Maybe California."

I wrinkled my nose before I could stop myself.

"Not a fan?" Kate asked, tilting her head. "I thought you lived there!"

"It's... expensive," I said carefully, not wanting to ruin the mood. "And I guess it's worth it if you like the beach. You could probably do better somewhere else."

Kate exchanged a look with Chase, then smiled. "We'll figure it out."

We settled around the small table, bowls of chili steaming in front of us. I took a cautious bite and was pleasantly surprised. It was hearty and full of flavor, with just the right amount of spice.

"This is amazing," I said, looking at Cole.

He grinned. "Family recipe. It's a good thing Trent's not here, or there wouldn't be enough for the rest of us."

Chase nodded. "That guy could eat his weight in chili and still ask for seconds."

I cleared my throat, setting my spoon down. "Speaking of Trent..."

Everyone looked at me expectantly.

"I was just wondering," I said, trying to sound casual. "Why doesn't Ridgeview market its beef as grass-fed and organic?"

Cole and Chase exchanged a glance. "What does Trent eating chili have to do with marketing cattle?" Cole wondered.

"Yeah, what do you mean?" Emily asked, her brow furrowing.

"Well, when Trent was showing me around yesterday, I noticed a lot of things that seem... different. Like the grazing rotations and the water systems. I don't know much about ranching, but it feels like Ridgeview is doing something special."

Cole shrugged, leaning back in his chair. "I guess it's not something we've thought much about. We aren't the only ones doing things like that."

"Well, what about Walker Ranch? They're a whole different kind of operation. Ridgeview feels more... personal. Custom, maybe.

Chase rolled his bite of cornbread around in his mouth so he could swallow it, then spoke up. "We all sell to the same buyers, so it hasn't seemed like a big deal."

"But it *is* different," I insisted. "You've got something unique—why not take advantage of that?"

Chase scratched his jaw, looking thoughtful. "Might be worth thinking about. We'd need to talk to Trent and Gage, though. They're the ones really running the operations there, so they'd have to be on board."

"Trent?" I asked, raising an eyebrow. "Can't imagine he'd be thrilled about the idea."

Cole chuckled. "Yeah, well, that's just Trent. But if it's good for the ranch, he'll listen."

I nodded, though my thoughts were already spinning. Ridgeview had something special, and it seemed like no one even realized it. The ideas were coming faster now, but I bit my tongue. One step at a time.

Trent

THE SMELL OF CHILI greeted me as I stepped into the kitchen, Gage just a step behind. The warmth hit like a wall after the biting cold outside, and I shrugged off my jacket, hanging it on the hook by the door.

Mom was at the table, her reading glasses perched on her nose as she squinted at the computer screen. A half-eaten bowl of chili sat beside her, forgotten, while she typed numbers into a spreadsheet.

"Boys," she said without looking up, "there's chili on the stove. Grab some before it gets cold."

"We'll take it," Gage said, his voice tired.

The day had been long. Too long. I could feel it in every joint, and the ache in my shoulders hadn't let up since we'd wrestled that busted gate back into place after dinner.

I filled a bowl and handed one to Gage, then poured myself a glass of milk. We ate standing at the counter, too tired to bother with plates or the table.

"You hear anything from Ethan or Liam?" I asked between bites.

"Not since earlier," Mom said, her tone distracted as she clicked at the keyboard. "Liam was brushing Hickory after chores. Ethan was tinkering with something in the shed. I told them to be in by nine, but I haven't seen them since."

I grunted. "Well, at least they did most of their chores."

"That's a win," Gage said, shoveling another spoonful of chili into his mouth.

When the bowls were empty, we both shuffled into the living room and sank onto the couch. The cushions were worn so thin you could feel the frame through them, but right then, it felt like the most comfortable seat in the world.

Gage stretched his legs out, tipping his head back. "You know," he started, "Evan Walker offered to sell me some cows."

I raised an eyebrow and lifted my head off the pillow—felt like I was pulling up an anchor chain with my ab muscles. "Evan Walker?"

"Yeah," Gage said, sitting up a little, too. "He's got some good breeding stock that he wants to cycle out of his herds—get some fresh blood into the mix. It'd be different genetics for us, too, solid additions to what we've got."

I leaned back, rubbing a hand over my face. "Feels like we're a long way from thinking about that right now."

He sighed, nodding. "Yeah. But it's worth keeping in mind."

The sound of a car pulling up outside broke the quiet, the headlights sweeping across the front window.

Gage frowned, turning his head toward the door. "You expecting anyone?"

"Nope."

We exchanged a glance, and I motioned toward the window. "Maybe the truant officer's here to pick up Ethan and Liam."

Gage snorted. "Not on a Saturday night."

Before either of us could get up to check, the door opened, and the sound of boots on the floor filled the entryway. Cole and Emily walked in first, brushing snow off their jackets. Chase and Kate followed, their laughter cutting through the quiet, and then... Lauren.

I stood up slowly, crossing my arms as I watched the group file in like they owned the place.

"What's this about?" I asked.

Cole grinned, clapping me on the shoulder. "We've got an idea to run by you."

"An idea?" Gage asked, hooking his thumbs in his belt.

Emily nodded, her cheeks pink from the cold. "Lauren had a thought about the ranch. Something we think could really work."

I glanced at Lauren, who was standing near the door, her arms crossed and her gaze fixed somewhere between the floor and the table.

I exhaled, tilting my head toward the table. "All right. Let's hear it."

I T WAS LIKE DEJA Vu when we stepped inside. The house smelled like chili and fresh-baked cornbread—did they plan that?—but the cozy warmth didn't do much to calm my nerves.

Trent had a faint scowl on his face, though I was starting to think that was just his neutral expression. Nora bustled in behind me, carrying a notepad and pen, filling the room like sunshine.

"What's this about an idea? I'm all ears."

Trent frowned at his mom. "You must have insider information."

"Emily *might* have texted me that they were on their way a few minutes ago. Sit down, Lauren," Nora said brightly, gesturing to a chair where there were already mugs set out beside a steaming teakettle. Apparently, she was excited to see us. That made one person, anyway.

I hesitated, trying not to let on that I suddenly had butterflies in my stomach. Why was I so tense? It wasn't like I hadn't pitched big ideas before—back in San Diego, I'd presented plans to executives who controlled multimillion-dollar budgets.

But this wasn't an executive boardroom. This was Ridgeview, and somehow, sharing this idea with regular people—people who would take everything I said personally—felt harder than it should've.

"Coffee?" Nora asked, already pouring a mug. "It's decaf. And don't you start," she said, pointing a finger at her two older sons.

Gage held up both hands in surrender, but Trent rolled his eyes and mumbled something about tasting like lukewarm dishwater.

But it would give me something to do with my hands while I talked, so I took the cup.

"Sure, thanks." I fiddled with my phone while she set the mug in front of me, her warm smile doing little to calm my nerves.

Trent dragged out an opposite chair and crossed his arms on the tabletop as he sat. "So, what's this idea Emily said you've been cooking up?"

"It's not a fully formed idea," I said quickly, swiping my phone screen to open my planning app. "More of a... suggestion."

Nora finished pouring coffee and sat down beside me. "Well, we'd love to hear it. Go on, honey."

I glanced between them—Nora, open and encouraging; Trent, skeptical and quiet—and took a deep breath.

"Okay," I started, typing on my phone screen as I talked. "So, yesterday, when you were showing me around, I noticed how Ridgeview does things differently. The grazing rotations, the solar-powered watering systems, the grass-fed-only approach—it's unique. And people, especially urban customers, care about that kind of thing. They're willing to pay for it."

Trent's brow furrowed, but he didn't interrupt.

I pressed on. "Right now, you're selling your beef through contracts and middlemen who take a big cut. But if you marketed directly to consumers—people in cities who want premium, locally raised, grass-fed beef—you could create a new revenue stream."

He raised an eyebrow. "Market directly? Like what, door-to-door sales?"

"Not exactly," I said, forcing a small smile. "Social media, a website with a clear brand story, maybe even subscription boxes for high-end cuts. You'd be giving people something they can't find at a grocery store."

Trent tapped his fingers on the table, and his eyes shifted up to bounce over each of his brothers. "And who's running this magical new operation? Because I'll tell you right now, we don't have the time or manpower for something like that."

I hesitated, glancing at Nora, who was nodding thoughtfully.

"Lauren's got a point," Nora said, tapping her pen against the table. "People *are* looking for more transparency these days. They want to know where their food's coming from. Some with food sensitivities don't want the grain-fed beef. And with the way you boys run this place, you've got a good story to tell."

"That doesn't answer my question," Trent said.

I squared my shoulders. "I can help. At least while I'm here. It's what I do for a living—building brand stories, creating marketing strategies. I could at least get you started."

Trent's eyes narrowed slightly, his skepticism clear. "And you're just going to do this for free? Take time out of your vacation to help a ranch you barely know?"

"I'm here," I said firmly, lifting my chin. "I'm not doing much else, and I'd like to help if I can. You're my sister's family now, so..."

The room went quiet, the only sound the faint hum of the refrigerator. Trent studied me for a long moment, his expression unreadable, and I had to resist the urge to fidget under his gaze.

"I'll think about it," he said finally, leaning back in his chair.

The knot in my stomach loosened slightly, but I wasn't sure if it was relief or just the fact that I'd survived the conversation.

"That's all I'm asking," I said, taking a sip of coffee to hide the way my hands were trembling. "Let me show you what I was going to suggest..."

I WANTED TO SHUT this crazy idea down right then and there, but the words didn't come.

Instead, I stared at her phone, not really understanding what she was trying to show me, but it didn't matter, anyway. My mind was already spinning with the logistics.

Who was supposed to pack this meat? We didn't exactly have a state-of-the-art processing facility. Refrigeration? Shipping? That was a whole separate business, and the overhead would bleed us dry before we even got started.

And then what? Let's say it worked—what kind of margins could we even expect? Not enough to justify the gamble. What if we couldn't move the product fast enough? What if it sat in freezers until we were eating the losses in fuel and power costs?

And what if it didn't work at all? We'd be losing valuable time and missing market deadlines. Once you pass up on the usual buyers, you can't just crawl back and expect them to take your stock later when they're too big for prime.

"This isn't realistic," I said finally, leaning back and crossing my arms. "What you're talking about—it's not how things work. There's a reason everyone uses the same market. It's predictable. It works."

Lauren tilted her head, her eyes narrowing slightly. "Does it, though? Because from what I'm hearing, it sounds like 'predictable' isn't cutting it anymore."

I frowned, her words striking closer to home than I wanted to admit.

She leaned forward, resting her elbows on the table. "Look, I get it. You think I don't know what I'm talking about because I'm a city girl who doesn't know the first thing about ranching."

I opened my mouth, but she cut me off with a pointed look. "But I *do* know how to get people's attention. That's my job. And I'm good at it."

"Good enough to pull this off?" I asked, arching a skeptical brow.

"Good enough to prove it to you," she shot back. Her tone was sharp, almost challenging, and for the first time, I saw a flash of the ambition that must've gotten her where she was in her career.

I frowned over at Gage, but he just shrugged. "Go on."

"I'll make you a bet," she said. "If you cooperate—give me access to the ranch, answer my questions, and trust me—I'll have Ridgeview's social media following over ten thousand by the end of the week."

I blinked. "Ten... *thousand?*"

She smirked. "Easily."

"That's impossible," I said flatly.

"Then try me," she said, sitting back with a self-assured shrug.

I glanced at Mom, who had been quietly listening the whole time. She twisted her untouched coffee mug between her hands, looking more serious than I'd seen her in weeks.

"She's got a point, Trent. I just finished going over the bills, and let me tell you—this ranch can't survive another year of 'predictable.' Not the way we're running now. We've had a few things break our way lately, but so far, it's just drops in the ocean. Something big has to change."

I opened my mouth to argue, but Mom held up a hand. "This might be a risk, but so is doing nothing. We've got to go big or quit. And I don't think any of us are ready to quit."

I looked at Gage, but he just shrugged. "She's right. What's the harm in trying?"

What was the harm? Sudden death rather than a slow, agonizing one, I guess. I sighed, running a hand over my face. Lauren was watching me, her smirk gone, her expression sharp and focused.

"Fine," I said finally, throwing up my hands. "Let's give the internet a show. At least if we go under, we'll go out with a bang."

Lauren's lips twitched, like she was suppressing a triumphant grin. I wasn't about to let her see me crack, so I focused on my empty coffee cup instead.

"Glad that's settled," Chase said suddenly. "Because we got somethin' better to talk about."

Everyone turned to look at him as he grinned and nodded toward Kate. She smiled, lifting her hand to show off a sparkling ring on her finger.

Mom gasped, clapping her hands together as she jumped up from her chair. "Oh my gosh! You're engaged!"

Kate giggled as she nodded. "Chase proposed Thursday night."

Squeals and hugs erupted, and Mom threw her arms around both of them at once, peppering them with questions about the wedding plans.

I stayed in my seat, glancing across the table at Lauren. She was smiling, but it didn't quite reach her eyes, and I realized I was doing the same thing.

We stared at each other for a moment, each of us holding on to a fake smile, before I finally looked away.

Eight

Trent

G AGE JABBED THE BUTTER knife into the dish, scooping out a chunk like it owed him money. He slapped it onto his toast, the knife scraping loud enough to make me wince.

"You're gonna break the plate if you're not careful," I said, my coffee mug halfway to my lips.

He didn't look up, just spread the butter in jerky motions. "We're really doing this?"

The smell of bacon frying on the stove mingled with the heavy silence hanging over the kitchen. Mom hummed to herself in the background, but Gage's question lingered like an unwelcome guest.

I grunted, leaning back in my chair. "Looks that way."

Gage finally glanced up, his eyes narrowing. "I don't get it. We've been running this place for years without someone swooping in to tell us how to sell our beef. Why do we need to change the plan now?"

Before I could answer, Mom stepped in from the pantry, wiping her hands on a towel. She gave us both a sharp look.

"You need a new plan. Or I can just shut the books down and call it quits."

The room went quiet except for the hiss of bacon in the skillet.

Gage sighed heavily, slapping his toast onto his plate. "Fine. But don't blame me if this whole thing blows up in our faces."

Mom raised an eyebrow. "It's not going to blow up if you actually listen and give it a shot. That girl knows what she's doing."

Gage muttered something under his breath, but he didn't argue further. He just pushed his chair back and stood, his plate still half-full.

"Where are you going?" I asked, frowning as he started toward the door.

"Chores," he said over his shoulder. "Some of us still have work to do."

"Wait a second—"

Gage paused in the doorway, glancing back with a crooked grin. "Ethan! Liam! Let's go."

The boys appeared from the hallway, already shrugging into their jackets. They didn't say a word, just shuffled toward the door like they'd been sentenced to a long day of manual labor.

"Hold on," I said, pushing my chair back. "I should be doing chores, too."

Gage stopped, turning back with a look I didn't like. "No, no," he said, holding up a hand. "You're the pretty one. You should be the one to deal with this."

I blinked. "What's that supposed to mean?"

Gage huffed, jamming his hands into his coat pockets. "It means you're the charming one, the one who knows how to talk to people. You're the perfect poster child for Ridgeview Ranch. This is your wheelhouse, not mine."

"Charming?" I repeated, more offended than flattered.

"Don't pretend you don't know it," Gage said, his grin widening. "I saw how heavy you were pouring it on with Cassie last summer.

Remember that rodeo? All those girls she had to beat out just to be the one on your arm? You were practically sparkling."

I bristled, crossing my arms. "That was different."

"Hope so," Gage said, winking before stepping out onto the porch.

The door clicked shut behind him, leaving me sitting there with my jaw tight and my coffee cooling in my hand.

Cassie. The name alone was enough to set my teeth on edge.

I muttered a curse under my breath, draining the rest of my coffee in one bitter gulp.

Charming. Right.

If Gage thought this was my wheelhouse, he was about to find out just how wrong he was.

B Y THE TIME HER car pulled up, I'd already made up my mind that this was going to be a colossal waste of time.

I leaned back against the porch railing, arms crossed, watching as the little compact skidded to a stop in front of the house. The thing looked even more ridiculous out here than it had stuck in the snowbank, its tires slipping every time she tried to crank the wheel.

Lauren climbed out, her hair perfectly smooth and shiny like she'd just stepped out of a salon, even though it was barely above freezing. She adjusted her coat and glanced up at me, her expression equal parts determination and annoyance.

"Morning," I called, my voice just loud enough to carry.

She slammed the car door and marched up the steps, heels clicking on the wood. "Let's get something straight," she said, pointing a finger at me. "I'm only here because Emily asked me to be. Don't make me regret it."

"Didn't say a word," I replied, holding my hands up in mock surrender.

Her eyes narrowed, but she didn't take the bait. Instead, she brushed past me, stepping into the house like she owned the place.

We sat at the kitchen table, the same one where Gage and I had been arguing over breakfast. Lauren set her laptop on the table, her polished nails tapping against the lid as she opened it.

"Okay," she said briskly. "Let's start with what makes Ridgeview unique."

I raised an eyebrow, leaning back in my chair. "You're the expert. Shouldn't you be telling me that?"

She shot me a look that could've melted a frozen water trough, but put on a sweet, professional smile. "I need to hear it from you. What do you think sets your ranch apart?"

I shrugged. "We don't do anything special. We just keep the herd healthy and try not to go broke in the process."

"That's what every ranch says. But not every ranch is grass-fed, no-grain, and uses sustainable practices like you do. Those things matter."

"To who?" I asked. "The buyers don't care. They're just looking at weight and quality."

Lauren leaned forward, her eyes sharp. "They don't care because you're not telling them to care. If you market your beef as grass-fed and organic, you'll attract a whole different kind of buyer—people who are willing to pay more for something they believe is better."

"And how do we even do that?" I asked, frowning. "We don't have the time or the manpower to drive around selling directly to people."

"You don't need to," she said, clicking her laptop open. The screen lit up, displaying a sleek website template. "That's the point of this. You build an online presence, connect with people through social media, and create a brand that stands out. People in cities—places like California or New York—will pay a premium for beef that's marketed the right way."

I rubbed a hand over my face, trying to keep up. "That sounds great in theory, but how do we even start? We don't have the resources to hire someone to run a website, let alone keep up with social media."

Lauren smirked, a little too smug for my liking. "That's where I come in."

"So, you're saying you'll do all this for us? Out of the goodness of your heart?"

Her smirk faltered, and for the first time, she looked a little uncomfortable. "I'm helping because Emily asked me to," she said, her tone stiff. "And because I think you have potential here. But if you don't want my help, just say so."

I studied her for a moment, watching the way her jaw tightened and her fingers curled slightly around the edge of the laptop. There was something else there—something she wasn't saying.

"Well," I said, leaning forward, "if you're the expert, prove it. Tell me how this actually works. Step by step."

Her eyes flashed, and I almost smiled. Almost.

"Fine. First, we'll take inventory of what you have—photos, videos, anything that tells Ridgeview's story. Then, we'll build a simple website. Nothing fancy, just something clean and professional. After that, we'll start creating content for social media—pictures, short videos, things that show what makes Ridgeview different."

"And who's doing all that?" I asked. "You or us?"

"We'll do it together," she said firmly. "I'll handle the technical side, but I'll need you to cooperate. You know this place better than anyone, so I'll need your input to make it work."

I leaned back again, crossing my arms. "So, you're saying I'll be doing most of the work."

Lauren exhaled sharply, pinching the bridge of her nose. "I'm saying it's a partnership. If you can't handle that, then this won't work."

For a moment, we just stared at each other.

Finally, from around the corner of the kitchen wall, Gage let out a low whistle. I hadn't even heard him come back in. "I like her," he said, grinning. "She's got guts."

Lauren shot him a glare, and I couldn't help but chuckle.

"All right," I said, holding up a hand. "We'll give it a shot. But if this turns into a waste of time—"

"It won't."

I scowled. She wasn't going to make it easy on me. And my family was going to hold my feet to the fire unless I cooperated, so I might as well get it over with.

"Fine," I said finally. "Let's get started."

Lauren

THE WIND HAD PICKED up by the time Trent and I stepped out of the barn. I clutched my coat tighter, wishing I'd opted for something thicker, but Trent seemed unfazed as he strode ahead, his boots kicking up loose clods of fresh snow so I could walk on the broken path.

"This," he said, pointing to a covered feed bin near the equipment shed, "is where we keep the grain for emergencies. Don't use it much since we're grass-fed, but it's good to have on hand if we have some bad doers."

I followed, trying to look interested as he launched into an explanation about how feed prices had been fluctuating for years and how that affected margins.

"Most folks around here use silage or a mix of grain and forage," he said, running a gloved hand along the edge of the bin. "It's cheaper up front, but long term, we stick to grass with some hay to supplement."

"Right," I said, scribbling notes on the little notepad I'd brought along. Not that I planned to use most of this information, but I needed to look like I was paying attention.

He led me toward the equipment shed, gesturing to a line of vehicles that looked like they'd seen better days.

"Tractor's down again," he said, frowning. "Water pump's shot. Parts are getting harder to find for this model, but we make do."

I glanced at the tractor in question, its hood open and guts exposed like it was waiting for surgery. "Doesn't seem ideal."

"It's not," he said, his tone flat. "But buying new isn't an option right now."

I hesitated, watching as he kicked a clump of snow off his boot. "Look, Trent," I said finally, "The broken tractor is interesting, but I don't think we need to feature every detail of your feed routines or repair logs in this project."

He turned to me, one eyebrow raised. "You don't?"

"No. What we need is personality. People don't connect with numbers and statistics—they connect with stories, with people. We need to show them what makes Ridgeview special, and that starts with you."

"Me?" he asked, his tone skeptical.

"Yes, you," I said, crossing my arms. "You're the one who knows this place inside and out. You're the one doing the work. That's what people want to see—someone they can root for."

He stared at me for a moment, then shook his head. "You've got the wrong guy for that. Gage is better at—"

"You," I interrupted. "Not Gage, not your mom, not your brothers. *You*."

Before he could argue, a loud *clang* echoed from the other side of the shed.

Trent's face altered from cynical to near disgust. "What now?" he muttered, striding toward the sound.

I followed, rounding the corner just in time to see Ethan crouched beside the tractor, a wrench in one hand.

"Thought I told you to finish cleaning the stalls," Trent snapped.

Ethan barely glanced up. "I did. And then I came here because this thing's been bugging me since yesterday."

Trent folded his arms, his jaw tight. "You're not supposed to mess with the equipment."

Ethan rolled his eyes. "Relax. I didn't break anything. Actually, I think I fixed it."

"Fixed it?" Trent repeated, stepping closer.

Ethan grinned, dropping the wrench and standing. "Yeah. Try it."

Trent shot him a skeptical look, but climbed into the tractor's cab. He turned the key, and after a sputter, the engine roared to life.

I covered my ears as the noise echoed through the shed. Trent cut the engine and hopped down, his expression a mix of surprise and irritation.

"What'd you do?" he asked, narrowing his eyes at Ethan.

"Cleaned out the line and adjusted the belt," Ethan said, shrugging like it was no big deal. "Wasn't that hard."

Trent stared at him for a beat, then nodded slowly. "Huh. Good work."

Ethan's grin widened, but he tried to hide it by grabbing his coat and walking away. "Told you I could fix it," he muttered.

As he disappeared into the barn, I turned to Trent. "Looks like you've got a mechanic in the making."

He shook his head, but there was a faint smile tugging at the corner of his mouth. "We'll see."

We were heading back toward the house when movement behind a little pine tree caught my eye. It wasn't human. Not a tractor, either. It was... I squinted. It looked like a horse's behind, if I was any judge. Just then, a scraggy tail flicked, erasing all doubt.

"Uh... is that horse supposed to be out?" I asked, pointing to the yard.

Trent followed my gaze and groaned. "Marty."

"Who's Marty?"

Trent started toward the animal, shaking his head. "Only the biggest pain in the tuchus you ever saw. He's twenty-nine this winter, but he thinks he's a dad-blamed colt."

The big, shaggy horse was ambling across the snow-covered yard like he didn't have a care in the world. A red feed bucket dangled from his mouth, swaying with every step.

"Does he always... escape like this?" I asked as Trent strode after him.

"Only when he feels like it," Trent grumbled. "Must've gotten bored again. He's a menace, that's what he is. Always getting into something, but we mostly just let 'im be. Keeps the lawn mowed in the summer. Mom's no help because she's always got some apple peelings or something for him on the porch."

"Why do you keep such a problem horse around here?"

Trent shot me a look over his shoulder. "What else are we supposed to do with him? What, were you looking for a pet to take back to California?"

"No, I just meant..." Trent was walking faster now, and I had to hurry to keep up. "If he's that old, and he gets into trouble..."

"He's healthy. And he was Dad's horse," Trent retorted, with a hint of softness in his voice at those last words. "You old miscreant," he muttered to the horse. "I thought I fixed that latch."

Marty stopped by the porch, dropping the bucket and nosing at the door like he was planning to let himself in.

"No treats today, buddy," Trent said, grabbing the horse by the mane and steering him back toward the barn.

Marty snorted but followed willingly, even though Trent had no halter or rope. He just plodded along, his steps slow and deliberate.

As I watched them, an idea started forming in my head. *This*. This was what people wanted to see—the unpolished, real moments that made Ridgeview unique.

When Trent returned, brushing snow off his gloves, I was ready.

"That," I said, pointing to the barn. "That's what we need."

He frowned. "What are you talking about?"

"You," I said, gesturing to the horse. "Marty. The kid who fixed the tractor. The way you handle things around here. That's what's going to sell this place—not spreadsheets or feed bins. Just you being you."

Trent stared at me like I'd grown a second head. "You think people want to see me chasing a horse around?"

"Yes," I said, grinning. "Is he going to get out again?"

He scratched the back of his neck, pushing his hat forward a little. "Probably. Old buggar broke the latch I just fixed."

"Perfect. We're filming that."

Nine

Trent

THE FOUR-WHEELER GRUMBLED TO life beneath me as I pulled it out of the shed, the engine's low hum vibrating up through the seat. I glanced over my shoulder at Lauren, who was adjusting her scarf and checking her phone at the same time.

"You sure you're ready?" I asked.

She tucked her phone into her pocket and looked up. "Are you?"

I rolled my eyes, but I didn't argue. She climbed onto the back of the four-wheeler, her knees brushing against the backs of my legs as she settled in. We were both bundled up better than yesterday—she'd traded her city boots for something a little sturdier, though they were still too shiny to have seen much dirt. I'd bet money that Emily took her to the farm store yesterday and made her buy them.

"Same route as before?" I asked, kicking the machine into gear.

"Same route," she said, pulling her phone back out of her coat pocket. "But slower this time. And don't worry about getting it per-fect—I'll edit it later."

I grunted and eased us forward.

The first stop was the pasture, where the cattle were clustered around the windbreak, grazing through patches of snow. Lauren hopped off the four-wheeler as soon as we stopped, raising the camera.

"Okay," she said, turning to me. "Go ahead and explain what they're doing here."

I glanced at the camera, then back at the cows. "Uh... they're grazing."

She lowered the camera, giving me a look. "You're going to have to give me more than that."

"They're eating the grass we left standing in the summer," I said, shifting my weight uncomfortably. "It's called stockpiling. Saves us money on hay, keeps the land healthier—"

"Look at me, not the cows," she interrupted, gesturing with her hand. "And don't overthink it. Just talk like you're explaining it to a friend."

I tried again, fumbling over the same points but getting halfway through before stopping. "Wait, can I start over?"

"No," she said firmly, lowering the camera.

"No?"

"I want the mistakes. They make it real. If people wanted a polished ad, they'd watch a commercial. This is better."

I stared at her, my brow furrowed. "You want me to sound like an idiot?"

"Not like an idiot," she said, rolling her eyes. "Like a human."

"Well, I can't very well sound like a dog, can I? What exactly do you want?"

She stepped closer, the camera still in her hand but lowered to her side. "Relax," she said softly. "You don't have to impress anyone. Just be yourself."

Her gloved hand rested briefly on my arm, and I froze, caught off guard by the light touch. Even through the layers of fabric, it was enough to send a flicker of warmth up my arm.

Our eyes met, and for a second, the cold air around us seemed to disappear. Her gaze softened, and I thought I saw a hint of something—sympathy, maybe, or understanding.

"Just talk," she said. "You're good at this, even if you don't think you are."

I cleared my throat. "Fine. But don't say I didn't warn you."

We went through the rest of the tour at what felt like a snail's pace. Every time I stopped to explain something—the water trough, the grazing rotations, the windbreaks—Lauren was there with the camera, pointing it at me like she was hunting for the perfect shot.

"Why do you rotate the cows like this?" she asked at one point, holding the camera steady, her gloved hands wrapped tightly around it.

I shifted my weight, glancing between her and the cattle. They were clustered together, heads down, grazing in the snow-dappled pasture. "Gives the grass time to recover," I said. "If you let them graze wherever they want all the time, they'd kill it off. This way, the pasture stays productive longer."

She nodded slightly, but her gaze didn't waver from me. "And how do you decide when to move them?"

"It depends on the season," I said, kicking at a clump of frozen mud with the toe of my boot. "In summer, it's about how much they've grazed and how fast the grass is growing. In winter, it's about keeping them on the stockpiled forage as long as we can before we have to break into the hay stores."

"Stockpiled forage," she repeated. "That's just the grass you let grow tall before winter, right?"

"Yeah," I said, nodding. "You let it grow, then leave it standing. The snow actually helps insulate it, so it stays fresher longer. The cows dig through the snow to get to it."

She adjusted the camera slightly, zooming in on the cattle. "And that works better than feeding hay all winter?"

I growled and folded my arms. "Look, didn't we already do this? I've said all this before. Like six times."

Lauren paused the camera and gave me an exasperated look. "Yeah, and I'm going to take this all back and edit it. Chop it up, decide which bits sound the most authentic, and put them together to make a story."

"What if I don't want to be a 'story?' What's wrong with just... just being a guy trying to raise his cows?"

She sucked in a long sigh, her eyes tripping heavenward as she bit her lower lip. Probably trying to keep from biting my head off. "Nothing. That's *exactly* what I want. I want you to be the guy you were yesterday, when you were just showing me what you do. Don't act like I've heard it before, okay? *This*—" she held up her phone— "*hasn't* heard it. So, just... do your thing. Stop worrying about looking good or bad because that part is my job.

I stuck my tongue in my cheek, trying to come up with a good argument, but darn it if she didn't make sense. "Fine. Where were we?"

Lauren put her phone back up and hit the record button. "Stock-piling grass. You said it works better for you than feeding hay all winter."

I made myself swallow and release a breath. "For us, yeah. Hay's expensive to grow and even more expensive to buy. Stockpiling saves us money, and the cows stay healthier. They're eating what they're meant to eat, they're moving more, and they're not as exposed to parasites and mud."

Lauren lowered the camera for a moment, her brow furrowing as she processed what I'd said. "So, it's cheaper, healthier, and better for the land?"

"Exactly."

"Then why isn't every ranch doing it?"

I shrugged. "Takes planning. Takes more acres per cow, and it takes time. You've got to manage your pastures carefully all year round and stick to the rotations, or it won't work. A lot of folks just don't have the time, or they've got operations too big to make it practical."

She smiled, lowering the camera for a moment. "See? That wasn't so hard."

I shook my head, muttering under my breath as I turned back to the four-wheeler.

Lauren scurried to catch up, but she was slow to hop on behind me. She was swiping the screen of her phone, playing back snippets of the video like she was already piecing together the story she wanted to tell.

At the next stop, the solar-powered water trough, Lauren was back to firing off questions before I even had both feet on the ground.

"Explain how this works," she said, panning the camera over the trough as I walked up to it.

"It's motion-activated," I said, crouching beside the insulated basin. The words came out on autopilot, a repeat of what I'd told her yesterday, but this time, my attention wasn't on the trough. It was on her.

Lauren had her camera steady in one hand, the other tucked into her coat pocket. Her face was set in concentration, her brows drawing together just enough to make her look serious but not harsh.

"When the cows come close, the sensor triggers and the water fills up here," I continued, tapping the upper basin with a gloved finger.

She tilted her head slightly, her curls peeking out from under the edge of her knit hat. Her eyes flicked from the trough to me, and for a second, it felt like she was watching me more than the thing I was explaining.

"And once they're done drinking," I said, my voice faltering just a little under her gaze, "uh... the water drains back into the lower part, where it, uh, stays warm and fresh."

Lauren gave the faintest nod, her lips curving in approval. She didn't say anything, but the way her expression softened made it clear she thought I was doing fine. Better than fine, maybe.

"Warm?" she asked, her voice pulling me back. "Even in this weather?"

"It's designed to do that. *Especially* in this weather," I said, straightening up. "If the water's too cold, they don't drink as much, and that messes with their digestion." I paused, glancing at her again. Her cheeks were pink from the cold, her breath forming faint clouds in the air, but she didn't look like she felt the chill. "Keeping it warm encourages them to drink more."

She nodded again, zooming in on the trough. "And you don't need heaters or anything? Just the solar power?"

"Just the solar and the movement of the water in the chamber," I said, though my focus was wandering now. She was tilting her head again, the movement small but deliberate, her curls brushing the edge of her coat collar.

"That's incredible," she murmured, almost to herself.

I didn't reply right away, watching as she lowered the camera and took a step closer to the trough. Her boots skidded a little in the packed snow, and for a moment, she just stared at the water like it was the most fascinating thing she'd ever seen.

Her face was so open now, her usual sharp edges smoothed away by something I couldn't quite name. It wasn't just curiosity—it was respect, like she actually cared about what we were doing here.

I cleared my throat, breaking the silence. "Ready for the next stop?"

She turned back to me, her eyes meeting mine, and for a moment, I forgot what I'd just asked.

"Ready," she said, her voice steady but light, like the smile tugging at the corners of her mouth.

I nodded, turning back to the four-wheeler before I let myself smile too much. The last thing I needed was to get distracted now, but her face lingered in my mind as I started the engine, soft and serious all at once.

The windbreak came into view as we crested the hill, the bare trees standing in a neat line against the snow-covered pasture. The sight of them usually gave me a quiet sense of pride—a reminder that some things we'd done right, even when everything else felt like a gamble.

Lauren raised her camera, angling it toward the trunks. "These are young. When did you plant them?"

"Six years ago," I said, slowing the four-wheeler to a stop. "The last project my dad was here for, actually. They're just starting to make a difference now."

I hopped off, glancing at her as I gestured toward the trees. Her camera followed me, but her eyes didn't leave my face.

"In the winter, they block the wind," I said. "Keeps the cows warmer. In the summer, they give shade. It's a small thing, but it helps."

"Helps the cattle?"

"Helps everything," I said, crouching to brush the snow off a patch of frozen grass near the base of the nearest trunk. "Less wind means less erosion. The roots hold the soil in place, and the trees hold moisture, which helps the grass grow better."

I stood and dusted my gloves off, watching as she tilted her head, her gaze shifting from the trees to me.

"You've really thought this all through," she said, the camera momentarily forgotten in her hand.

I let out a short laugh, shaking my head. "It's not about being clever. It's about staying in business. If we don't take care of the land, it won't take care of us."

Her eyes lingered on me, soft and steady, like she was seeing past the words. For the first time all day, she didn't have a follow-up question.

I cleared my throat, suddenly uncomfortable under her gaze. There was something about the way she looked at me—not judgmental, not skeptical, just... understanding. Like she got it, or at least wanted to.

She shifted her weight, finally breaking eye contact as she glanced back at the trees. "You make it sound so simple."

"It's not," I said, my voice coming out rougher than I intended. "Most days, it's anything but."

She nodded, her camera still rolling like she was hoping to catch me saying something else, and for a moment, we just stood there in the cold.

Her scarf had slipped slightly, revealing the edge of her jaw, pink from the wind. The curls escaping from under her hat danced in the breeze, catching the last light of the day.

I looked away quickly, turning my attention back to the trees. "Anything else you need to see?"

"Not right now."

I glanced at her again, half-expecting her to start firing off another round of questions, but she just smiled faintly, her expression thoughtful.

"All right," I said, climbing back onto the four-wheeler. "Let's head back."

Lauren was still fiddling with her phone as she settled behind me, and she had to pause mid-way, resting one hand on my shoulder to steady herself. It was like that time when Gage threw me into the electric fence—a bolt of fire racing from the roots of my hair all the way to my toes. My hand slipped on the clutch, and I accidentally killed the engine.

Lauren didn't seem to notice that I had suddenly turned into a lightning rod. She just settled behind me—feeling a *lot* warmer against my back than she did earlier.

"Good grief, it's cold," she said with a hiss and a shiver. "You're really out here all the time? We need to make sure to show that in the videos." And then she burrowed a little, against my shoulder, hiding her face from the wind.

I tried to swallow, but my throat broke. "I... um... yeah." I flexed my hand and fired up the quad again. "Every day."

"We're totally using that." And that was when she just... put her arms around my middle.

I blinked, and my mouth hung open until I felt my tongue starting to get frostbite. She just... Why wasn't she using the cargo rails like before? They were still there, right? She could just...

"Oh, that's better," she announced. "Much warmer—hope you don't mind. It's a wonder you have fingers and toes left, working out here all the time. Do you have more to do out here, or can we go back now?"

Go back. Right. Good idea. "Uh... Yeah." I cleared my throat and eased the throttle and the clutch, hoping I didn't kill it again like a bonehead.

"This was good," she said over the engine noise. "I think we got a lot of great material."

I snorted and turned my head back a little to reply. "I felt like an idiot half the time."

I felt her body rocking against me—she must have been shaking her head. "You weren't. You're a natural, even if you don't know it yet."

I rolled my eyes but didn't argue. There was something in her tone—something almost reassuring—that made me wonder if she believed that more than I did.

"Just wait until you see the footage," she said, leaning... oh, man, she was leaning *closer*, just so I could hear her. "You're going to love it."

"Doubt it," I muttered, but I just kept driving.

By the time we got to the barn, I felt like a frog trying to hop out of its own skin. How could a guy be a popsicle on the outside but boiling lava on the inside at the same time? I'd need a quick hose-down in the shower, but I couldn't make up my mind whether it should be hot or cold.

It didn't help that now, every time I looked at Lauren, I got nervous about that blasted camera of hers. I'd lost count of how many times I'd stumbled over my words or forgotten what I was supposed to say, and Lauren didn't let a single one of those moments slide.

"Let's get one more shot of you moving the cows," she said, blowing some warm air up inside her gloves before she fished her phone back out of her coat pocket. "Why are these up here by the house when the others are far out in the field?"

"They gotta go somewhere," I reasoned. "'Sides, these are the ones getting closer to market weight. We're giving them some haylage just to finish them, but they're grazing, too."

"Great. Show me how you take care of them."

I sighed, opening the gate and stepping into the pen. The cows lumbered toward me, their breath fogging in the cold air as they jostled to follow me.

"Don't forget to smile," she called.

I glared at her over the gate. "Only an insane man smiles when he's working cows. Want me to get locked up in the looney bin?"

"Just... act like you like them!"

"I do. I like to eat them."

Lauren rolled her eyes. "Come on, Trent. Stop trying to play the macho cowboy. I saw you treating a huge old horse like a big teddy bear and checking each cow like you know its name, its mother, and where it likes to be scratched."

I blinked at her. "Because I do."

"Then show it!"

My scowl deepened. "I'm telling you, this is ridiculous."

"It's perfect," she said, the camera focused squarely on me.

I muttered something under my breath and opened the gate. The cows sprang through, with awkward bucks and kicks and even a few jumping up to push their fellows through faster. They'd be out on that field for the next couple of days. I wasn't planning to move them until tomorrow, but... well, they could just as well go now, and Lauren was standing there with that camera of hers, and... anyway, it was fine. I could play along for the camera. Wasn't like anything was going to come of it, anyway.

Lauren lowered the camera, a satisfied grin on her face. "See? You're a natural."

"Yeah, sure," I said, brushing the frost off my gloves from the metal gate. "Remind me to never do this again."

She laughed, tucking the camera into her pocket. "You're going to thank me when this all works out."

I didn't say anything, but as we walked back toward the house, I found myself glancing at her out of the corner of my eye. For all her city polish and big ideas, there was something about her that was starting to make sense.

Maybe.

Ten

Lauren

Back at my mom's apartment that evening, I kicked off my new mud boots by the door and dropped my bag onto the floor. Every part of me felt heavy—from my legs to my eyelids—but my mind wouldn't slow down.

I flopped onto the couch with a groan, throwing an arm over my face.

"Rough afternoon?" Mom asked from the kitchen. The clink of mugs and the hum of the kettle told me she was making her evening tea.

I peeked out from under my arm. "Let's just say Trent Langton is officially the most stubborn human being I've ever met."

She chuckled, coming over to set a steaming mug on the coffee table. "Give him time. That boy's been through a lot. He just needs to trust you."

"Trust me?" I propped myself up on one elbow. "He barely looks at me without rolling his eyes."

Mom raised an eyebrow, her expression annoyingly serene. "Well, then prove him wrong."

"Sure, easy," I muttered as she headed back into the kitchen.

The tea smelled like chamomile, but I didn't touch it. Instead, I pulled out my laptop, determined to make some progress on the footage.

The screen glowed to life, and I opened the folder where I'd dumped the videos from today's tour. There were over a hundred clips, some just a few seconds long, others stretching several minutes. I clicked on the first one and watched as Trent's face filled the screen.

He was explaining the water trough, crouched beside it with his gloves dusted in snow and his hat tilted just enough to shade his eyes. The words he'd fumbled earlier sounded smoother now as I listened, his low voice grounding even the most mundane details.

I paused the video, leaning closer. His face was frozen mid-sentence, his lips slightly parted, and his eyes intent on the trough. There was a warmth to his expression, subtle but real—like he was talking to someone he trusted, even if he didn't realize it.

I hit play again, fast-forwarding through a few scenes that looked solid, but I wasn't seeing that *thing* I needed to see.

The next clip showed him standing by the barn, scratching that old black horse, Marty, behind the ears. Marty leaned into him, his massive head practically resting on Trent's shoulder.

"You're spoiled, you know that? I oughta make you earn your keep around here, you old plug," Trent muttered, but the smile tugging at his mouth betrayed him.

I slowed the playback, watching the way he ran his gloved hand down Marty's neck, the kind of easy affection you didn't fake. It was the same with the dogs in another clip—they circled his boots as he tossed a stick, their tails wagging furiously, and he laughed when one of them tripped over its own feet.

I found myself smiling without meaning to.

The next clip was back at the windbreak. Trent was explaining the roots and erosion, but I wasn't focused on his words. My attention was on the way his brows furrowed as he gestured toward the trees, his gloved hand cutting through the cold air. You could *see* how cold it was, and that was what I'd been hoping for. His hat had slipped forward because he'd been rubbing the back of his neck, the way he did whenever I made him repeat something. He pushed it back absently, his gaze flicking toward the camera once before darting away.

I paused again, zooming in slightly. The lighting wasn't great—late afternoon shadows had turned everything a little gray—but there was something in the way his eyes crinkled at the corners that caught me.

I leaned closer, debating whether to tweak the brightness or leave it as it was. My finger hovered over the editing tool when I heard Mom's footsteps behind me.

"What're you working on?" she asked, peering over my shoulder.

I jumped, snapping the laptop shut instinctively. "Nothing!"

She crossed her arms, smirking. "Didn't look like nothing."

"It's just footage from today," I said, my voice a little too high-pitched. "I was—uh—fixing the lighting."

"Fixing the lighting?" she repeated, arching a brow. "Or staring at that cowboy's face like you're ready to frame it and hang it over the mantel?"

I felt heat rush to my cheeks. "Mom!"

She laughed, backing away with her hands raised. "All right, all right. I'll leave you to your... lighting adjustments."

I groaned, burying my face in my hands as she disappeared into the other room.

When I reopened the laptop, Trent's face was still frozen on the screen. I stared at it for a second longer, my mom's teasing words echoing in my head.

I wasn't drooling over him.

I *wasn't.*

Before I could defend myself further, my laptop chimed with a notification. The corner of the screen lit up with a new email, and the sender's name made my breath hitch.

Rebecca.

I clicked it open, the teasing moment with Mom already fading into the background.

Lauren,

Just wanted to give you an update. Things are looking somewhat better on our end. Still some rough patches to smooth out with some of our clients, but overall, I'm optimistic. Let's connect early next week to discuss where we stand.

Rebecca

The tight knot in my stomach loosened slightly. "Looking somewhat better" wasn't exactly a glowing endorsement, but it wasn't a disaster, either.

I leaned back in my chair, rereading the email as if the words might magically change into something more concrete. When they didn't, I sighed and let my eyes drift to the rest of my inbox.

Another email caught my attention, this one from Stacy—her signature in the preview standing out in its usual cheery, bold font. I clicked on it, bracing myself for her blend of gossip and unsolicited advice.

*Girl, you won't believe this. I was talking to Darren in Legal (yes, **that** Darren), and guess what? He says he's had a thing for you for a while now. Why didn't you tell me he was so into you?! It was that post that did it, you know. He thought you were seeing someone, and when he saw that, he said he figured he might as well ask you out before I set you up on another blind date. Anyway, I'm thinking we set something* *up when you get back. Drinks? Dinner? Something fun. I'll be nice and bring Ryan along, we'll make it a double date. Let me know what you think.*

-Stacy

I stared at the email, torn between amusement and disbelief. Darren? The polished, confident lawyer with the killer smile. Any other time, the idea might have intrigued me.

But now? I glanced back at Rebecca's email, the words "rough patches" and "discuss where we stand" still lingering in my mind. And Stacy wanted me to just... jump back in. Like I hadn't torpedoed—or nearly torpedoed—my whole career. Sure, just go out with the successful guy with a straight avenue to the top. No problem. That wouldn't look desperate at *all*.

I shook my head, closing the email and pushing the laptop a little farther away. Drinks with Darren could wait. All of it could wait.

I was here, in Big River Valley, and for better or worse, I had something else in front of me.

My fingers hovered over the keyboard, then slowly pulled the laptop back toward me. The screen lit up again, the paused frame of Trent's face filling the monitor.

His expression was caught mid-smile, one of those rare, fleeting moments when the tension left his features, and something softer took its place.

I hesitated for half a second, then hit play.

The rest of the evening passed in a blur of editing. I clipped together moments that highlighted the ranch's quirks: Marty's escape, the dogs' antics, the windbreak's trees swaying in the cold breeze.

And Trent.

I didn't mean to focus on him so much, but every time he laughed, every time his expression mellowed into something deep and thoughtful, it added something to the story I was trying to tell.

It wasn't just about the ranch. It was about the people who made it what it was.

I leaned back, rubbing my eyes as I watched the rough cut one more time. Trent's voice filled the room, deep and thoughtful, and I couldn't help but think Mom might be right about one thing.

Maybe *I* wasn't the one who needed to earn *his* trust.

Maybe Trent needed a chance to see himself the way I was starting to see him.

S UNLIGHT STREAMED THROUGH THE curtains, brighter than I wanted it to be. I groaned, rolling over and squinting at the clock. Almost nine.

I hadn't meant to sleep this late, but after staying up past midnight editing video footage, I'd completely crashed.

Dragging myself out of bed, I grabbed my robe and padded to the window. Down below, the shop's "Open" sign, the one hanging from the metal frame someone had welded for Mom, swayed gently over the sidewalk. If I held my breath, I could hear my mom bustling around downstairs, probably sweeping up and moving racks into position for the day. Guilt scalded my brain. She was already down working, and I was just barely rolling out of bed.

I'd been here days already and hadn't spent more than a few fleeting hours with her. That had been the one good thing about this enforced "holiday"—reconnecting with the mom I'd hardly seen in the last five years. But between trips to Ridgeview and getting sucked into work, I'd let her fend for herself during one of her busiest weeks of the year.

No more excuses.

After throwing on jeans and a sweater, I made my way downstairs. The faint smell of cinnamon pinecones wafted over me as I stepped into the shop. Mom was already in full swing, chatting with a customer over a rack of sweaters while she carefully folded some scarves.

She glanced up when she saw me. "Morning, sleepyhead!"

"Morning," I said sheepishly. "Need any help?"

Her eyebrows lifted in surprise, but she smiled. "Sure. I've got a pile of clothes in the back that need tagging. They're already sorted in piles by price, so you should be able to find what's what. And if you're feeling brave, you can tackle the Christmas display by the window. I don't know, it just looks kind of slap-dash. It's been bothering me all week."

"On it," I said, grabbing the tagging gun from the counter.

For the next hour, I worked my way through a mountain of clothes, attaching price tags and organizing the racks. The shop had that comfortable, cluttered charm that was right out of some cheesy movie—a mix of clothes, books, old toys, and Christmas decorations, all crammed into the small space in a way that somehow worked.

As I sorted through a box of ornaments, my thoughts drifted to Ridgeview. The footage I'd edited last night was solid, but I needed to think bigger if this was going to work.

A website was a no-brainer—simple, clean, and focused on their story. Then there were the social media platforms. Instagram for the photos and reels, definitely. Facebook for the local crowd, and maybe TikTok if I could convince Trent to go along with it. Twitter was probably a waste of time for a ranch like Ridgeview, but Pinterest could be useful for recipe ideas featuring grass-fed beef. Nora Langton would be the face of that project.

I mentally sketched out the first few steps: set up the accounts, choose a consistent logo and handle, create a batch of introductory posts, and schedule them to go live over the next two weeks. It would take some work to gain traction, but I knew how to build momentum.

The door jingled, but I wasn't waiting on customers. I'd be terrible at that—didn't really know where anything was, and if someone wanted to haggle, I'd be in over my head. I just kept on working.

"Morning, Cassie," my mom said, her voice friendly but not overly warm.

I glanced up briefly. The woman who'd just walked in looked every bit the cowgirl—tight jeans, a rhinestone belt, and a jacket that screamed "rodeo circuit." Her nails were painted a bright, glossy red, and she carried herself with a kind of restless energy, like she'd rather be anywhere else but had soiled herself to come here.

She barely acknowledged Mom's greeting, heading straight for a rack of jeans and flipping through them with quick, impatient movements.

I returned to tagging clothes, but I couldn't help noticing how she kept glancing toward the window, her shoulders tense.

"Find what you're looking for?" Mom asked after a few minutes.

"Yeah," Cassie muttered, pulling a pair of jeans off the rack and walking to the counter.

I busied myself organizing some scarves, but I could hear every word of their exchange.

"That'll be fifteen," Mom said, ringing her up.

Cassie fished some crumpled bills out of her pocket and handed them over, avoiding eye contact.

The door jingled again, and I looked up to see Emily walking in, her face brightening when she spotted me.

"There you are!" she said, striding toward me.

"Hey, Em," I said, smiling.

Before I could say more, Emily's gaze shifted to the counter, and her smile faltered. "Oh. Hi, Cassie."

Cassie stiffened, gripping the bag Mom handed her. "Emily," she said flatly, her tone giving nothing away.

"Good to see you," Emily said, her voice careful. "How've you been?"

"Fine," Cassie said shortly.

An awkward silence hung between them for a moment before Cassie nodded at Mom, muttered a quick "Thanks," and bolted for the door.

The bell jingled as it swung shut behind her, and I let out a low whistle. "What's her problem?"

Emily shook her head, looking half-amused, half-uncomfortable. "That's Cassie. She's... complicated."

I raised an eyebrow. "Complicated how?"

Emily hesitated, then shrugged. "She and Trent used to date."

My head snapped toward the window, where a banged-up red compact car was wheeling and skidding out of the icy parking lot. "*Her?*"

Mom was wagging her head with a knowing... and somewhat disapproving... frown. "Crazy, right? He got the looks and brains in the divorce. She got all the angst."

"Mom!" Emily laughed. "Don't make it sound like they were serious." She whirled to me, pointing at my chest. "They *weren't* serious. Just clearing that up. They only dated for like six months, and it should've been a lot less than that."

I held up my hands. "Why do I care?"

Emily shrugged. "I didn't say you did."

"Well, I don't."

"Good. Hey, how about a coffee break? I stopped by Kelli's place—she gives me discounts." Emily pointed at the counter, and I hadn't realized until just then that there was a drink holder with three disposable cups sitting there. "Whaddaya say, Laur? Iced oat milk Americano with a splash of vanilla for you, right? Don't know how you drink cold coffee when it's this cold outside, but whatever. I got Mom a pumpkin spice, and I..." She pulled the cups out, handing them each to us in turn. "I got the peppermint mocha."

"Mmmm...." Mom put the plastic lid to her lips and just inhaled that coffee like it was nourishing her soul. "Nobody does pumpkin spice like the Coffee Wagon."

I wrinkled my nose as I sucked on my straw. "You can have it. I'd go into a sugar coma."

Emily groaned as she tried the first sip of hers. "It's not the sugar. It's the *cream*. You gotta try this."

I grinned, shaking my head and raising my brows at my little sister. Well... not so little anymore. She was married and seemed to have her life figured out better than I did. But she still chugged her coffee like a teenager.

I lowered my cup, watching them, and smiled when Emily came up for air. "So..." I hesitated. "You're not kidding me, right? *That* twitchy chick... and Trent Langton?"

Emily's laugh was short and almost sheepish. "I know, right? Some things just don't make sense."

"Yeah, no kidding," I muttered, glancing toward the door where Cassie had just disappeared.

Eleven

Trent

THE TRACTOR WAS STILL sitting in the same spot it had been for two weeks. It started now, thanks to Ethan, but something was still wrong. I hadn't had time to mess with it, or the money to hire Bobby Eckhart to come fix it, so I'd been using the smaller one that barely got the job done. Meanwhile, a hundred-grand piece of equipment was just sitting there, half-covered in snow and waiting for a miracle—or for me to find time to figure out what was wrong. At least, that's what I'd resigned myself to before walking out this morning and seeing Ethan elbow-deep in the engine compartment.

The kid didn't even flinch when I came up behind him.

"You know it's not polite to mess with a man's equipment without asking," I said, folding my arms.

Ethan glanced over his shoulder, a wrench in one hand and a streak of grease on his cheek. "Figured you'd just say no."

I couldn't argue with that. "What're you trying to do?"

"Adjust the timing belt," he muttered, turning back to the engine. "I looked it up online. Think it's part of why it's not firing right."

I raised an eyebrow. "You looked it up?"

He shrugged like it was no big deal, but I could see the faint twitch of pride in his expression. "Yeah. It's not that hard to figure out."

I leaned in, watching him work. He moved with surprising confidence, his hands steady even as he navigated the mess of parts. "You're not bad at this," I admitted.

Ethan didn't respond, but the corner of his mouth twitched.

We worked in silence for a while, passing tools back and forth as I gave him pointers here and there. For a kid who barely said a word most days, Ethan was focused and quick to catch on. His movements were careful but confident, like he'd spent more time fixing things than anyone had given him credit for.

"Hold that steady," I said, watching as he tightened a bolt on the timing belt. He nodded without looking up, his lips pressed into a thin line.

After a while, I straightened, brushing the snow off my gloves. "I'm going to feed the stock. You go ahead with what you're doing. Just... don't blow anything up."

He smirked faintly, a rare glimmer of humor flashing across his face.

I headed off toward the barn, the cold making my ears hurt as I trudged across the yard. I hadn't bundled up for this. Feeding wasn't supposed to be my chore today, but if the kid was making himself useful elsewhere, I figured I'd pick up the slack. The horses were banging on their stall doors, waiting with all the patience of a squirrel as I forked out hay from the stacks.

It didn't take long, but by the time I made it back to the tractor, Ethan hadn't budged. He was still crouched by the engine, his breath puffing in the cold air as he worked.

"Didn't lose any fingers, did you?" I asked, stepping up beside him.

"Not yet," he muttered, glancing at me briefly before returning his attention to the wrench in his hand.

I crouched beside him, watching as he adjusted the belt with practiced precision. He worked like a kid who didn't have much else to rely on—like fixing the tractor was a puzzle he could solve if he just tried hard enough.

After a few minutes, I grabbed another tool and joined him. The minutes stretched into an hour, then another. Neither of us said much, but the quiet was comfortable.

"Hand me that socket," I said, gesturing toward the pile of tools. Ethan passed it to me without hesitation, wiping his grease-streaked hands on his jeans.

"You've done this before," I said after a while—more observation than question.

He shrugged. "Messed around with dirt bikes back at the group home. One of the guys there taught me how to fix 'em up."

"Dirt bikes, huh?" I said, glancing at him.

"Yeah. Nothing fancy. Just junkers people didn't want anymore. This is... a bit bigger."

I nodded, tightening a bolt. "Still. It's good work. Takes patience."

He didn't respond, but his posture seemed to relax slightly.

It wasn't until I leaned back to check my watch that I realized how much time had passed.

"Wait... it's Monday. What time's your bus come through?" I asked, brushing the snow off my gloves again.

Ethan froze, his hand stilling on the wrench.

"Ethan," I said, narrowing my eyes. "What time?"

"...Seven thirty," he muttered, not meeting my gaze.

I stared at him. "And what time is it now?"

He hesitated, then glanced at the faint sunlight creeping higher over the horizon. "... Probably... after nine?"

I groaned, standing up and shaking my head. "Kid, why didn't you say something?"

Ethan shrugged, avoiding my eyes. "Didn't think you'd care."

"Well, I do. Get your stuff. I'll drive you."

He hesitated, like he wasn't sure if I meant it, then finally wiped his hands on his jeans and grabbed his backpack from the porch steps.

THE DRIVE TO THE school was quiet at first. Ethan slumped in the passenger seat, staring out the window as the fields blurred by. I kept my eyes on the road, letting him have the silence if that's what he needed.

Halfway there, he spoke. "One time, when I missed the bus, my mom drove me."

I glanced at him, careful not to say anything that might make him shut down. "Yeah?"

"She was mad, though," he added, his voice flat. "Said it was my fault for not waking up on time. Liam made it, but I didn't. Didn't talk to me the whole way."

I tightened my grip on the wheel. "Sounds rough."

Ethan shrugged, the motion stiff, like the memory was caught somewhere between shame and defiance. "Wasn't the first time. She... she just had a lot going on."

I waited, my grip easing on the wheel as he stared out the window, his reflection blurred in the glass. "A lot going on" was the kind of phrase kids used when they didn't know how to explain the adults in their lives.

"She always came through, though," he said suddenly, his voice quieter now, like he wasn't sure if he believed it himself. "Even when she was mad, she always got me there."

I nodded slowly. "That's something."

"Yeah," he said, but his tone was hollow. He shifted in his seat, crossing his arms as his gaze dropped to the floorboard. "She'd stop at the gas station on the way, get one of those coffee things in a can, you know?"

"Yeah."

"She'd get me one of those powdered donuts, the little white ones," he continued, his words coming faster now. "She said they were my reward for being a pain in her butt." He gave a short, humorless laugh, like he wasn't sure if it was supposed to be funny or not.

I didn't say anything, just let him talk.

"She'd blast music the whole way, stuff from when she was a teenager—some band I can't even remember. And she'd smoke out the window, but sometimes the wind would blow it back in, and I'd complain about it, and she'd tell me to quit whining. But she did throw her smoke out and roll the window up."

There was a small pause, and then he added, "That was a good day, I guess."

A good day.

I didn't know what to say to that. From the sound of it, his "good days" were the kind most kids would want to forget. But I could hear it in his voice—the thread of longing, like he was holding onto that memory because it was one of the only ones he had.

"She, uh..." I coughed. Good grief, what could I say? "... Sounds like she did her best."

"She tried," he said finally. "I think she really tried. She just... couldn't."

My throat tightened, but I kept my face neutral. "That's hard," I said quietly.

Ethan didn't respond. His jaw clenched, and his hands balled into fists on his lap. The moment passed, and the door slammed shut on whatever he'd been willing to share.

By the time we reached the school, his usual guarded expression was firmly back in place. He opened the door and hopped out, slinging his bag over one shoulder.

"Thanks," he said without looking at me.

"Hey, Ethan," I called before he shut the door.

He paused, glancing back at me, his eyes shadowed but searching.

"You did good with the tractor."

He stared at me for a second, like he was trying to decide if I meant it. Then he nodded once, quick and small, and disappeared into the building.

T HE DRIVE BACK TO Ridgeview was uneventful—until I hit Main Street and noticed a familiar little white compact car pulling out behind me.

I frowned, checking my mirrors as I turned onto the highway. The car stayed behind me, close enough to make my skin crawl.

When I turned off the main road toward the ranch, it followed.

"Figures," I muttered under my breath, gripping the wheel tighter.

By the time I pulled into the yard, the compact had come to a stop behind me. Lauren stepped out, her coat flapping in the wind, one hand clutching her bag.

"Morning," she called, her voice carrying over the squeaking of her boots on the snow.

"Morning," I said cautiously, climbing out of the truck.

She came closer, brushing a strand of hair out of her face. "I've got something to show you. Do you have a few minutes?"

I hesitated, glancing toward the house. Mom was probably inside, and the last thing I needed was for this to feel like some kind of social visit. Lauren... I could handle Lauren by herself, but Mom would get ideas.

"There's an office in the barn," I said, jerking my head in that direction. "Chase set it up for his drafting work. It's got heat."

"Works for me," Lauren said with a shrug, following me across the yard.

Inside the barn, the makeshift office was a small space walled off near the tack room. Chase had left a folding table, a couple of chairs, and an old space heater that hummed softly in the corner when I plugged it in.

Lauren set her bag on the table, pulling out her laptop and a stack of notes. "I've edited a few of the videos we shot, and I think they're starting to come together."

I leaned against the wall, crossing my arms as she powered up the laptop. Her fingers moved quickly over the keyboard, her brow furrowed in concentration.

"You really don't waste any time, do you?"

She glanced up briefly, her lips quirking. "Efficiency is key. That and timing. You've got to... what's that saying? Strike while the iron is hot?"

"Uh-huh," I muttered, watching as she pulled up a video file.

Before she could hit play, the barn door creaked open, and Mom's voice cut through the quiet. "Didn't know anyone was in here."

Lauren straightened, glancing over her shoulder as Mom appeared, a bucket of vet supplies in one hand.

"Just showing Trent some ideas," Lauren said.

Mom's gaze flicked between us, her eyes twinkling with something that made my neck heat up. "Well, don't let me interrupt," she said with a grin, disappearing back into the barn.

Lauren turned back to the laptop, but the corner of her mouth twitched like she was holding back a laugh.

"Something funny?" I asked, narrowing my eyes.

"Nothing at all," she said innocently, hitting play on the video.

Lauren

T HE BARN OFFICE SMELLED like old hay and motor oil, and the little space heater in the corner wheezed like it was on its last legs. I couldn't imagine how Chase ever got any drafting done out here, but it would have to do.

Trent leaned back in the metal chair across from me, his arms crossed over his chest. His hat was tipped low enough to cast a shadow over his eyes, but the hard set of his jaw told me everything I needed to know.

"You've got a plan," he said flatly. "Let's hear it."

I tapped the laptop's trackpad, pulling up a few notes I'd jotted down. "Okay, first step is building Ridgeview's online presence. Social media, a website, the works. I already have a draft of that, but I want you to look at it. We need to get your story out there—the ranch, the cattle, the family behind it all. People want to feel connected to what they're buying."

Trent's eyes didn't flicker. "And you think people are gonna care about a ranch in the middle of nowhere?"

I bit back a sigh. "Yes. People care about quality, especially when it comes to food. You've got a unique product, and it's a niche market that's growing like crazy."

He tilted his head, one eyebrow lifting. "Growing like crazy? That sounds real nice, but how many ranches around here are doing this already?"

"Not many," I shot back. "That's the point. Ridgeview can stand out, but only if you're willing to take a chance."

Trent let out a low, skeptical grunt, his arms tightening across his chest. "I still don't know. Sounds expensive."

I closed my laptop with more force than necessary. "Of course, it's expensive. It's called an investment, Trent."

His gaze sharpened at my tone, but I didn't care. I'd done enough of these pitches to know when someone was just being stubborn.

"I've done this before," I said, doing all I could to keep my voice professional even though my patience was fraying. "I know what I'm talking about."

"Do you?" he countered. "Because all I'm hearing is you telling me to trust you without giving me a reason why."

My pulse jumped, and before I could second-guess myself, I yanked my phone out of my bag.

"Fine," I said, flicking through my photos. "You want proof? Here's proof."

I opened my portfolio app, flipping to the accounts I'd worked on back in California. First, the boutique coffee roaster whose Instagram following had tripled in three months. Then, the farm-to-table restaurant that had doubled its revenue after the campaign I'd run. And finally, the national wellness brand whose social media presence I'd helped overhaul. And those were just my headliners.

I slid the phone across the table to him. "Take a look."

He hesitated, his fingers brushing the edge of the phone before he picked it up. For a long moment, he scrolled silently, his eyes narrowing as he took in the analytics, the photos, the engagement numbers I'd built from the ground up.

When he finally looked up, I caught the faintest flicker of surprise in his expression.

"You're good," he said grudgingly, handing the phone back.

I couldn't help the sharp laugh that escaped me. "Wow, a compliment from Trent Langton. I should frame it."

He ignored that, leaning back in his chair again. "Doesn't mean this is gonna work for us, though."

I exhaled slowly, fighting the urge to throw my hands in the air. "What exactly are you worried about?"

"Packing," he said immediately, ticking the points off on his fingers. "Refrigeration. Distribution. Getting the product to the people you're talking about. It's not like we can just load up the truck and deliver beef to L.A."

I crossed my arms, tilting my head. "You must know people."

He scratched the back of his neck, and sure enough, his hat tipped forward. I found myself staring for a second too long, wondering why the sight of him doing something so ordinary suddenly felt... endearing.

"Sure, I know people," he said after a pause. "Doesn't mean they'll want to work with us."

"Why not?"

He sighed, leaning back in his chair. "Okay, for packing, there's Morrison Meats up in Baker City. They've got the facilities for what you're talking about—vacuum-sealed packaging, custom cuts, all that. But they're swamped half the time. I'd have to book processing dates months in advance, and even then, there's no guarantee they'd prioritize us over their bigger accounts."

"Okay," I said, nodding thoughtfully. "That's one issue. What else?"

"Refrigeration," he said, ticking off another finger. "We've got one walk-in freezer that's already pushing capacity. Anything bigger, and we'd need to upgrade the electrical system to handle it. Not cheap, not fast."

I could feel my jaw tightening, but I forced myself to stay calm. "And distribution?"

Trent's mouth pulled into a grim line. "Closest cold-storage trucking company is in Twin Falls. We could probably get them to haul for us, but the mileage costs alone would eat into the profits. And if we're shipping to major hubs, we'd need a reliable receiving partner on the other end. That's a whole other level of coordination."

Okay, he had me there. These were the kind of logistical problems that didn't come with easy answers.

But I wasn't about to let him off the hook. "Okay," I said, crossing my arms tighter. "So, you've got connections. People who can do packing, trucking, and receiving. Maybe they won't all work out, but they're a place to start, right?"

He hesitated, his hand brushing the brim of his hat again. "Maybe."

"Call them."

Trent's eyes narrowed, like he was weighing whether or not to argue. "You think you can just will this into working, don't you?"

"No," I said firmly. "I think we can figure it out if you stop listing reasons it won't work and start trying to make it happen."

He snorted softly, but there was a faint flicker of something—maybe amusement, maybe respect—in his expression. "You're pushy, you know that?"

I shrugged. "And you're stubborn. Looks like we're even."

For a long moment, he just stared at me, the tension in the room shifting slightly. Then he nodded, almost to himself, and I felt a spark of satisfaction.

"Fine. I'll make some calls."

Twelve

Trent

T HE BARN OFFICE FELT smaller than ever as I paced the length of the room, my phone pressed to my ear. The chair I'd been sitting in earlier creaked behind me, but I ignored it, too caught up in the string of disappointments I'd hit so far.

"Appreciate it, Jeff," I said, "but if you've got a backlog like that, there's no way we could—"

The line went dead before I could finish. I muttered a curse under my breath, lowering the phone and glaring at it like it was responsible for the string of dead ends.

Behind me, Lauren was hunched over her laptop, her fingers flying over the keys. She hadn't said much since I'd started making calls, just the occasional murmured "uh-huh" or "that's interesting" to herself, like she was having a conversation no one else could hear.

"What're you working on over there?" I asked.

She glanced up, one eyebrow raised. "Building out your social media framework."

I grunted, pacing back toward the window. "Oh, a 'framework,' huh? Great. Whatever that means. Glad one of us is getting something done."

She didn't rise to the bait, just went back to typing. I pressed the next number in my call log and braced myself.

"Yeah, good to hear from you, Trent," came the gravelly voice on the other end. "But we're full up till April. Sorry, bud."

I hung up and threw a glance at Lauren. She didn't look up, but her cheek twitched, like she could feel me stewing.

"Let me guess," she said, not bothering to pause her typing. "Another dead end?"

"Something like that," I muttered, scrubbing a hand over my face.

The next two calls weren't much better. One guy didn't even bother to apologize before saying he was too busy and hanging up, and the other rambled for ten minutes about his own operation before saying he couldn't help. By the time I hit the fifth number on the list, my patience was wearing thin.

I leaned against the wall, tapping my boot against the floor as the phone rang. Just when I was about to give up, a voice crackled through the speaker.

"Trent Langton? Long time, no hear! What can I do for you?"

My pulse jumped, and I straightened. "Hey, Scott. Yeah, it's been a while. I was hoping you could help me out with something."

Scott listened as I explained the situation, his occasional "uh-huhs" giving me just enough hope to keep going. When I finished, there was a pause, and I braced for the usual brush-off.

"Well," he said slowly, "I can't take on anything new right now, but I've got a buddy who might be able to. Runs a smaller packing plant out in Caldwell, and he's looking to expand. I can give you his number, if you want."

My heart kicked into gear. "Yeah, that'd be great. Thanks, Scott."

"Don't thank me yet," he said with a chuckle. "This guy's a little picky about who he works with, but if you drop my name, he'll at least take your call."

He rattled off the number, and I jotted it down on the notepad by the window. When the call ended, I turned to Lauren, holding the paper up with a grin.

"Success," I mouthed, feeling an unexpected rush of excitement.

She looked up, her eyes narrowing as she tilted her head. "Seriously?"

I nodded, unable to keep the grin off my face.

"Finally," she said, a small smile tugging at her lips. "Told you this would work."

I didn't respond, but a spark of something I couldn't quite name flared in my chest. Maybe it was the fact that I'd finally gotten a lead, or maybe it was the way Lauren's eyes lit up like she'd been rooting for me all along.

Either way, for the first time since we'd started this whole thing, it felt like we might actually pull it off.

I punched in the number Scott had given me and waited as the line rang. Lauren had her head buried behind her laptop again, typing away like she was solving the world's problems one keystroke at a time. I couldn't help stealing a glance at her every so often—just to see if she was listening.

When the voice on the other end picked up, I straightened instinctively. "Hi, this is Trent Langton from Ridgeview Ranch. Scott Hawkins gave me your number."

There was a pause, followed by, "Yeah, I just got a text from Scott—he mentioned you might call. What can I do for you?"

I launched into a summary of what we were trying to do—local, grass-fed beef, aiming to reach new markets. I didn't even stop for breath because I figured I might as well get to the rejection part as soon as possible. Get it over with. But when I finished, he said something that stopped me short.

"Well, we could probably make something work. And if you're looking for storage, we've got an overflow freezer that's not being used right now. It's not huge, but it might help get you started."

"Wait, you'd let us use your freezer?"

"For a fair price. But yeah, I'd be open to it."

I was already scribbling down notes when he added, "And, just so you know, I lost a client last week—big order canceled on me. That's why the freezer's empty. I've got capacity for a quick turnaround if you've got anything you can send my way by the end of this week."

I froze, the pen hovering over the notepad. "This week?"

"Yeah," he said easily, like he was offering to lend me a wrench instead of asking me to bet the entire ranch.

My pulse jumped as I scrambled to pull myself together. "Yeah, we—we've got a truckload we were planning to sell soon. I can make it work."

It wasn't a total lie. We did have a load ready, but we'd been planning to send it to the auction for a flat price. Guaranteed revenue to pay the bills this month. This? This was a gamble. If we didn't hit the right buyers fast enough, it could sink us.

"Good," he said. "Let me know by tomorrow so I can schedule the time."

We hung up, and I stared at the phone in my hand, my heartbeat pounding in my ears.

"Something wrong?" Lauren's voice cut through my thoughts, pulling my attention to where she sat with her laptop.

I shook my head, trying to calm the storm brewing in my chest. "Not wrong. Just... fast. He needs a shipment by the end of the week."

Her eyes lit up, and she leaned forward. "That's perfect!"

"Perfect?" I gave her a look, my voice dripping with skepticism. "It's a risk. If we don't sell this at the right price, we're toast. And if your plan doesn't come together in record time..."

"It will," she said firmly, cutting me off. Her confidence was like a slap to the face—in a good way.

"Better hope so," I muttered, though deep down, a spark of hope flickered to life.

This wasn't just a chance. It was our shot.

If only my hands would quit shaking.

"What about storage?" she asked—eyes back on the screen as she kept clicking on something, but I could tell she was managing to somehow juggle my conversation with whatever else she was doing.

I gulped. "Uh, yeah. Storage. He's got storage space he'll rent us."

She paused her typing and looked up. "Seriously?"

I nodded, my excitement getting the better of me. "Yeah. They've got a freezer we can use."

"That's amazing!"

"I know!" Before I knew what I was doing, I held up my hand. It was instinct, a reaction to the rush of relief and adrenaline coursing through me.

Lauren hesitated for just a second, then she rose to her feet, and her palm met mine in a solid smack. Her hand was warm against mine, her skin soft in a way that surprised me.

We lingered there for a heartbeat too long. It wasn't just the high-five—it was the way her eyes lit up when she smiled, the way she leaned just slightly into the moment... the way her fingers curled around my hand, like she felt something, too.

I dropped my hand, clearing my throat as a heat that had nothing to do with the little space heater in the corner climbed up my neck.

"Good job, partner," she said with a grin, her voice teasing but light, like she didn't realize what that small touch had done to me.

I laughed softly, more out of self-defense than humor, and looked away. "Yeah, well, let's not celebrate yet. Still a long way to go."

But as I busied myself picking up the notepad, my hand still tingled where hers had touched it. It had only lasted a second, but it felt longer. Long enough for me to regret it. Not because it wasn't a good moment, but because it felt like more than a good moment.

"Okay," Lauren said, shifting her laptop. "My turn with the news. I want to show you your new Ridgeview Ranch website."

Lauren turned the screen toward me, and I leaned closer, my eyes narrowing as the website loaded.

It was stunning. Clean white backgrounds with soft greens and browns that mirrored the fields and timberland around the ranch. Across the top of the page, "Ridgeview Ranch" was written in bold, simple letters, flanked by an animated herd of cows that trotted across the screen whenever a new page was loading.

She clicked on a bio section, and a family photo filled the screen. It was from Cole and Emily's wedding—a shot of all of us standing on the lawn, dressed up but still looking like ourselves.

Another click, and a smudgy, faded old photo appeared of Mom and Dad in the middle of a herd of cows. They looked so young it made my chest ache. Gage and I were barely toddlers, perched on a hay bale behind them, grinning at the camera like we didn't have a care in the world.

"Where'd you get that?" I asked, my voice tight.

She glanced at me. "The photo wall in the house—it's in a frame on the way to the bathroom. I thought it fit."

I couldn't speak. My throat felt thick, and I looked away, sucking in a deep breath.

"Trent?" Lauren's voice softened, and when I looked back, she'd stood, her brow furrowed with concern. "What's wrong?"

"Nothing," I said, forcing a smile. "Just... I owe you something for this. Even if it goes nowhere. A worker's worth their wages, as the Good Book says."

Her brow creased further. "You don't have to—"

"I'd like to take you to dinner," I said, cutting her off.

Her mouth hung open for a second, mid-protest, before her cheeks turned faintly pink. "What?"

"Dinner," I repeated, shrugging like it wasn't a big deal even though my heart was hammering. "Do you like steak?"

"Uh..." She blinked, clearly trying to process. "Yeah?"

"Good," I said. "Because Beaufort's Steakhouse buys beef from Ridgeview."

Her eyes rounded. "Really?"

"Not really," I said with a grin. "But it sounded good, didn't it?"

She burst out laughing, the sound light and real. "You're terrible."

"I'll take that as a yes," I said, standing and grabbing my coat.

She snapped her laptop shut and tucked it under her arm. "Well, I am getting pretty hungry..."

I opened the door for her, the cold air rushing in. "Then let's fix that."

Thirteen

Lauren

"DO YOU ALWAYS DRIVE like that?" I asked as I slammed the car door shut, yanking my coat tighter against the cold.

Trent leaned casually against his truck, his breath clouding the air. "Like what?"

"Like you're in a race with the clock." I gestured toward the road we'd just come from. "I thought you were going to leave me in the dust."

He shrugged, a hint of a smirk tugging at his mouth. "Figured you'd keep up."

"Barely," I muttered, stepping past him toward the steakhouse doors. "I thought I'd end up in a snowbank again."

"And I'd get to pull you out again."

I looked at him—the smug grin he was sporting, the way one eyebrow teased its way up under his hat brim... and decided that there might be worse things than having a cute cowboy dig my car out of the snow for me. Even if he *was* a pain in the tush.

Trent held the door open for me—polite but not showy— and the warmth inside Beaufort's washed over me like a wave, along with the smell of grilling meat and baked bread. The place was rustic in the most charming way: wooden beams, leather booths, and antlers mounted on the walls. A wagon wheel chandelier hung overhead, casting a golden glow over the crowd of diners.

A hostess greeted us, menus in hand. "Table for two?"

Trent nodded, and she led us to a corner booth near the fireplace. As I slid into my seat, the leather creaked, and I couldn't help but notice how comfortable Trent looked, like he'd been here a hundred times before.

"What's good here?" I asked, scanning the menu.

He didn't even look at it. "Ribeye. Medium rare."

"Let me guess," I said, raising an eyebrow. "Baked potato, green beans on the side?"

"Obviously," he said, leaning back in the booth. "And don't forget the roll with butter."

I grinned despite myself. "You're predictable."

"And you're ordering... what? Some salad with dressing on the side?"

I rolled my eyes. "I'll have you know I'm getting the sirloin. And maybe a salad. But definitely not with dressing on the side."

"You know..." He flipped his menu over and pointed at the seasonal specials on the back. "They've still got Turkey Dinner through the end of December. Might get you some cranberry sauce to round out the deal."

I laughed. "Like I'd trust you within a mile of me with cranberry sauce!"

The waitress brought our drinks first—a water for me and iced tea for him. She set them down with a practiced smile and pulled out her notepad.

"Know what you want, or do you need a minute?" she asked.

We made our orders—Trent added an appetizer of some sort of fried onion with chipotle dipping sauce, and I went out on a limb and asked for mashed potatoes and gravy.

"Got it," she said, snapping the pad shut. "I'll get that going for you."

As she walked away, Trent leaned back, eyeing me over the rim of his glass. "Mashed potatoes, huh? Didn't figure you for a gravy girl."

I shrugged. "It sounded good, and I'm betting it's better than the fries. Fewer calories, at least, although probably not by much."

"Ah, I see. Calorie counting. Playing it safe, huh?"

I raised an eyebrow. "Says the guy who orders the same thing every time."

"It's not the same every time. Sometimes I get fries instead of green beans."

"Oh, so adventurous."

"Hey, I know what I like."

"Clearly," I said, taking a sip of my water.

We sat in silence for a moment, the buzz of the restaurant filling the space between us. A family at the next table was laughing about something, the kids fighting over who got the last roll. Across the room, a server was lighting a birthday candle, the flame flickering in the dim light.

"So," I said, breaking the quiet. "Do you ever get tired of it?"

He frowned slightly. "Tired of what?"

"Ranch life. The routine. Cows, grass, repeat."

Trent shrugged, setting his glass down. "It's not just cows and grass. There's a lot more to it than people think. And no, I don't get tired of it. This place—it's home. It's not perfect, but it's worth it."

I studied him, his expression serious but not defensive. He really did love the ranch, even if he grumbled about it half the time.

"What about you?" he asked, turning the question back on me. "You like the chaos of the city?"

I hesitated, my fingers tracing the condensation on my glass. "I used to. Lately, though..." I shrugged. "It feels more like noise than anything else."

He tilted his head, watching me with an unreadable expression. "So why go back?"

"I'm not sure I have a choice," I said honestly. "My career's there. My life's there."

"Maybe," he said, swirling the ice in his glass. "But that doesn't mean it's the only place you can build a life."

I blinked, caught off guard by the weight of his words. "Oh, so now you're a life coach?"

He smirked, leaning back in his seat. "Just saying. You don't seem like you're itching to get back there."

I hesitated, the condensation on my glass suddenly fascinating. "It's not that simple. If I want to advance my career, do all the things I'm good at... My... everything is there."

He tilted his head, watching me closely. "Everything, huh? Like what? A fancy apartment? An office with your name on the door?"

"Something like that," I said lightly, though the edge of truth in his words stung.

"What about people?" he asked, his voice casual, but his eyes a little too intent. "Anyone special waiting for you back there?"

I looked up sharply, catching the faintest flicker of curiosity—or something like it—in his expression. A laugh bubbled up before I could stop it.

"Wow, subtle," I teased, resting my chin on my hand. "That's your big move? Fishing for my relationship status over a steak dinner?"

His smirk deepened, but I caught the faintest hint of red creeping up his neck. "Just making conversation."

"Uh-huh," I said, narrowing my eyes. "For your information, no. There's no one special waiting for me."

He nodded, like he was filing that information away, then raised an eyebrow. "What about your family? Your dad's still out there, right?"

"Yeah. He's there. But it's not like we're close. He's got his girl-friend, and I've got my career."

"And that's enough for you?"

I paused, the question hanging in the air. Was it? It had been, for a while. The job, the city, the constant grind—it had filled the gaps left by the things I didn't want to think about. But now...

"It's not perfect," I admitted. "But it's what I've got. My career's the one thing I can count on."

His gaze stayed on me, steady and unflinching, and for a moment, I wondered if I should tell him. About the post. The fallout. The uncertainty hanging over my head like a storm cloud.

I opened my mouth to start, but just then, the door from the kitchen banged open, and Trent caught the motion from the corner of his eye. It must have been some sort of sixth sense or something—that feeling you get when it's your food coming out next, so you sit up and move stuff around to make room. And it was just as well—I wasn't sure I really needed to tell him everything.

We both turned as a waitress emerged, balancing a tray so over-loaded with plates that it tilted dangerously to one side. More than just our plates, probably.

"That doesn't look good," I murmured, watching as she headed straight for our table.

Sure enough, just as she reached us, the tray wobbled. The baked potato from Trent's plate launched off the edge and landed squarely on his lap, sour cream and all.

"Oh no!" the waitress gasped.

Trent froze for a second, then slowly looked down at the mess on his jeans.

"Well," he said, picking up the offending potato and placing it back on the tray, "that's one way to stay regular."

I burst out laughing, clapping a hand over my mouth as the waitress apologized profusely. Trent waved her off, his tone calm as he asked for a napkin and assured her it was fine.

"Oh, my gosh... Let me get you another potato!" The waitress spun around, her tray still wobbling a bit until she found one of her co-workers to help her unload it. She dropped my plate in front of me—and it did look delicious—then her friend took off with what was left on the tray while our waitress ran back to the kitchen.

Trent had given up on the napkin, and now he had a spoon to glop big scoops of sour cream and butter from his lap onto the side plate. "You handled that way better than I would've," I said.

"It's just a potato," he said, going for another scoop. "Not something that's going to stain... like cranberry sauce."

That got me laughing again, hiding my face behind my napkin and sniggering until tears ran down my cheeks. Why in the world was that so funny? Probably because he was so stinking cute, the way he kept glancing up at me and grinning every time he plopped another spoonful of sour cream on the plate.

When Trent's fresh plate finally arrived—sans flying potatoes—I finally picked up my knife and fork and couldn't help but make a show of inspecting my steak.

"Looks good," Trent said, eyeing it with mock seriousness.

"Better be," I replied. "I didn't risk life and limb on the drive over here for subpar steak."

"Why would it be subpar? Beaufort's is the best steakhouse in town."

"Maybe," I said, leaning forward with a grin. "But they don't get their beef from you, so I have to wonder if it's any good."

He rolled his eyes with a chuckle. "You're still hung up on that?"

"Let's just say my job is to convince people that they need what I have to show them. And it works best if I believe it first."

"Ah. Well, then, if it helps you at all, just pretend this is our beef. Because nobody grills a ribeye like Beaufort's."

I sliced into my food, and at the first bite... oh, goodness, he was right. I closed my eyes and savored my sirloin like it was a juicy cut of prime rib. Just... wow.

"Well, what do you know?" Trent's voice made me open my eyes.

I swallowed and arched a brow innocently. "Hmm?"

He looked down as he cut his own steak. "I gotta say, I had my doubts. After all, Emily says you take oat milk in your coffee, and real steak lovers don't usually get sirloin."

I narrowed my eyes. "What are you getting at?"

He shrugged. "Thought maybe you were a closet vegetarian. It's okay, I won't tell anyone."

I popped another bite of steak in my mouth. "Tried it. Not for me. My dad's girlfriend does that, though."

"Ah. Guilt by association. Welcome back to real food, then."

We ate and laughed, and lingered over the last bites of our food like we didn't want to admit that the bare white of our plates was getting bigger with each moment. Finally, Trent pushed his plate aside, leaning back in the booth like a man who didn't often let himself relax.

"So," he said, "did Beaufort's steak live up to the hype?"

I smirked. "It was decent."

"Just decent? I'll bet they're practically starving you out in California, and you say that's just 'decent'?"

I laced my fingers together and framed my chin on them, leaning forward. "Would have been better if it was all local beef—"

"It was," he interrupted. "I didn't tell you they buy from Walkers."

"...And grass-fed. It wasn't grass-fed."

Trent shrugged. "It mostly was. They do grain and silage finishing, but it's mostly—"

"That still matters. Work with me, here, Trent."

His chuckle was low and easy, and for a moment, the guarded edge I'd come to expect from him wasn't there. "Fine. Guess I'll give you credit for that."

I rolled my eyes but couldn't help smiling.

The waitress returned with the check, and Trent didn't hesitate to grab it, sliding his card across the table before I could object.

"You don't have to do that," I said, frowning.

"I know," he said, meeting my gaze. "But I told you—my way of trying to repay you something."

I quirked an eyebrow. "So, you're sold on the idea now?"

He chuckled softly, shaking his head. "Not quite. But I'm getting there."

I leaned back, studying him for a moment. For all his rough edges and skeptical comments, there was something about him that felt... dependable. Like he carried the weight of his world without ever making it someone else's problem.

"Thanks," I said softly. "For the steak. And the potato-free lap."

He shook his head, a quiet laugh escaping him. "Don't mention it."

As we gathered our things and stepped out into the cold, I couldn't help but feel a strange sense of ease. For all his gruffness and skepticism, Trent Langton had a way of making the world feel smaller. Simpler.

And maybe—just maybe—that wasn't such a bad thing.

He walked me to my car—how sweet was that? His truck was only a few spaces away, and it wasn't like I was alone in a bad part of town. But he stood by, waiting until I got the door open and the engine running. The first thing I did was crank up the heater, but then I rolled down the window and looked up at him. "Guess I'll see you tomorrow?"

He nodded, his breath a cloud in the night air. "See you tomorrow."

I rolled my window back up and sat there in my idling rental, watching him through the tiny defrosted spot in my windshield as he walked to his truck.

And I wonder how I'd never noticed before that those tight jeans looked... pretty good on him. Even if they did have sour cream on them.

Fourteen

Trent

G AGE SLAMMED THE COFFEE pot down on the table, sloshing a bit over the rim of his mug. "You look like you're trying to solve world hunger over there."

I blinked, pulled from my thoughts, and glanced at him. "What?"

"You've been staring into that coffee like it insulted your mama," he said as he slid into his chair. "What's eating you?"

"Nothing," I muttered, shifting in my seat and taking a sip. The bitterness hit harder than usual, but it was easier to focus on that than the tangled mess of thoughts I couldn't shake.

Gage raised an eyebrow, clearly not buying it. "This wouldn't have anything to do with your fancy steak dinner last night, would it?"

Of course it didn't. Last night wasn't supposed to feel like... whatever that was. Dinner with Lauren had been about business—thanking her for everything she'd done so far. Nothing more.

Except it had felt like more.

I'd replayed the way she'd laughed at the potato fiasco, her eyes lighting up with something genuine, not the polished city-girl shield she wore most of the time. And the way she'd teased me—it wasn't mean-spirited, just sharp enough to keep me on my toes. I'd gone to bed trying to push the memory away, but it had stuck like burrs to my boots.

The creak of the kitchen chair brought me back to the present. Gage was rubbing his face, his hair sticking up in every direction like he hadn't seen a shower yet today. "You're brooding," he said.

"I'm thinking," I corrected.

"Same difference. So, you haven't answered my question. How was dinner?"

"It was fine."

"Fine?" His eyebrows rose. "She didn't dump her salad on you or something? Figure she owes you one..."

"Drop it, Gage," I muttered, sipping my coffee.

"What's all this about dinner?" Mom walked in, carrying a basket of eggs from the henhouse. She set it on the counter and turned, her gaze zeroing in on me.

"Nothing," I said quickly, but Gage was already grinning like a fool.

"Trent took Lauren to Beaufort's last night," he announced.

Mom's eyebrows went up, her hands pausing as she started to crack an egg into the skillet. "You did? That's nice."

"It wasn't like that," I said, feeling the heat rise in my neck. "It was just a thank-you for the work she's doing."

"Uh-huh." Gage leaned forward, resting his chin in his hand, his grin as wide as the barn door. "So, did you thank her before or after you gazed into her eyes across the candlelight?"

"You're asking the wrong questions," I snapped, pushing back from the table hard enough to rattle the silverware. "How about asking what her actual plans are? Or how we're going to handle all the logistics of this crazy idea?"

Gage leaned back, looking more amused than chastised. "All right, Mr. Serious. Enlighten us. What's the big plan?"

I sighed, running a hand through my hair. "Lauren's got this whole marketing strategy—social media, a website, the works. She showed me he website—looks good. I've got an arrangement with a packing plant to handle the processing, and they're going to help us with storage. It's a good start, but we've still got to figure out distribution and make sure we can even get the product to market on time."

Mom turned from the stove, her brow furrowing slightly as she listened. "That sounds like progress."

"It is," I admitted, though the words tasted grudging in my mouth. "But it's also a huge risk. We're betting on people wanting to buy directly from us instead of going through the usual system. If it flops, we're out a truckload of beef and the money that comes with it."

Gage shrugged, still toting that smirk I wanted to wipe off his face. "Doesn't sound like a candlelit romance to me."

"Exactly," I shot back, leveling a glare at him.

Mom cleared her throat, giving Gage a pointed look that had him holding up his hands in mock surrender. She turned her attention back to me, her voice softer now. "It sounds like you're putting a lot of thought into this, Trent. That's good. But maybe you're focusing too much on the questions instead of the answers."

I rolled my eyes, slumping back in my chair. "Whatever that means."

Before she could explain, Gage burst out laughing, and Mom shooed him toward the door. "Go on, both of you. You've got work to do, and I've got breakfast to make. Ethan and Liam, do not miss the bus again today. Better hop to your chores."

The table cleared as everyone scattered to their tasks, leaving me alone with my coffee. I sighed, drained the last sip, and grabbed my jacket.

Lauren

I TAPPED MY FINGERS against the edge of the laptop, glancing at my phone for the tenth time in as many minutes. Still no reply. Letting out a huff, I leaned back in the chair and grabbed my phone again, firing off another text.

Everything's ready. Are we good to go?

I set the phone down a little harder than I meant to and turned back to the screen. The website was perfect—at least, as perfect as it could be. Clean layout, simple navigation, photos that practically screamed authenticity. The storefront was stocked and gleaming with options: grass-fed beef bundles, holiday roasts, specialty cuts.

All it needed was Trent's okay.

The phone buzzed, and I snatched it up like it might disappear.

Let me think for a minute.

I groaned, letting my head thunk softly against the table. "Come on, cowboy," I muttered, glaring at the phone like that might speed things up. "Make up your mind."

The minutes stretched painfully long. I opened my email, scrolled aimlessly, and checked my work messages just to feel busy. I clicked over to the Instagram page I'd set up for Ridgeview, just to see where it was at, and my heart did a little skip. Starting to get results! Not that I didn't expect it, but it's always a thrill when it happens. Now we just needed that website to go live...

My fingers hovered over the keyboard, itching to do something.

Finally, the screen lit up again with a message from Trent. *Okay. Let's do it.*

"Yes!" I practically shouted, pumping a fist in the air.

I clicked the "Go Live" button before he could change his mind, watching as the site shifted from draft mode to live. The little notification in the corner confirmed it—Ridgeview Ranch was officially open for business.

"Done," I said aloud, even though no one was listening.

The satisfaction was immediate, but it didn't last long. I glanced at the time. It'd be hours, maybe a full day before I'd know if people were clicking through or making orders. For now, there wasn't much else I could do. I guess I might as well hang out with my sister.

I scrolled through my contacts, landing on Emily's name. Tapping out a message, I asked:*Hey, what are you up to today?*

Her response came quickly.*Doing chores at home. Cole's feeding horses, I'm tackling the tack room. Wanna come hang out?*

I smiled. It wasn't like I had pressing plans.*Sure. Brace yourself for a roadside service call—I'm bringing the sketchy compact up that mountain.*

Brave woman. See you soon.

I laughed, shoving my phone into my pocket and grabbing my keys. If the rental car could handle the Ridgeview driveway, it could handle the hilly, icy highway up to White Pines.

Probably.

The air outside was sharp and cold, my breath clouding as I slid into the car. As the engine sputtered to life, I muttered a small prayer. "Don't fail me now, little car. We've got work to do."

The studded tires popped and ground over the frosty asphalt, and I turned onto the main road, aiming for White Pines. It felt good to have a plan again—even if it just meant tackling the next few hours.

"**O**KAY, SO THIS IS the main barn," Emily said, waving a hand as we walked down the snow-packed path. "Most of the therapy horses live here, along with the tack and the feed for their specific routines. We've got a smaller barn out back for overflow or horses out on furlough."

The barn doors creaked as she pushed them open, revealing the warm, hay-scented interior. Horses shifted in their stalls, the occasional soft whicker breaking the quiet. Kate followed us in, her sharp eyes scanning everything like she'd know if one horse had a single hair out of place. She probably would.

"You're gonna love Amber," Emily said as we walked past a stall with a big bay horse munching on hay. "She's basically Morgan's right-hand woman and knows everything about this place."

"She sounds busy," I said, tucking my gloves into my coat pockets.

Kate grinned as she piped up. "Busy doesn't even cover it. She keeps this place running, and the clients love her."

We rounded the corner into the tack room, where a woman was sitting on a small bench, her face buried in her hands. Her reddish chestnut hair was pulled into a loose ponytail, but a few strands had slipped free, framing her flushed cheeks. She looked up at the sound of our footsteps, her hazel eyes red-rimmed like she'd been crying.

"Oh, hey," Emily said gently, her smile softening. "You okay?"

Amber straightened, wiping her hands quickly over her face. "Yeah, fine. Just a long morning."

Emily hesitated, then stepped forward, her voice low. "Something happen?"

Amber shook her head and stood, brushing imaginary dust off her jeans. "Nothing big. Just one of those days where everything feels like it's going sideways." Her voice was steady—over the phone, no one would have noticed a thing, but the exhaustion in her eyes told a different story. She didn't give Emily a chance to ask again, though, because her gaze flicked curiously to me.

"Oh. This is my sister, Lauren," Emily said, gesturing toward me. "Lauren, this is Amber."

Amber gave me a polite smile, but it didn't do much to shift that tired look off her face. "Right, the sister from California. Emily talks about you a lot. Nice to meet you."

"You too," I said, stepping forward to shake her hand. Her grip was firm, but her fingers were ice-cold. "Everything okay?"

Amber's smile wavered, and for a moment, I thought she might actually answer. But then she shrugged, her walls snapping back into place. "It's fine. Just clients canceling last minute, a horse pulling a shoe, and me realizing I haven't eaten since breakfast—which was a black coffee. Nothing new."

"That sounds like a lot," I said.

Amber's gaze flicked to Emily, who was leaning against the wall with her arms crossed, giving her a skeptical look. Amber let out a long sigh, the kind that seemed to carry more weight than the list of chores she'd rattled off. "Okay, fine. That's not all."

Emily tilted her head, eyebrows raised as if to say, *Obviously*.

Amber hesitated, gripping the edge of the tack bench like it was the only thing holding her upright. "I just got off the phone with my sister and brother-in-law. We... had a fight over Thanksgiving dinner, and now it's turning into this whole family thing."

Emily straightened, her expression softening. "What kind of fight?"

"They want to move my parents into assisted living. They found this place near them in Missoula and are acting like it's all settled. But they haven't talked to my parents yet." She sighed. "I know them. They'll go, if Shauna makes them, because what choice do they have? They need support, and if she's not willing to give it..." She shrugged. "But they'd hate it. It would kill Mom."

"So, what's your plan?" Emily asked gently.

Amber rubbed her temples, looking both frustrated and exhausted. "I told them I'd bring Mom and Dad here. They can live with me. I've got space, and they'd be able to see the mountains. Mom will die if she can't see the mountains."

Emily blinked. "Here? Like... in Big River Valley? In your house?"

"Yes, my house, where else?" Amber snapped, then sighed again. "Sorry. I just... I have spent days arguing this already. I think it's the right thing. But my sister doesn't agree. She thinks it's too much for me to take on."

Lauren glanced at Emily, then back at Amber. "Is it?"

Amber gave a dry laugh. "Probably. But they're my parents. What am I supposed to do? Just let them waste away in a place they don't want to be?"

"No," Emily said softly, moving closer to sit beside her. "You're not wrong to want to keep them close. But have you asked them what they want?"

Amber hesitated, her hands tightening into fists in her lap. "Not yet. I was planning to, but now I feel like I'm stuck in the middle. If I ask and they agree with me, my sister's just going to get angrier."

Emily nodded slowly. "And if they don't agree?"

Amber's shoulders slumped, the fight in her fading. "Then either they're just rolling over to please my sister, or... I guess I'm wrong. And I don't know what to do with that."

I cleared my throat, drawing both their attention. "You'll figure it out," I said simply. "You don't seem like the type to back down from something important, and this... this sounds important."

Amber gave me a faint, tired smile. "Thanks. I guess I just needed to vent."

"That's what friends are for," Emily said, wrapping an arm around her shoulders.

Amber shot her a look, but there was warmth in it now. "Thanks. Both of you."

Emily nudged Amber playfully. "You're always running yourself ragged. I've told you to take a break, haven't I?"

"Yeah, yeah," Amber muttered, but her lips twitched into the faintest grin.

Kate had vanished a minute or two ago, but she suddenly appeared around the corner of the tack room door, brandishing a banged-up travel mug. "Hey, good news! We still had cocoa mix in the office. And you look like a woman who needs a peppermint cocoa."

Amber's eyes widened as she took the cup. "Oh, bless you. I take back every mean thing I've ever said about you."

Kate snorted. "Like you'd ever dare. You'd have to saddle all the horses and wrangle volunteers yourself."

"You got me there." Amber took a sip, visibly relaxing as the warmth seeped into her hands.

"So, what's the plan for today?" she asked, glancing at Emily.

"Giving Lauren the grand tour," Emily said, looping an arm through mine. "She's in town for Christmas and thought she'd see what we do out here."

Amber nodded, her smile a little more genuine now. "Well, welcome to the chaos. Let me know if you have any questions—or if you want to see the real work, not just the pretty parts."

I grinned. "I might take you up on that."

Amber laughed softly, then gestured toward the barn door. "I'd better get back out there before Morgan sends a search party. Nice meeting you, Lauren."

"You too," I said, watching as she marched down the aisle, knocking back that cocoa mug every few steps, like it was her only fuel to get through the rest of the day. Maybe it was.

Emily leaned closer, her voice low. "Amber's kind of all business, all the time. I've never seen her like that—usually she's the toughest nut you never could crack. She's kind of too-serious sometimes, but Amber's the best. You'll love her once you get to know her."

"I think I already do," I said with a small smile.

Trent

I JOGGED INTO THE barn, my boots clomping against the packed dirt floor. The air smelled of leather and horses, and I found Gage bent over a bay mare's hoof, his tools scattered around him like he was setting up shop.

"We gotta go," I said, pulling my gloves off and tucking them into my pocket.

"Go where?" Gage muttered, not looking up as he worked the rasp over the hoof.

"Caldwell," I said, pacing a few steps and running a hand through my hair. "The website's up, the orders are gonna start rolling in any second, and we've got to get that load to the packer. It's go time."

"*We?*" Gage straightened, wiping sweat off his brow with the back of his hand. Amazing how he could still sweat in twenty-nine degrees, but shoeing always did it. "You've got a truck and two good hands. What do you need me for?"

"It's a big deal," I said, trying not to sound desperate. "I'd feel better if you were there."

Gage raised an eyebrow, crossing his arms. "You've done hauls a hundred times before. What's so special about this one?"

"It's not just the haul!" I snapped, then groaned, rubbing the back of my neck. "This is the first load to the custom packer. If something goes wrong, it all goes down with it. I don't want it all on me."

"Then don't screw it up," Gage said, shrugging as he turned back to the mare.

"Gage—"

"Trent." He cut me off, holding up a hand. "I've got a backlog of horses to shoe. Got Mrs. Wilson bringing her show horses over this afternoon, too, because her farrier up and quit on her, and I won't say no to the cash. I'm not gonna drop everything because you've got butterflies about a beef order. Take Mom with you if you want someone to yak at."

I glared at him, but he just shrugged, already back to his work.

"Fine," I muttered, spinning on my heel and stalking toward the truck.

The herd was already sorted, the steers ready to go, but it took longer than I wanted to get them loaded. I checked the latches twice, then climbed into the cab, letting out a long sigh. The truck had been idling for ten minutes but air inside was still cold, and for a second, I just sat there, staring at the steering wheel.

My phone buzzed in my pocket. I pulled it out, swiping at the screen, and froze.

Lauren had sent me a message: a screenshot of one of the social media pages she'd set up for Ridgeview. The follower count wasn't just good—it was ridiculous. Over two thousand people had already clicked the little button. I rubbed my eyes. Was… was I *seeing* this right?

Another message popped up right after, this time a different screenshot. Five custom beef orders, all placed since the page went live, like two hours ago.

My stomach flipped. Five orders already? I wasn't even ready!

My thumbs hovered over the keyboard as I tried to text her back. My hands were shaking, and I couldn't seem to figure out what to say. Finally, I managed to type: *This is incredible. I can't believe it.*

The little dots popped up, then disappeared. Then came back. Then vanished again. Then: *Did you doubt me, cowboy?*

I swallowed before I typed back. *Not anymore*

I sat there, staring at the screen like it might explode. Then, before I could stop myself, I started typing again.

Do you want to ride to Caldwell with me?

I stared at the message, my thumb hovering over the send button. It felt ridiculous. Why would she want to spend all day in a truck with me, hauling cattle?

I almost deleted it. Then I sent it.

The phone sat silent in my hand for what felt like forever. The little dots appeared again, but this time they didn't disappear.

Her response popped up.

Sure.

I swallowed hard, my pulse jumping like I'd just run a mile.

What had I done?

Fifteen

Lauren

"**D**O YOU ALWAYS GRIP the door like it's about to fall off?" Trent asked, just enough teasing in his voice to pull my eyes away from the snow-dusted hills stretching into the distance.

I glanced down at my hand, still clenched around the door handle. "Oh," I muttered, letting go and shaking out my fingers. "Guess I'm not used to trucks this big."

He smirked, shifting gears with a smoothness that seemed effortless. "You're in good hands. Done this a thousand times."

The cab jostled slightly as the semi rolled over a patch of uneven road, but Trent didn't seem fazed. His hands were steady on the wheel, his eyes scanning the icy road ahead like he could see the best path carved out for miles.

I relaxed a fraction, though the sheer size of the truck still felt overwhelming. The high vantage point offered a sweeping view of the valley, its rolling white fields glistening under the winter sun. "Well, this is a first for me," I said. "You really just drive these things like it's nothing, huh?"

Trent shifted gears effortlessly, one hand on the wheel, his eyes scanning the road like he could read it. His movements were smooth, practiced, like he'd been born in the driver's seat. "Every rancher who hauls does. My dad taught me how to drive one of these when I was fifteen. Said if I was gonna work the ranch, I'd better know every part of it, including getting the cows to market."

"Fifteen? That seems young to be handling something this size."

He chuckled, eyes flicking to the rearview mirror. "He figured if I could handle this, I could handle just about anything. Got my CDL as soon as I turned eighteen, though." He chuckled. "Sheriff Wyatt caught me out on the highway hauling a load—a little too fast—and said he'd write me a ticket, or I could go sign up for a class."

"He should've given you a ticket. You mean to say you were hauling loads this size for three years before you were even eligible to get the CDL?"

Trent shrugged. "There's an exemption for farmers' kids. He was just messin' with me, tryin' to scare me straight."

"Ah." I sighed. "Did it work?"

"Never got caught speeding again. *Caught* being the operative word." I watched as he navigated a curve with precision, the truck barely swaying despite the icy road. "Dad woulda had my head." His voice changed to a goofy deep mimic, and he tilted his head. "'I taught you to drive a truck, not fly a plane,' he'd have said."

I laughed. "Well, he did a good job. You look like you've been doing this your whole life."

"Feels like it sometimes," he admitted, tapping the wheel with his fingers.

We fell into silence again, and I took the chance to glance around the cab. It was clean but functional, with a few tools tucked into compartments and a faint smell of hay and diesel.

After a moment, I cleared my throat. "You know, if this plan works, you're going to have to hire someone else to do this."

He glanced at me, one eyebrow raised. "Why's that?"

"Because you'll have too much hauling to do," I said, matter-of-factly. "You're not going to be able to keep up with demand and run the ranch at the same time."

He laughed, a deep, easy sound that made my stomach flip unexpectedly. "We're a long way from that kind of problem. I don't even have enough cows to sell for that."

"*Yet*," I said, leaning back and crossing my arms. "But I heard a rumor that Gage wants to buy some new breeding stock from Walker Ranch. If this pays off the way I think it will, you won't have a choice. You'll *have* to buy more cattle."

He shook his head, but there was a faint smile on his lips. "You think big, don't you?"

I shrugged, smiling a little myself. "It's part of the job."

The truck hit a straight stretch, and he relaxed a bit, leaning back in his seat. "Speaking of jobs, how'd you end up doing what you do? I mean, digital marketing? Sounds like a long way from here."

I glanced at him, debating how much to say. But his tone was casual, curious, not judgmental, and that made it easier to answer.

"It is a long way," I admitted. "But I always liked creative stuff—art, writing, things like that. After college, I interned at a marketing agency and realized I loved the strategy side of it, too. It's like a puzzle—figuring out what makes people tick and how to connect them to something they didn't even know they wanted."

He nodded, his attention flicking between me and the road. "And that brought you to California?"

I hesitated, fiddling with the zipper on my coat. "Sort of. My dad moved out there after the divorce, and I followed him. I thought... I don't know, maybe I'd find a big career and a new start."

"Did you?"

I thought about the disaster that had brought me here and tried to push it out of my mind. "For a while. I was doing really well—working on big accounts, climbing the ladder. It's... it's great. Not always what I thought it would be, but still good, you know?"

He nodded slowly. "Yeah. I get that."

I glanced at him, surprised. "You do?"

He shrugged, his hands steady on the wheel. "I thought I'd be running this ranch with my dad and brothers forever. Then Dad passed, Cole took a job working for Cody, Chase started thinking about leaving, and everything changed. Took me a while to figure out what I wanted out of it all."

I watched him, something about his honesty catching me off guard. "And did you?"

His lips pressed into a thoughtful line. "I think so. But there are still days when it feels like I'm figuring it out as I go."

"Sounds familiar."

We drove in silence for a few moments, the truck rumbling steadily along. It wasn't the kind of silence that felt awkward or strained, though. Trent shifted gears again, the semi humming steadily as it took the incline with ease.

"So," I started hesitantly, watching his expression. "Are you... seeing anyone?"

He flicked his eyes toward me, then back to the road, his jaw tightening just a fraction. "Pass."

I probably should've left it alone—I mean, I already kind of knew the answer, but I wanted to hear it from him, not hearsay. "Oh, come on. You asked me back at Beaufort's, remember? Fair's fair."

He sighed, his grip tightening briefly on the wheel. "Fine. I was seeing someone, but it didn't work out."

I pretended to look surprised. "Why not?"

He glanced at me again, his brows drawing together. "You're full of questions today."

"It's a long drive," I said with a small shrug. "Plenty of time for stories."

He smirked faintly, but his tone was guarded. "Cassie. We met at a rodeo last summer. She was... well, let's just say it started out fine, but it didn't take long to figure out we... uh... we weren't a good match."

"Was she clingy?"

Chase shot me a funny look. "How'd you guess?"

I shrugged. "Stubborn cowboy like you? I can't think of anything that would drive you crazy faster."

He narrowed his eyes.

"Okay." I cleared my throat and looked down. "Uh, to be honest, she came into my mom's shop the other day. Emily pointed her out. The rest was just a guess."

His lips quirked, like he wasn't sure if he wanted to laugh or groan. "Oh, so you were bluffing! Not wrong, though."

I frowned. "Yeah, I didn't think I was."

"Let's just say she had her own... challenges. Things got messy fast."

I watched him, waiting for more.

"She broke up with me over text," he added after a moment, his voice flat.

I blinked. "*What?*"

"Yep." He glanced my way, clearly expecting me to laugh it off or poke fun.

Instead, I crossed my arms. "That's awful. I mean, breaking up is one thing, but to do it over a text? That's just..." I trailed off, shaking my head. "That's cheap and dirty."

Trent shot me a sidelong glance. "You seem a lot more worked up about it than I was. What, bad breakup stories of your own?"

"Not exactly. I've never gotten far enough to get to the breaking up part."

His brow furrowed. "Really? Why's that?"

I hesitated, biting my lip. But he seemed genuinely curious, and his tone wasn't mocking, so I relented. "Most of my dates have been disasters. My friend Stacy keeps setting me up, and her picks are... let's just say they're more *interesting* than compatible."

"Interesting how?"

"There was one guy who wouldn't stop talking about his crypto investments. Another one kept showing me pictures of his cats—like, not even cute ones, just weird close-ups of their noses." I shook my head, letting out a little laugh despite myself. "And don't even get me started on the guy who showed up in flip-flops to a steakhouse."

Trent let out a low chuckle, shaking his head. "Sounds like you've been through it."

"Understatement," I said, rolling my eyes. "But hey, at least I get some good stories out of it, right?"

"Guess that's one way to look at it," he said, his grin softening as he glanced my way again.

For a moment, the cab was quiet except for the rumble of the engine. I caught him looking at me out of the corner of my eye, like he wanted to ask something else but couldn't quite figure out how to say it.

"What?" I asked, raising an eyebrow.

He shook his head, the grin turning sheepish. "Nothing. Just glad you didn't bring up cats or crypto when we had dinner."

I laughed, the sound echoing in the cab. "Trust me, I'd never make that mistake."

Trent

T HE LOADING DOCK AT Silver Creek Packers was bustling with activity, steam curling into the icy air as workers moved crates and equipment like a well-oiled machine. I parked the truck and climbed out, my boots crunching on the frosted gravel. For all the nerves I'd felt on the way here, I forced myself to square my shoulders and step up to the dock like I belonged.

"Trent Langton?" a voice called.

I turned to see a man in his forties, stocky with an openly friendly face that didn't quite match the firm handshake he offered. "That's me," I said, gripping his hand.

"Mike Henderson. We spoke on the phone. Glad you could make it."

"Glad you were willing to take us on," I said, releasing his hand. This wasn't just a handshake—it was a gamble.

Mike waved me toward the truck. "Let's take a look at what you've got."

We spent the next twenty minutes going over the cattle, Mike checking tags and asking shop-talk-type questions about our feed and grazing practices. I answered every one, thankful for the years of knowledge that had been drilled into me by Dad and my own experience. By the end, he nodded, looking impressed.

"You've got quality here," he said, stepping back from the cattle. "We'll process this load right away. We do a seven-day hang, and your cuts will be ready for shipping by next week. Freezer space is set aside, like we discussed."

I nodded, gripping his hand firmly. "Appreciate it."

He hesitated, giving me a look that felt more like a challenge than encouragement. "I don't usually see ranches around here going this route. You're taking a risk with the direct-to-consumer thing. You sure you're ready for it?"

I tightened my grip on the handshake, holding his gaze. "I have to be."

"Well, you've got the product for it. Let's see what you can do."

The words were both an opportunity and a warning. "I'll make it work."

By the time I got back to the truck, Lauren was leaning against the passenger door, her phone in hand. She looked up as I approached, her cheeks pink from the cold.

"How'd it go?" she asked, slipping her phone into her coat pocket.

"Good," I said, climbing into the driver's seat. "Better than I thought, actually."

She grinned as I started the engine. "Told you."

I glanced at her, the corner of my mouth twitching. "Yeah, yeah. You want credit for everything, don't you?"

She shrugged, pulling out her phone again. "Speaking of credit, I made some calls while you were out there. Got cold shipping sorted for the orders we've got so far."

I paused, my hand hovering over the gear shift. "Already?"

"Thirteen orders," she said, showing me the screen. "And counting. We're shipping to Idaho, Washington, and even one to California."

I let out a low whistle, leaning back in the seat as I stared at the screen. "Thirteen? Already?"

"That's what happens when you go viral," she said, her grin widening.

"*Viral?*" I repeated, half in awe, half in disbelief.

She nodded, scrolling to another screen. "Your social media page. Over five thousand followers now. And they're engaged, Trent. Comments, likes, shares. People love what Ridgeview is about."

I stared at the screen, my heart pounding. For the first time, it hit me just how big this could be.

"Five thousand," I muttered, shaking my head. "That's... incredible."

Lauren tucked her phone away, her expression softening. "It's a start."

A start. The words hung in the air, heavy with promise. As I pulled the truck back onto the road, I couldn't help but feel like we'd just opened a door I hadn't even known existed.

THE HOUSE WAS LIT up like a beacon in the night as I pulled the truck into the driveway. Inside, I could hear the muffled hum of voices and laughter, the warm glow spilling through the windows making it look like a holiday postcard.

I glanced at Lauren as I shut off the engine. She had one hand on the door handle, hesitating like she wasn't sure what to do next.

"Want to come in?" I asked, trying to sound casual. "It's dinner time. You've gotta be starving by now."

Her fingers tightened on the handle, her brows drawing together in that way they did when she was overthinking. "I don't want to intrude."

"You wouldn't be," I said, opening my door. "Come on. You've already survived one Langton family dinner. What's one more?"

That got a faint smile out of her, and after a second, she followed me out of the truck.

The smell of roasted chicken and potatoes sucked us in like a vacuum, rich and warm and exactly the kind of thing you wanted to come home to after a long day.

"Look who decided to bring company!" Gage hollered from the table, pointing a fork at us with a grin.

"Don't start," I muttered, shaking off my hat and hanging it by the door.

Mom looked up from her seat, her face brightening when she saw Lauren. "Lauren! Come in, come in. Sit down—you must be starving after a long day like today."

"I don't want to impose," Lauren started, but Mom waved her hand like she hadn't even heard it.

"Nonsense. There's plenty of food. Grab a plate."

Lauren gave me a sidelong glance, like she was still debating her options, but I just gestured toward the table. "Might as well. Mom won't take no for an answer."

Before long, she was sitting between me and Gage, a steaming plate of food in front of her. Ethan and Liam were down at the far end, sneaking glances at her and whispering back and forth like they thought no one could hear them.

"What?" Ethan said when I gave him a look. "We were just saying how fancy your lady friend looks."

I groaned, scrubbing a hand down my face. "Knock it off, Ethan. Go back to eating."

The boys snickered but obeyed, though I didn't miss the grin Liam shot in my direction.

"They're starting to warm up," Mom said quietly, her eyes soft as she watched them.

She was right. Those boys were... well, they smiled once in a while now. I'd overheard the social worker tell Mom on her last check that she'd never seen Ethan when he wasn't trying to hit someone. Guess that was a good sign.

Dinner passed in a blur of conversation and laughter, Lauren's occasional quips blending seamlessly with the family dynamic. For someone who'd grown up in such a different world, she fit better than I'd expected, almost like she'd always been part of it.

By the time we finished, plates were stacked high on the counter, and Mom sat back with her coffee, giving Lauren a curious look. "So, what exactly are you posting on social media to rake in all these followers? I haven't had a chance to look yet, but from what Trent says, it's impressive."

Lauren blinked, mid-sip of her water, and set the glass down. "Oh, it's nothing fancy. Just videos and pictures, mostly."

"Videos and pictures," Gage repeated, smirking. "Wow, ground-breaking."

Lauren shot him a mock glare. "It's more about how you use them, wise guy."

"Well, enlighten us, then," Gage said, leaning back in his chair with an exaggerated wave of his hand.

Lauren pulled her phone out of her pocket, unlocking it as she spoke. "It's all about engagement—keeping things short, sweet, and optimized for attention spans that rival goldfish." She swiped through the Ridgeview Ranch profile and turned the screen toward Mom.

The first video showed Marty, trotting across the yard with his tail flagged high like he owned the place. Lauren had paired it with upbeat music and a caption that read: "Meet Marty, the King of Ridgeview Ranch. Crown optional."

Mom chuckled, leaning closer. "Oh, he does look like a little king, doesn't he?"

The next clip was of Ethan and Liam tossing hay while the dogs darted around their legs. Lauren had added a voiceover—her voice—explaining how chores taught responsibility and built a connection to the land. She'd been careful not to use names or show their faces, but the point was clear.

"You made that sound like we're running a youth camp," I said, narrowing my eyes at her.

"You kind of are," she shot back with a grin.

The third clip was me talking about the water trough system. The shot was tight on my face, showing the steam rising from my breath in the cold air. My voice played over the video as I explained how the system worked and why it was good for the cattle.

"Wait, wait," I said, holding up a hand. "You posted that one?"

"It's one of my favorites," Lauren said, turning the screen toward me.

"I look like I'm auditioning for a survival show."

"You look like you care about what you're doing," she corrected, her tone softer now. "That's what people are connecting with."

Mom touched my arm lightly, her eyes warm. "She's right, Trent. You come across as... well, authentic. Like someone people can trust."

The room went quiet for a beat as everyone digested that. Then Gage broke the silence with a laugh. "Authentic, huh? I knew those grumpy looks of yours would come in handy someday."

"Pipe down," I muttered, my ears burning. "Is that really what my voice sounds like?"

"Literally *everyone* says that," she laughed as she swiped to another video. "And yes, it is."

This one showed me again, tossing hay into a stall, laughing at something offscreen. The camera panned to Gage, dumping a round block of ice out of a bucket he'd accidentally left out overnight, his grin so wide it looked like it might split his face.

"Wow," Mom said softly. "You really saw *him*, didn't you?"

Lauren looked up, her eyes meeting mine for just a second before she glanced away. "It's easy when there's a good story to tell."

Mom gave me a sly look, but I ignored it, focusing on the coffee cup in front of me because my face was on fire. She was right, though. Lauren had... seen *me*. Somehow.

"You got all that from a few hours of filming?" I asked.

She nodded, her fingers swiping across the screen. "That's the magic of editing. I mix things up to keep the content fresh, even if the footage comes from the same day."

"Doesn't that get repetitive?" Gage asked, squinting at the phone.

"Not if you do it right. It's not about the footage itself—it's about the stories it tells."

The room went quiet as we all watched her work, her explanations falling into the background. What struck me wasn't just how polished and yet raw the videos were—it was how much they captured us. The ranch, the animals, the land. Me. She'd taken a few hours of chaos and turned it into something... meaningful.

Lauren leaned down and put her phone away in the pocket of her jeans, but when she looked up, her eyes shifted suddenly, and she burst into a laugh.

"What?" I asked, following her gaze toward the window.

She pointed, her smile wide. "Is that... Marty?"

Sure enough, the old horse was standing just beyond the porch, his ears perked forward like he was trying to join in on the conversation. His breath puffed out in the cold, and he tilted his head, staring straight at us through the glass like he was offended no one had invited him in.

I groaned. "Yup."

"He always stare in windows like that?"

"Only when he wants something," I said, grinning. "Come on, let's put him back where he belongs."

Outside, Marty greeted us with a snort, his breath visible in the frosty air. "You wanna lead him?" I asked.

Lauren stopped in the snow and stared at me like I had just spoken a foreign language. "Me?"

"Here," I said, taking her hand and placing it behind Marty's jaw. "Just guide him like this. He'll follow you. And even if he doesn't, he's too old to outrun you. Just catch him again."

She hesitated for a second, glancing back at me like she was waiting for reassurance. I nodded, and her grip on Marty's jaw steadied. Slowly, she started walking toward the barn, and Marty followed her without a fuss, his ears twirling like he was enjoying the attention.

"You're a natural," I said, trailing behind them with my hands stuffed in my coat pockets.

Lauren glanced over her shoulder, a faint grin on her lips. "I think he's just humoring me."

By the time we reached the barn, Marty had settled into her pace like he had figured she was his best new buddy. Once he was in his stall, she leaned on the edge of the door, running a hand over his thick winter coat. Her fingers tangled in his mane, the dim light catching the way her breath puffed in soft clouds.

"I never had a horse."

I leaned on the stall door. "Did you want one?"

She shrugged. "What little girl doesn't? But I wasn't obsessed with performance and training and bloodlines like Emily. I just... I guess I'd have wanted a friend, is all."

My eyes narrowed. "That sounds kind of sad, Lauren."

She gave Marty another pat and lowered her hand, turning back to me. "I didn't mean I was that lonely. But if I had a horse, it'd be one like him."

"Marty?" I walked closer, tugging affectionately at the old gelding's mane. "A washed-up old coot who won't stay where he's put and is a giant pain in my—"

"No!" she laughed. "I mean... Funny, sweet, always up to something crazy... and probably a little useless on a working ranch."

I chuckled, stepping closer to rest my arm on the stall door. "He's not useless. Just... specialized."

"Specialized?" she repeated, raising an eyebrow.

"Yeah. He's got a talent for being himself," I said, shrugging. "Sometimes, that's enough."

Lauren laughed softly, her hand still absently stroking Marty's neck. "Well, then maybe I'd fit in better around here than I thought."

I didn't respond right away, my eyes on the way Marty leaned into her touch like he'd known her forever. "You'd fit just fine. And by the way, you're anything but useless."

She looked up, startled, her hand pausing mid-stroke in Marty's mane. "Why would you say that?"

I leaned a little closer, resting one hand on the edge of the stall door. "Because you're brilliant. Amazing. You've brought something here that no one else ever has."

Her eyes searched mine, something unsure flickering there, but she didn't back away. "I don't know about all that," she said, her voice softer now. "I'm just doing my job."

"It's more than that," I said, stepping closer. I could feel the warmth of her even in the chill of the barn. "You've made people see Ridgeview the way I see it. The way it's always been, but I couldn't figure out how to show anyone."

She blinked, her lips parting slightly, like she wanted to say something but couldn't quite find the words.

"You see things," I continued, my voice dropping to something more quiet, more serious. "You see me in a way I didn't think anyone could."

Her gaze locked on mine, and for a moment, we just stood there, the air between us charged with something I couldn't put a name to. Her hand drifted down from Marty's mane, and she shifted slightly toward me.

"Trent—"

Before she could say anything else, I stepped closer, cupped her cheek, and kissed her.

Sixteen

Lauren

I KICKED THE DOOR shut behind me and tossed my bag onto the couch before peeling off my coat. The apartment was quiet except for the hum of the radiator kicking on in the corner. My mom was downstairs, bustling around the shop like always, and the apartment above it seemed too small, too calm after the constant noise of the ranch.

I settled at the kitchen table, opening my laptop. My fingers hovered over the keys for a second before I finally pulled up the footage. There he was. Marty.

On the screen, the old black horse moved with that lazy, confident charm that had already made him a fan favorite. The late afternoon sunlight turned his coat sleek as he trotted across the frame, his tail swishing and ears twitching as if he was on a mission to show the world exactly who he was.

I hit pause and leaned closer to the screen, staring at the still frame. Everything about him screamed personality—like he'd known I was filming and decided to give me his best side.

A small, satisfied smile tugged at my lips. It wasn't much, but it was something. A win.

The rest of the day had been... well, it had been something else entirely. Spending the afternoon at Ridgeview had been fun in a way I wasn't ready to admit out loud. The laughs, the filming, the way Nora Langton had brought me in to cook up a storm so I could video her ranch cooking, and then... Trent.

The memory of his lips sent a jolt through me, so vivid it was like he'd just kissed me again. My hand brushed my mouth absently, as if it could still feel the warmth of his. My cheeks heated, and I shook my head, trying to focus on the footage in front of me.

But there was no forgetting it.

Last night in the barn had been a shock—a stolen moment that left me blinking at him, unsure if it had even really happened. But today?

Today was deliberate. His hand had lingered on mine as I climbed off the four-wheeler, his thumb brushing my knuckles just long enough to send my pulse skittering. And then he leaned in, slow enough that I could have pulled away, but fast enough to catch me off guard.

It wasn't just a kiss this time. It was... *something*.

The way his hand lingered against my cheek, his thumb brushing lightly along my jaw—it wasn't rushed, like he'd been swept up in the moment. It was steady, intentional, like he wanted to make sure I felt it. His other hand had rested against my back, warm and firm, grounding me as the icy wind swirled around us.

When he pulled back, his eyes searched mine, like he was waiting for something—an answer, a reaction, maybe even a rejection. I didn't know what he saw there, but he didn't let go right away.

It wasn't just a kiss. It was a question. And I wasn't sure I knew the answer.

I bit my lip, half-laughing at myself as I pushed back from the table. "Get a grip, Lauren," I muttered under my breath, pacing to the window and back.

And yet, no matter how much I told myself to snap out of it, I couldn't shake the giddy rush bubbling under my skin.

What had he meant by it? Did it even mean anything? Or was this just one of those moments that didn't fit neatly into a box?

The thought sent a ripple of unease through me, and I clicked back to the editing screen, trying to ignore it. I clicked play, forcing myself to focus on Marty on the screen and not on the way Trent's hand had lingered on mine when he helped me off the four-wheeler.

This was work. A project. Nothing more. I couldn't afford to let my feelings get tangled up in this.

My phone buzzed on the table, snapping me out of it. Rebecca's name lit up the screen.

Perfect timing, I thought dryly, reaching for it. Nothing like a little professional reality to drag me back down to earth.

I picked up. "Hi, Rebecca."

"Lauren! Glad I caught you," she said, her tone bright but brisk, like she was packing her day into ten-minute increments. "How's your trip?"

"It's... good," I replied, faltering. How did I explain the whirlwind of the last few days without sounding like I was losing focus? "A nice change of pace."

"Glad to hear it," she said, though her tone made me doubt she cared much about the pace of my life. "I just wanted to touch base. I know things have been a little rocky lately, but the team is optimistic we can smooth things over. We're in the middle of some important contract negotiations, and I wanted to remind you how crucial it is to keep a low profile right now."

The words hit like a weight to the chest, and I gripped the edge of the table. "Of course. I understand."

"Good. We'll circle back after the holiday to discuss next steps. Hang in there, okay?"

"Thanks, Rebecca," I murmured.

The call ended, leaving an empty silence in its wake. Why did she bother calling just to repeat what she said a few days ago in an email? I stared at the phone for a long moment. *Keep a low profile. Smooth things over. Crucial.* The buzzwords sounded polished, corporate, and completely devoid of the security I'd spent years working for.

She didn't...? I squinted at the screen. Rebecca hadn't caught on to my work for Ridgeview, had she? There was no way she could. I wasn't using my work accounts for anything. None of their licensed software. My contract said I wasn't supposed to take side work, thus competing with my employers, but I wasn't being paid for this, so it didn't count, right?

The laptop screen dimmed in front of me, and I tapped the touch-pad to wake it up. Marty's frozen frame reappeared, and the flicker of satisfaction I'd felt earlier was gone, replaced by a gnawing doubt.

What was I even doing here? Helping Ridgeview Ranch wasn't going to fix my career—or my reputation. Rebecca's voice was a reminder of where my priorities should be, but somehow, they weren't where I'd left them.

I exhaled heavily, leaning my elbows on the table. As much as I hated to admit it, there was something about this project that didn't feel like a distraction. It felt different. Capturing cows grazing in the pasture, piecing together videos of the Langtons, brainstorming ideas to tell their story—it felt...

Real.

The thought startled me. I pushed it away as quickly as it came, shaking my head and closing the laptop. Real or not, this wasn't my life. My life was in California, with its deadlines, meetings, and Rebecca's voice in my ear. That's where I belonged.

At least, that's what I told myself as I shut off the lights and headed for bed. But when I closed my eyes, it wasn't California deadlines that filled my thoughts. It was Ridgeview. Marty. Trent. And for the first time in a long while, I wasn't sure what belonging was supposed to feel like.

Trent

T HE CLANK OF METAL and a muffled curse carried across the yard as Ethan wrestled with the hood of the tractor. I leaned against the barn door, arms crossed, watching him struggle for a second before deciding to step in.

"Need a hand?" I called.

Ethan glanced up, his hair sticking out from under his cap, his face smeared with grease. "I got it," he grumbled, but his shoulders sagged with relief when I moved closer.

Together, we got the hood open, the rusty hinges protesting loudly. Ethan wiped his hands on an old rag and pointed at the engine. "I was thinking... if we replace this housing here, we could add a secondary filter. It'd run cleaner, and you wouldn't have to mess with the injectors as much."

I raised an eyebrow, leaning in to inspect the engine. "Not a bad idea. Where'd you learn about that?"

He shrugged, avoiding eye contact. "Read it somewhere. Figured it couldn't hurt to try."

I studied him for a moment. He'd come a long way since the day he'd arrived, angry at the world and refusing to speak. Now here he was, throwing out ideas like he'd been fixing tractors his whole life.

"Go ahead," I said finally. "Just don't break anything we can't replace."

Ethan's face lit up in a way that was almost foreign. He nodded quickly, diving back into the engine like I hadn't just given him permission to mess with one of the most expensive pieces of equipment on the ranch.

I stepped back, leaving him to it, and headed toward the barn. From a distance, I kept an eye on him, watching as he worked with a focus that reminded me a little too much of myself at his age.

"You look like a proud dad," Mom's voice teased from behind me.

I turned, catching the knowing smile on her face as she joined me. "Don't start," I said, shaking my head.

"What? I can't be impressed?" She nudged me with her elbow. "That boy's got more determination than I thought. Maybe I was right to bring him here after all."

"Right?" I shot her a look. "You dragged us all into it, Mom. Chase, Gage, and I said it wouldn't work. Remember?"

Her smirk widened, unapologetic as always. "And yet, here we are. Liam's bonding with Hickory, Ethan's elbow-deep in that tractor, and none of you have packed your bags yet."

I opened my mouth to point out the obvious, but she pointed at me with a grin. "And before you say it, Chase doesn't count. Admit it. Seems like I might've known what I was doing."

I rolled my eyes but couldn't argue. "Don't get ahead of yourself. We'll see if the tractor still runs when he's done with it."

"Oh, don't be so hard on him." Her tone softened, her gaze flicking to Ethan, who was hunched over the engine, lost in his work. "Sometimes, just gotta give things a chance, Trent. Even things that seem... unlikely."

I shot her a look, catching the way her smile had shifted into something more pointed. "What's that supposed to mean?"

"Oh, I don't know." She tilted her head innocently, her eyes sparkling with mischief. "Just thinking about how great this idea of Lauren's seems to be. And how often she's around lately."

I stiffened, already regretting not walking away when I had the chance. "She's helping the ranch. That's it."

"Is she?" Mom's voice was light, but her gaze was sharp. "Seems to me like she's helping a certain someone lighten up, too."

I rubbed the back of my neck, glancing toward the horizon like it might offer a way out of this conversation. "Mom..."

"What? She's a good fit, Trent. For the ranch. For the family. Maybe even for you."

I sighed, shoving my hands into my coat pockets. "She's not staying, Mom. She's got a life in California. A career. This is just a project for her."

Mom studied me for a long moment before giving a small, knowing smile. "Maybe. But it's okay to hope for more, you know."

I didn't respond, and she didn't say any more. Instead, she patted my arm and walked back toward the house, leaving me to wrestle with the truth she'd just laid bare.

Lauren's laugh echoed in my memory, unbidden, as clear as if she'd just said something snarky over her shoulder.

I shook my head, muttering to myself. "Get a grip, Trent."

It wasn't like me to get caught up in someone. Sure, she was gorgeous, but that wasn't it—not entirely. There was something else about her that made it hard to think straight when she was around.

Maybe it was the way she lit up when she talked about her work, her eyes bright with enthusiasm. That fire she had, the drive to take something from an idea to a fully realized plan—it felt familiar. It reminded me of the hours I spent pouring over ranch books, analyzing feed prices, testing new systems. She understood what it was to invest everything in a goal, even when the odds weren't in your favor.

I reached the barn and stopped short, leaning against the weathered wall. The boys had cleared out earlier, leaving the place unusually quiet. I tipped my hat back and stared at the far end of the pasture, the grazing cattle barely visible in the dimming light.

I couldn't afford to be distracted.

Lauren wasn't sticking around. I'd said it to Mom, and it was the truth. Her life was in California, and everything about her—the way she dressed, the way she carried herself—made that clear. She was classy, polished, completely opposite of the small-town chaos I'd grown up with.

And yet, that wasn't what kept me drawn to her. It wasn't just the way her curls caught the light or how her laugh felt like it cut through the noise in my head. It was something else.

Lauren had a loneliness about her. Not the kind people could see from the outside—she was too put-together for that. But it was there, in the moments she thought no one was looking. The way she hesitated before answering questions about herself. The way she seemed surprised when people cared what she thought.

It was a loneliness I knew too well.

Even with my family, even with people depending on me, I'd spent the last year feeling like it all came down to me. Like one wrong step would send everything tumbling. And she... she got that.

I ran a hand over my face and sighed. "Doesn't matter."

The low bellow of a cow pulled me out of my thoughts, and I shoved myself off the wall, heading toward the equipment shed. There was always something that needed fixing or feeding. Maybe keeping my hands busy would get my head straight.

By the time I finished the evening chores, the sun had dipped behind the hills, painting the horizon in muted oranges and purples. I was reaching for the barn door when my phone buzzed in my pocket.

Lauren.

I pulled it out and saw the screen light up with a screenshot of one of our new social media pages. The following had climbed higher than I ever would've expected. Underneath it, she'd added a simple message: "Told you this would work."

A grin tugged at the corner of my mouth despite myself.

Before I could think twice, I typed back: "Guess I owe you another dinner for that."

I hesitated for a second, staring at the message. Then, with a shrug, I hit send. Whatever this was, I wasn't ready to walk away from it just y et.

Seventeen

Lauren

"Y OU'RE EARLY."

Trent's voice caught my attention as I parked my car by the barn. The morning sun was already bright, the frost sparkling on the fields like someone had sprinkled glitter over the whole valley, so I'd been fixated on the scenery when I drove up.

But the cowboy waiting for me looked pretty nice this morning, too.

I stepped out of my car and grabbed my bag from the passenger seat. I'd brought my good camera today, in hopes that we could get some quality promo stills. Trent was leaning against the side of the barn, a thermos in one hand, watching me with that cute cowboy smirk he always seemed to wear. I paused, pulled my camera out, and snapped him before he could move.

"Didn't know there was a set time," I replied, slinging the strap of my bag over my shoulder as I walked toward him.

He tipped his hat back slightly as he fell into step beside me. "There's not. Just not used to people showing up before they're expected. And not used to stealth photography, either. What're you gonna do with that?"

"Guess I'm breaking the mold," I said, brushing past him and heading into the barn. "And as for the picture... you'll see."

Inside, Gage was hunched over the workbench, sorting through a clutter of tools like he was on the verge of giving up. He glanced up when I came in and grinned. "Well, look who it is. Our social media superstar."

"Good morning to you too, Gage," I said, setting my bag down on a bale of hay.

Gage straightened and leaned against the bench, wiping his hands on a rag. "You making us famous yet, or do we still have to work for a living?"

"Depends on how well you take direction," I shot back, pulling out my laptop.

"Oh, Trent loves taking direction. Don't you, little brother?"

"Don't start," Trent muttered, stepping inside and closing the door behind him.

I flipped open the laptop and pulled up the latest stats. "Alright, jokes aside, here's where we stand. Overnight, we picked up nearly two thousand followers across all platforms, and ten more orders came in. The storefront's gaining traction faster than I expected."

Trent moved closer, his brow furrowing as he looked over my shoulder. "Ten orders?"

"That's on top of the first wave," I said, nodding. "Momentum's building. But we need to keep it going. I've got ideas for today—"

"Hold on," Gage interrupted, holding up a hand. "Before you start firing off plans, let's talk logistics. If this keeps growing, do we even have the stock to keep up?"

I glanced at Trent, waiting for his input, but he didn't say anything right away.

"We'll figure it out as we go."

Gage blinked. "Alright then," he said, tossing a wrench onto the bench. "Guess we'll see how this goes."

As he wandered off, I bit back a smile, glancing up at Trent. "Thanks for the vote of confidence."

"Don't get used to it," he said, but there was a trace of warmth in his voice that made me want to grin.

I tapped my screen, bringing up the schedule. "Alright, then. Ready to film more?"

He groaned like I'd asked him to shovel snow with his bare hands, but he nodded. "Fine. But no four-wheeler this time."

I laughed. "Deal."

"TELL ME SOMETHING," I said, snapping the camera closed and slinging the strap back around my neck.

Trent glanced over, the sunlight catching the edge of his jawline as he turned. "What now?"

"What's the best part of ranching for you? I don't mean the grass or the cows—I mean you. Why do you do it?"

He frowned, his hand tightening on the post as he looked out at the field. For a long moment, he didn't answer.

Finally, he spoke. "It's in my blood, I guess. This land—it's been in my family for three generations. My dad used to say it was more than a job. It's a responsibility."

I tilted my head, watching him closely. "That's noble, but is it enough? Just because your dad said so?"

He shot me a look, not annoyed, but thoughtful. "I guess it's more than that. There's something about being out here—working with your hands, knowing you're part of something bigger than yourself. It's... something that will last."

I nodded, lowering the camera a little. "I get that. Kind of."

His brow lifted. "Kind of?"

"Well, I don't have a family legacy to preserve or anything," I admitted. "But I do know what it's like to throw everything you have into something and hope it works. I guess for me, it's not the land—it's the stories. Showing people something they didn't even know they needed to see."

"Like a rancher explaining how cows eat?" he teased, a small smile tugging at the corner of his mouth.

"Exactly," I said, grinning. "Don't knock it. People eat that stuff up."

He chuckled. "I still don't get it, but I'll take your word for it."

"I mean it. Lots of people don't get to see this up close. The work, the planning, the satisfaction..."

"They'll think I'm crazy. Like I got nothing better to do with myself."

I laughed. "Kind of funny, isn't it?"

"What is?"

"Well, I mean..." I turned the camera off completely. "*Do* you ever feel like the crazy one?"

His brow furrowed. "All the time, but why do you ask?"

I shrugged. "I guess I think about it sometimes. Our *younger* siblings have it all figured out, and here we are..." I trailed off, motioning between us.

"Floundering?"

"Still searching for our footing," I corrected with mock indignation, though I couldn't help but laugh. "I mean, seriously. Emily and Cole? They're, what, twenty-one? *So* young, but they've already built something to last. Something human and personal."

Trent's smirk softened into something more reflective. "Yeah, they have."

"It's kind of surreal," I admitted, turning my gaze to the horizon. "I remember Emily sneaking out to ride bareback on some poor, unsuspecting pony she wasn't supposed to touch. Now she's married, training horses, and she has all her dreams in her sights. Meanwhile..."

"Meanwhile, you're flying blind, and I'm trying to keep a ship from sinking."

I smiled, meeting his gaze. "That about sums it up."

For a moment, we just walked, heading back for the quad, but Trent kept glancing at me.

"Honestly, that's part of why I tried so hard to make things work with Cassie," Trent said suddenly.

I stopped. "Really?"

He nodded, his hands shoved deep into his jacket pockets. "At the time, it felt like the right thing to do. She was... fun, I guess. Kept things interesting. And I thought maybe if I stuck it out, I could build something solid. Figured it was time I got serious about something."

"But it didn't work out."

"Turns out, you can't force something that doesn't fit. Cassie wasn't exactly... grounded."

I tilted my head, watching him carefully. "So, why didn't you break it off sooner?"

Trent hesitated, then sighed. "Because every time I thought about it, she'd pull the rug out from under me. Start talking about how I was the only one who understood her, how nobody else ever cared. Made me feel like walking away would wreck her."

I frowned, my heart squeezing with something uncomfortably close to sympathy. "That's called manipulation, Trent."

He shrugged, but his jaw tightened. "It's over now. Guess I learned my lesson."

"Which is?"

"Don't try to build a life with someone who doesn't want the same things you do," he said simply, glancing at me with a faint, almost apologetic smile.

I didn't respond right away. How could I? Trent's words hung in the cold air between us, simple and unassuming, but they might as well have been carved into stone.

Don't try to build a life with someone who doesn't want the same things you do.

I'd never thought about my life in those terms. I'd always assumed I could find someone, fall in love, and everything else would work itself out. But Trent was right. Wanting the same things mattered—maybe more than anything else.

Except... what *did* I want?

A city career used to make sense, but one little mistake, and look how precarious it was? I had a sleek apartment in San Diego, but I came home to nothing but silence and work emails. My friends were all work friends, and I didn't even want to see them right now. Must mean they were great friends, right?

I glanced at Trent out of the corner of my eye. He was walking just ahead of me now, his hands stuffed in his jacket pockets, his broad shoulders cutting a steady path through the frost. The life he'd built was nothing like mine—gritty, hands-on, rooted in the kind of determination I wasn't sure I'd ever had.

And yet...

Another kiss or two with that cute cowboy seemed like the perfect way to straighten out my thoughts.

I shook my head, trying to clear it. Wanting Trent wasn't enough. Not if it came with a life I wasn't sure I could handle.

"Hey." His voice broke into my thoughts, and I realized he'd stopped walking. He turned to look at me, his expression softer now. "You okay?"

"Yeah," I said quickly, forcing a smile. "Just... thinking."

"Dangerous pastime," he teased, the faintest smile tugging at the corners of his mouth.

"Maybe," I said, my voice lighter than I felt.

We reached the barn, and he pushed the door open, gesturing for me to go inside. The warmth and the familiar scent of hay enveloped me as I stepped in, and for a moment, I was grateful for the distraction.

"You want to call it a day?" he asked, leaning against the stall door where Marty was waiting, his ears flicking at the sound of Trent's voice.

I nodded, glancing at the horse. "Probably a good idea. I've got more editing to do anyway."

Trent nodded, his gaze lingering on me just a second too long. "Thanks for... well, for everything, Lauren. Means a lot."

"You know..." I started, meeting his gaze as I leaned my shoulder against Marty's stall. The words danced on the edge of my tongue, but I hesitated, suddenly shy under the weight of his attention.

He raised an eyebrow, his expression softening. "What?"

"There is *one* thing you can do to thank me," I said, the corners of my mouth curving into a small smile.

His lips twitched into a half-smile, curiosity flickering in his eyes. "What's that?"

I stepped closer, tilting my head up to meet his gaze. "This."

Before I could second-guess myself, I reached up, sliding my hands to the collar of his jacket, and pulled him down into a kiss.

For half a second, he didn't move, and I thought I'd miscalculated. But then his arms wrapped around me, strong and steady, and he kissed me back.

It wasn't the kind of kiss I'd expected—if I'd even allowed myself to expect one at all. Especially not after that talk about being with someone who wanted the same things out of life, and we definitely did *not*.

But kissing Trent... well, that just felt like it was supposed to be. His touch was soft at first, almost tentative, like he wasn't sure he had the right. But then his hand found its way to the back of my neck, his fingers threading gently into my hair, and all hesitation melted away.

I didn't think about why I was doing this, or what it meant, or whether I was breaking every rule I'd ever made for myself. All I knew was how good it felt to be here, in his arms, his warmth chasing away the chill of the barn.

When we finally pulled apart, my breath was coming a little faster, and his eyes stayed locked on mine, searching for something I wasn't sure I had the words to give.

"Was that the thank-you you had in mind?" he asked softly.

I smiled, brushing a strand of hair out of my face. "It's a start."

He chuckled, his hand still resting lightly on my waist. For a moment, neither of us moved, the quiet hum of the barn and Marty's soft snort the only sounds between us.

"I should go," I whispered.

"Yeah," he murmured, though he didn't step back right away.

I forced myself to take a step, then another, until the cool evening air hit my cheeks as I walked out of the barn.

But even as I climbed into my car and drove away, the feel of his arms around me lingered, warm and impossible to ignore.

Trent

T HE BARN WAS QUIET now, the light from the setting sun filtering through the slats in the wall, casting long shadows across the stalls. Marty snorted softly, his breath visible in the chilly air as he leaned into my touch. I stroked his neck absently, my thoughts miles away.

Lauren.

I leaned against the stall door, staring out at nothing in particular. The kiss had been impulsive, like the handful before it, but it hadn't felt like a mistake. Not even close. But what was I doing? She wasn't staying, and I wasn't leaving.

"Don't try to build a life with someone who doesn't want the same things you do."

The words I'd said to her echoed in my head, sounding less like advice and more like a warning to myself now. I'd learned that lesson with Cassie—jumping in too fast, too soon, with someone who didn't fit into the bigger picture. It didn't end well.

So why did it feel so different with Lauren?

The barn door creaked open, pulling me out of my thoughts. Mom stepped inside, carrying a small bucket of feed. Her sharp eyes landed on me immediately, narrowing like she could see straight into my head.

"Evening," she said, setting the bucket down by one of the stalls.

"Evening," I replied, trying to keep my tone casual as I stepped back from Marty's stall.

She didn't move toward the feed right away, just stood there, leaning on the handle of the stall gate. "You look like you've got something on your mind."

I shook my head, attempting a shrug. "Just a long day."

Her knowing smile made it clear she wasn't buying it. "Long days don't usually leave you looking like you've been hit over the head with a sack of flour."

I huffed a laugh despite myself. "Thanks, Mom."

She crossed her arms, watching me closely. "It's her, isn't it? Lauren."

I froze, my hands stuffed deep into my coat pockets. "Why would you think that?"

"Call it a mother's intuition. Or maybe it's just the way you've been acting like a teenager with his first crush every time she's around."

I opened my mouth to argue, but she held up a hand.

"Relax, Trent. I'm not giving you a hard time. Just saying... sometimes the things we don't think are meant for us turn out to be exactly what we need."

I frowned, her words settling uneasily in my chest. "I'm not sure it's that simple."

She tilted her head, studying me. "It's rarely simple. Doesn't mean it's not worth it."

With that, she grabbed the bucket and moved to the next stall, leaving me alone with my thoughts and Marty's quiet, steady breathing.

I stayed there for a while longer, leaning against the stall door, trying to make sense of the mess in my head. Mom might've been right—things worth having didn't come easy.

But was I ready to take that risk again?

Marty nickered softly, nudging my arm, and I rubbed his nose absentmindedly. For the first time in a long time, the idea of taking that leap didn't feel so impossible.

.

Eighteen

Trent

I SLAMMED THE POST driver down, the clang echoing sharp against the frozen ground. The steel post sank another inch, and I stepped back, rolling my shoulders to shake off the stiffness. My gloves were starting to slip, and I yanked them tighter, ignoring the cold seeping through the worn leather.

The fence line ran straight along the edge of the south pasture, cutting a line between Ridgeview's land and the open hills beyond. It was a good fence—my dad and I had rebuilt most of it years ago—but winter had a way of testing everything. Between frost heaving and cattle rubbing against the posts, weak spots showed up fast.

I hauled another post from the pile at my feet, lining it up where the wire sagged between the last two. There wasn't much time to think when you were working with your hands, but that morning, my mind wouldn't quit running.

Lauren.

She was a force of nature, all confidence and ideas, her excitement bubbling over every time she talked about what we were building. What she was building. And I couldn't shake the way she'd looked at me yesterday, her lips curling into that teasing smile as she said, "You're welcome."

I shook my head and drove the post driver down hard, the clang echoing in the cold air. What was I doing, kissing her for fun whenever I felt like it? Sure, we were both adults. It wasn't like it was a crime, but the way we talked and teased and the way she felt in my arms... it wasn't just goofing around, either. And I wasn't sure I was okay with that.

She wasn't staying.

I lost track of how many times I'd warned myself of that. She might've come from around here, but California was her home. Her career, her whole life—it was all tied to a place a world away from Ridgeview.

And yet...

I adjusted the wire, pulling it taut and clipping it in place. The work was simple, the kind of thing you could do with your eyes closed, but I felt the knot of doubt tightening in my chest with every movement.

The ranch was starting to see traction thanks to her plan. Orders were coming in, the social media numbers were climbing, and the website was slicker than anything we'd ever imagined. But it wasn't just about the business.

Lauren made me feel something I hadn't let myself feel in years—like I wasn't just getting through the day, but actually moving toward something.

And that terrified me.

I stood back, eyeing the line of posts, and pulled off my gloves to rub the sting out of my fingers. The wind had picked up, whipping through the pasture and carrying with it a faint whistle from the barn.

My phone buzzed in my pocket, and I fished it out with a grimace, half-expecting another text from Gage about chores I should be doing. But it wasn't Gage.

The name on the screen made my stomach twist.

"Morning, Trent," the voice on the other end greeted. It was Bill Mattson, the shipping coordinator Lauren had lined up for the orders. His tone was brisk but polite, the way people sound when they're about to deliver bad news.

"Morning, Bill," I replied, already bracing myself. "What's going on?"

"Just wanted to give you a heads-up," he said. "We've had to adjust our rates effective next week. Fuel costs are up, and with the holidays, there's a demand surge for transportation. Unfortunately, we're passing some of those costs along."

I pinched the bridge of my nose. "You're raising prices? We just signed a contract."

"I know, I know," Bill said quickly, his voice taking on a slightly defensive edge. "But if you read the fine print, there's a clause that allows adjustments for fuel fluctuations. I'm giving you the courtesy of advance notice."

I closed my eyes, forcing myself to take a deep breath. "How much of an adjustment are we talking about?"

"Ten percent," he said after a slight hesitation.

"Ten percent," I repeated, the words heavy in my mouth. "Bill, that's going to kill my margins."

"I get it," he said, his tone more apologetic now. "Believe me, I do. But these are unprecedented times, and we've got to keep our fleet running. I'll email you the updated terms. Let me know if you have questions."

I stared at the phone for a second after the call ended, then shoved it back in my pocket with a muttered curse. Ten percent might not sound like much to most people, but in this business, it could mean the difference between breaking even and going under.

By the time I made it back to the barn, my thoughts were as tangled as the baling twine in the hayloft. I set the post driver down near the wall and leaned against a beam, staring out at the frost-covered fields.

We were doing everything right—or as close to it as we could manage. Lauren's plan, the social media push, the packing plant deal, all of it was supposed to make things better. But every step forward felt like it came with a new weight dragging us back.

I heard the barn door creak open behind me, followed by the sound of Mom's boots on the concrete floor.

"You've been scarce all morning. I was hoping you'd help me with..." She stopped when she got a good look at my face. "What's going on?"

"Prices are going up," I muttered. "Ten percent hike on shipping starting next week. Just found out."

Mom stepped closer, brushing hay off an overturned feed bucket before sitting down. "That's tough."

"Tough doesn't even cover it," I said, shaking my head. "We're gambling everything on this plan, and now the margins are getting tighter before we've even had a chance to prove it works."

She didn't answer right away, letting the silence settle between us like the dust in the sunbeams filtering through the rafters. "It's always a gamble, Trent," she said finally. "But you've got to trust that the work you're putting in will pay off."

"It's not just me," I said, turning to face her. "It's all of us. Gage, Chase, Cole... Emily and Kate, now. Even the boys. This ranch—it's on all of our shoulders, but I feel like I'm the one taking the risk with Lauren's plan. And if it doesn't work…"

"It will," she said firmly. "And if it doesn't? We'll figure it out together, like we always do."

I leaned back against the beam, crossing my arms. "You sound a lot more confident than I feel."

"That's because I've seen you handle worse," she said, her smile softening the edge of her words. "And because I know you, Trent. You won't let this ranch fail."

I didn't have a response to that, not one I could say without my voice giving away more than I wanted to admit. Lauren… I probably needed to talk to Lauren, to sort out how realistic this thing really was. She wasn't the kind to blow smoke up my rear just to pad her own ego. Impress the guy who never left his hometown, prove she was a big-time success in her world, and then disappear as soon as her little holiday was over…

Was she?

If she was, I wouldn't know until it was too late.

As if on cue, Lauren's name popped up on my phone. I stared at it for a second before answering.

"Yeah?"

"Hey," she said, her voice bright but businesslike. "I've got updates. The website's traffic is climbing, and I've got another lead on shipping logistics. Can I come by?"

I glanced at Mom, who raised an eyebrow but didn't say anything.

"Sure," I said after a pause. "I could definitely use a lead like that right now. See you soon."

When I hung up, Mom gave me a knowing smile.

"What's that saying? Something about the Lord closing a door and opening a window?" she asked.

"Maybe we just got a window, then," I muttered, pushing back from the table. "Or maybe we're just serving ourselves up on a platter for the bank."

T HE BARN WAS QUIETER than usual, save for the rustle of hay and the occasional stomp from Marty's stall. I'd been working through chores since Bill Mattson's call, trying to burn off the frustration, but it clung to me like a burr. I wasn't sure if it was the rising shipping costs, the doubt gnawing at my gut, or a mix of both, but my head was pounding, and my patience was running thin.

I shoved a pitchfork into a pile of hay, yanked it free, and accidentally sent half of it flying into the aisle. Marty snorted, craning his neck out to watch me with what looked suspiciously like amusement.

"Yeah, laugh it up," I muttered, crouching to scoop up the stray hay. My movements were jerky, my chest tight.

I'd bet the ranch—almost literally—on this plan. And now? Now I wasn't sure if I was a genius or an idiot.

The sound of that little compact car skidding on the snow outside snapped me out of it. A moment later, Lauren appeared in the barn doorway, bundled up and looking a little out of breath.

"Hey," she called, her cheeks flushed from the cold—or maybe from rushing.

"Hey," I answered, straightening up and brushing hay off my gloves. Her sudden appearance didn't exactly settle my nerves. "What's going on?"

She held up her laptop and a notepad like a trophy. "I've got something. A lead on a shipping company. But this is much more than a regular shipper."

Her excitement cut through my frustration like a sharp wind, and I gestured for her to come in. She stepped closer, her boots crunching against the straw as she set her stuff down on an overturned bucket.

"It's a logistics company," she began, flipping open her notepad. "I know we've already go something going for now, but this might be a better option going forward. They specialize in working with smaller operations like yours. Custom labels, expedited shipping... They've handled perishable goods before, including beef, and they're located about two hours away. I called to get some preliminary numbers, and their rates are competitive—much better than what you've been paying."

I folded my arms, leaning against the stall door. "What's the catch?"

She blinked at me, a little thrown. "Why does there have to be a catch?"

"Because nothing about this plan has been simple so far," I said. "What about reliability? Hidden fees? If we scale up, can they handle that?"

Lauren's expression shifted, and she gave me a look like I'd just issued a challenge. She reached for her laptop, pulling up a spreadsheet.

"I asked all of that," she said, spinning the screen toward me. "They have a good reputation—no delivery failures in the past three years. Their fees are transparent, and their contracts include optional scalability clauses. I did my homework, Trent."

I scanned the spreadsheet, my lips pressing into a thin line. I couldn't deny the numbers looked good. Better than I'd expected.

She crossed her arms, watching me. "Well?"

"It's promising," I admitted grudgingly.

Her eyebrows lifted. "Just promising?"

"Lauren," I said, rubbing the back of my neck, "I appreciate the work you're putting in. But you've gotta understand—this is a gamble. I'm risking everything. If this plan fails, it's not just me who's screwed. It's the ranch. My family."

Her gaze softened, and she stepped closer, her voice quieter now. "I get it. I do. But you've been gambling this whole time, haven't you? Running a ranch, keeping it alive—it's nothing but risks. You've been doing that long before I came along."

I stared at her, her words landing heavier than I wanted to admit. She was right. I hated it, but she was right.

"You didn't get here by playing it safe. And you didn't hire me just to quit halfway through."

"I didn't hire you at all," I muttered, unable to resist.

Her smile widened, and for a second, I forgot how much I hated taking risks.

"Fair point," she said. "But I'm here now. Let me help."

I exhaled, long and slow, feeling the weight on my shoulders shift just slightly. "Okay. Let's set up a call with them."

Her smile turned triumphant, and I couldn't help but feel a flicker of hope. Maybe, just maybe, this could work.

As she packed up her things, my gaze lingered on her. It sure seemed like she wasn't just doing this for the ego trip. Not trying to show off—at least, it didn't look that way. She believed in it, in the ranch, maybe even in me.

"Thanks, Lauren," I said before she left.

She paused in the doorway, glancing back at me with a grin. "Don't thank me yet. Save it for when this plan actually works."

I watched her disappear into the cold, a warmth I couldn't quite name settling in my chest.

"Hope she's right," I murmured to the barn, turning back to Marty.

Lauren

T HE TIRES SPUN USELESSLY as I tried to nudge the car forward, the steering wheel vibrating under my hands. I let out a
frustrated groan and slammed it into park. "Of course," I muttered,
glaring at the patch of icy road beneath the wheels.

This stupid car wasn't built for this kind of weather, and apparently, neither was this stupid town. Sure, the plows had come through,
but instead of laying down salt or sand like any self-respecting road
crew would, they'd left behind a slick, glassy layer of ice that was
practically begging for accidents.

I leaned back in my seat, muttering under my breath as I stared at
the glinting road. "Oh no, why bother keeping the streets safe when
you can just count on everyone to have snow tires or a death wish?"

My phone was sitting in the cupholder, and it *probably* had service.
Maybe. I glanced at it, torn between the urge to call for help and the
desire to tough it out. After all, this wasn't the first time this town's...
quirks had left me stranded.

I thought about the tow truck guy, who'd left my car outside my
mom's shop with the keys in the ignition like we lived in Mayberry.
Then there was the coffee shop that didn't open until nine, as if early
risers didn't exist. And now this—a town so small it didn't even believe
in treating its icy roads properly.

I let my head drop against the steering wheel, a deep sigh escaping as I resisted the urge to scream into the quiet of the car. Calling Trent was an option, sure, but the idea of adding one more "thing" to his growing list made my pride rear up. I didn't need to be another one of his problems.

I glanced at the phone again, the screen mocking me with its little service bars. "Great," I muttered. "Let's just add 'be a burden to Trent Langton' to my list of accomplishments today."

A sharp knock on the driver's side window startled me. I whipped my head around to find the sheriff standing there, his gloved hand raised in greeting. There was a name badge on his uniform that read Wyatt Dodds, and that did jog a memory. He'd been the sheriff around here since before I was born. How could the guy *still* be the sheriff? He'd pulled my dad over for a broken taillight the day we left this town with the moving van for California.

His breath puffed in the cold air as he motioned for me to roll the window down. I pressed the button, the glass squealing slightly as it slid down.

"You okay there, Miss?" he asked, leaning slightly to peer into the car.

"Not really," I admitted, my voice sharper than I intended. "This car can't handle the ice, and the roads aren't helping."

Wyatt chuckled, straightening up. "Looks like those tires aren't rated for winter driving. Half your studs are already popped out. You renting this thing?"

I nodded, my irritation flaring again. "Unfortunately. The SUV I reserved wasn't available, so I got stuck with this."

He gave the car an assessing glance, his expression somewhere between amusement and sympathy. "Well, let's get you back on the road. Stay put."

Before I could respond, Wyatt waved down a pickup truck that had just turned onto the street. The driver, a middle-aged man with a mustache and a friendly grin, hopped out and greeted Wyatt like an old friend. Together, they hooked a tow strap to my car and maneuvered it back onto the road with practiced ease.

Wyatt tapped on my window again once they were done. "You're good to go now, but take it slow. These roads are slick as sin."

"I noticed," I muttered, still gripping the wheel like it might slide out of my hands.

He grinned, unfazed by my mood. "I've seen that car parked outside the second-hand shop. My wife likes to shop there. You heading back there now?"

I nodded. "It's my mom's place."

"No kidding! Oh, that's right. Blake Walker was telling me that Cole's sister-in-law would be in town. That must be you. Told me to pull you over and make sure you got one of these."

My brow wrinkled as Sheriff Wyatt bent to pull something out of his pouch. Great... I was getting a ticket. What for? I hadn't done anything illegal, except get stuck. That wasn't illegal here, was it? Loitering or something?

But it wasn't a ticket that appeared out of his pocket. It was a stick of beef sausage, with a red ribbon twisting around the wrapping to make it look like a candy cane.

"Uh... thanks?"

"Don't mention it. Blake gave me a whole bucket of 'em to give out this month. Between you and me, I think he's just tryin' to get me to turn a blind eye when he takes that side-by-side of his out for a joy ride on the highway, but I've still got a ticket with his name on it. Already pre-filled-out," Wyatt chuckled. "Oh, and here's another sausage for your mom. Tell you what," he said, his voice kind but firm. "I'll follow you back, make sure you get there in one piece."

I opened my mouth to protest but stopped myself. What was the point? The roads were treacherous, and if the sheriff wanted to play escort, who was I to argue?

"That would be great."

He patted my windshield with a grin. "Take 'er easy, now. Hate to have to pull you out again."

As I pulled slowly back onto the street, Wyatt's cruiser idled behind me, its lights off but its presence reassuring in my rearview mirror. Maybe this town wasn't so bad after all. Or maybe I was just starting to get used to its quirks.

Nineteen

Lauren

T HE ICED COFFEE WAS bitter and it did nothing to warm me up, but I didn't care. I sat at my mom's kitchen table, staring at my laptop screen without really seeing it. My inbox was a mess of promotional emails, notifications, and a handful of work-related messages I wasn't quite ready to open. My fingers hovered over the touchpad, debating which digital fire to put out first.

Then my phone buzzed.

Rebecca's name lit up the screen, and my stomach did an anxious flip. I swallowed hard, setting the coffee aside and swiping to answer.

"Hi, Rebecca," I said, trying to sound chipper.

"Lauren! Glad I caught you," she said, her voice as brisk and professional as always. That clipped, bright tone usually meant she was softening the blow for something unpleasant. "How's your trip going?"

I leaned back in my chair, staring at the ceiling. "Still... good. Different."

"Glad to hear it," Rebecca said, but there was a pause before she continued. "Listen, Lauren, I wanted to touch base about the situation back here. You've probably heard through the grapevine that we lost a big client recently."

"I... no, I hadn't heard that." My heart started racing.

"Unfortunately, the Masterson account is taking their business elsewhere."

"Oh..." I closed my eyes. "Oh, that's not good."

"It's been a rough couple of weeks. The fallout has hit hard, and we've had to make some tough decisions. Unfortunately, we're going to need to downsize. You're not being let go," she added quickly, as if that would soften the blow. "But for now, we're putting you on indefinite furlough. It's not a reflection on your performance. You've done excellent work, and everyone recognizes that."

Indefinite furlough. The words echoed in my head like a bad joke. My grip on the phone tightened as I stared out the window, watching the snow pile up on the sill like nothing had changed.

"Lauren?" Rebecca's voice pulled me back to reality. "I know this isn't easy to hear."

"No kidding," I said, the words sharper than I'd intended. I winced at my own tone and took a steadying breath. "Sorry. I just... didn't see this coming."

Rebecca sighed, and for the first time, I thought I heard genuine sympathy in her voice. "I get it. Believe me, I do. This wasn't an easy call to make. But with the client fallout, we've had to make some tough decisions. You're not the only one impacted."

The words struck a nerve, and before I could stop myself, I asked, "The fallout—was that because of me?"

There was a pause, just long enough to make my stomach twist.

"Not entirely," she said carefully. "The deal was already on shaky ground. Your post... it didn't help, but it wasn't the sole reason."

"But it was the last straw," I finished for her, the weight of those words settling over me like lead. "They don't trust us anymore because of my screw-up."

"Lauren," Rebecca started, her tone softening. "It was a perfect storm of circumstances. The client had been looking for an excuse to walk away for months."

"And I handed them one," I said bitterly.

Rebecca hesitated, and that was all the confirmation I needed. My mistake—the one I'd spent two weeks trying to downplay in my own mind—had been the tipping point.

"Look," Rebecca said gently, "you're one of the best social media strategists I've ever worked with. This doesn't change that. What happened was unfortunate, but it doesn't define you. Take this time to reevaluate. Consider freelancing—you've got the talent to build something on your own. Or maybe... take a step back and think about what you really want. Sometimes, these setbacks lead to unexpected opportunities."

Her words were meant to soften the blow, but they only made the chaos in my chest worse. What I wanted? I didn't even know anymore. A big corporate career had been my dream for so long, but now that it was slipping through my fingers, I couldn't help wondering if it had ever really fit.

"Thanks," I managed, my voice tight. "I'll think about it."

"I mean it, Lauren," Rebecca pressed. "You're too good to let this knock you down. We'll touch base after the holidays, okay?"

"Okay," I murmured, though I wasn't sure if I believed her.

The call ended, and I set the phone down on the table, staring at it like it might explode. For a long moment, I just sat there, my thoughts a jumble of guilt and frustration.

I'd wanted to blame someone else—anyone else—for what had happened. But now, faced with the truth, all I could feel was the crushing weight of my own failure.

I dropped the phone onto the table and stared blankly at the laptop screen. Everything about my career had felt precarious since that humiliating post went viral, but this? This was different. It wasn't just the fallout from one mistake. It was the foundation I'd built my life on crumbling beneath me.

I needed to talk to someone.

Grabbing my coat and phone, I headed for the door.

E MILY OPENED THE DOOR with a mug of coffee in her hand and a worried look on her face. "Hey, you okay?"

"No," I said flatly, stepping inside.

Emily set her coffee down on the counter and waved me to the couch. "Talk to me."

I collapsed onto the cushions, pulling my knees up and wrapping my arms around them like I could hold myself together by sheer willpower. "I just got off the phone with Rebecca. They lost a big client and had to downsize. I'm on indefinite furlough."

Emily winced. "Ouch. That's tough."

"Tough?" I repeated, my voice breaking. "This is my career. Everything I've worked for. And now it's just... gone?"

"Hey, it's not gone," Emily said firmly, sitting beside me. "Furlough isn't the same as being fired. I bet they said they'd touch base after the holidays, right?"

"Yeah, but what does that even mean?" I buried my face in my hands. "Freelancing? Reevaluating my goals? That's just code for 'good luck out there, you're on your own.'"

Emily rubbed my back, almost like *she* was the big sister, and I was the shaky newbie just facing the real world for the first time. "You're not on your own, Lauren. You've got people who care about you."

I glanced at her, my eyes stinging. "I don't even know what I want anymore, Em. My job was everything. It was the one thing I was good at, and now I'm not even sure I want it back."

Emily tilted her head, studying me. "You know what I think? I think you're selling yourself short. Look at what you're doing for Ridgeview. You've taken this huge, crazy idea and made it real. That's no small thing, Lauren. You're good at more than just your job in California."

I shook my head, not ready to believe her.

Emily leaned closer, her voice softer now. "Maybe it's not about going back. Maybe it's about figuring out where you want to go next."

Her words hung in the air as I stared at the floor, trying to imagine what "next" could even look like.

Trent

THE SHARP CRACK OF frost-covered grass broke beneath the cows' hooves as I nudged them into the south pasture. They moved with that sluggish winter rhythm, their breath clouding the air. I glanced over the herd, counting out loud to keep my thoughts focused. But it wasn't working. Not today.

The night before had been a mess. Every time I tried to sleep, I kept thinking about Lauren—her voice, her confidence in what we were doing, the way her smile made it seem like we might actually pull this off.

The problem was, I wasn't sure I could believe in it as much as she did.

"Trent!" Gage's voice snapped me out of my thoughts. I turned to see him coming over the ridge, his hands jammed into his jacket pockets. "Truck's acting up again," he called. "Mom says we need it ready for Caldwell tomorrow. You know, if we're still doing that."

I muttered a curse under my breath. "Guess I know what I'm doing after this."

"Good thing you've got all this free time."

"Yeah, real funny," I shot back, shooing the last cow through the gate.

He leaned on the fence, watching as I latched it. "So, what's up? You've been quiet today."

"I'm always quiet," I said.

"No, this is different. This is brooding."

I rolled my eyes, shouldering past him. "Not everything's about feelings, Gage. Some of us actually work."

He laughed, jogging to catch up with me. "Whatever you say, man. But if this is about Lauren, maybe you oughta figure it out. She's not gonna be here forever."

I stopped in my tracks, the cold biting harder now. Gage didn't usually push like this. He must've seen something in me I hadn't realized I was showing.

"Leave it alone," I said, my voice clipped.

Gage raised his hands in mock surrender. "Whatever you say, man."

He veered off toward the barn, and I headed to the shop. The old truck was sitting there like a stubborn mule, and I grabbed a wrench, diving in.

Fixing things was something I could usually handle. It wasn't my gift—not like it seemed to be with Ethan—but it added up. A busted water pump, a bad spark plug—those were problems with clear solutions. But today, every bolt I turned just tightened the knot in my chest.

By the time I finished, the sun was dipping low, casting long shadows over the ranch. I wiped my hands on a rag and headed inside, hoping to avoid anyone until dinner.

No such luck.

Mom was in the kitchen, flour streaking her apron as she rolled out pie dough. She glanced up when I walked in, immediately narrowing her eyes. "What's that look?"

"Nothing," I said, dropping my gloves on the counter.

"That's not a nothing face."

Gage walked in behind me, grinning as he grabbed a glass of water. "He's been brooding all day."

"Gage," I growled, shooting him a glare.

Mom ignored the tension, dusting her hands off as she leaned against the counter. "Is this about Lauren?"

I froze, my jaw tightening. "Why would it be about Lauren?"

"You tell me. You've been different since she got here. Good different, mostly. But now..."

"She's not staying," I said flatly, cutting her off. "She's got a life in California. This is temporary."

Mom crossed her arms, watching me like she was trying to peel me apart with her eyes. "And that's enough for you? Just temporary?"

I didn't answer.

"Hmm," she said, turning back to the dough. "Funny thing about temporary—it has a way of sticking around when you least expect it."

Gage snorted. "Listen to her, Trent. She's got a PhD in rancher wisdom."

I shot him another glare, but this time, he just laughed and headed out.

LATER, I SAT IN my room, the soft creak of the house settling around me. The desk in front of me was as bare as my thoughts felt jumbled, except for the blank sheet of paper staring back at me like a challenge. The pen in my hand hovered, unmoving, while my mind spun in circles.

Dad used to say that when life felt tangled, writing it down was the way to make sense of it. "Get the thoughts out of your head and onto the page," he'd tell me. "Seeing them in black and white can show you what's missing."

I sighed, tapping the pen against the desk. It felt too simple—like a trick for someone who didn't have as much riding on every decision. But here I was, staring at a blank page and hoping that Dad was right.

Finally, I wrote at the top:

What do I want?

The words looked so small compared to the weight they carried. I leaned back in the chair, letting my gaze drift to the ceiling. For years, I thought I'd known the answer to that. Keep the ranch running. Take care of the family. Honor Dad's legacy. Those had been my guideposts, and I'd stuck to them like my life depended on it.

But now...

Now, there was Lauren.

I closed my eyes and saw her, unbidden. The way her face lit up when she caught a perfect shot on camera. The way her laugh filled the space around her, rare but rich, like it didn't need to happen often to be worth hearing. The way she'd looked at me—actually seen me—in a way I wasn't sure anyone else ever had.

She didn't belong here. I wasn't stupid. She had a life waiting for her in California, polished and bright and full of things I didn't even understand. I wasn't part of it. I couldn't be.

But that didn't stop me from wishing.

I leaned forward, resting my elbows on the desk as I stared at the page. I couldn't stop seeing her, even though I knew I should. She'd thrown everything out of balance, not because she tried to, but because she couldn't help it. She wasn't supposed to matter this much.

But she did.

I started tapping the pen again, replaying every moment of the last few days. The way she threw herself into this project. How her words came out in an excited rush when she talked about what Ridgeview could be. How she believed in what we were doing, maybe even more than I did.

She understood what it was like to give everything to something—to take that risk, even when it felt impossible.

My pen stilled, and I frowned down at the page. I wanted to believe there was a way to make it work, but every time I thought about it, the doubts crept in. She wasn't staying. I had to remember that. No matter what I wanted, it didn't change the reality.

And yet...

The pen moved before I realized I was writing:

Don't let her go without trying.

I sat back, staring at the words until they blurred. It wasn't the answer. It didn't solve anything. But it was something.

Twenty

Lauren

T HE COFFEE SHOP DOOR jingled behind me, a cheerful little chime that seemed at odds with the heavy knot in my chest. I clutched my laptop bag closer and stepped inside, immediately hit by the smell of espresso and freshly baked scones. I'd decided to try a new place today—Mrs. Finch's café, about a mile outside of town on a bend in the road. It was cozy, a mix of mismatched furniture and Christmas decorations that leaned more homemade than store-bought. A half-decorated tree stood in one corner, with a box of ornaments sitting nearby as if someone had started the project and wandered off.

I glanced around, searching for a quiet corner. Most of the tables were occupied—mothers with toddlers sharing muffins, older couples chatting over steaming mugs, and a trio of teenagers huddled together with their phones. Small-town life at its finest.

I found a spot near the window, set my laptop on the table, and dropped into the chair. Pulling out my phone, I opened my email, scanning for anything from Rebecca. Nothing. I gulped and shoved the phone aside, opting instead to boot up my laptop. If I had to sit here and job hunt all day, so be it.

No Wi-Fi... of course. I sighed and switched on my phone's hot spot.

The barista, a red-haired girl with a bright smile, brought over my iced oat milk Americano a few minutes later. "On the house today, hon. Merry early Christmas."

I blinked at her, startled. "Oh. Thank you."

She gave me a warm nod and returned to the counter, leaving me alone with my guilt. I hadn't done anything to deserve kindness, not from a stranger. Heck, I felt like a traitor even sitting here, because all the gang from Walker Ranch and White Pines and Ridgeview only got their coffee from Kelli's Coffee Wagon. Gotta support the family business, right? But the Coffee Wagon didn't have a warm place to sit down, and besides... I wasn't sure I wanted to be seen by anyone I knew. I had a mess to clean up, and all I'd done since arriving in Big River Valley was throw my life into more disarray than it had already been.

Halfway through scrolling a particularly grim list of marketing jobs that required relocation to cities I had no interest in, a familiar voice interrupted me.

"Mind if I join you, or are you solving world peace over here?"

I glanced up to see Amber standing next to my table, holding a paper cup and raising an eyebrow. Her auburn hair was twisted into a loose braid, and she had that effortless confidence that made her look like she belonged wherever she went. Which, apparently, was the same "off-brand" coffee shop that I was haunting today.

I hesitated, glancing at my laptop screen. "Uh... sure."

Amber pulled out a chair and sat down, leaning her elbows on the table. "So, what's the project? Spreadsheets? Marketing magic? A breakup playlist?"

That last one made me laugh despite myself. "Job hunting, actually."

Her face softened, and she took a sip of her coffee. "Tough market?"

"You could say that," I muttered, staring at the swirling foam in my cup.

Amber gestured toward the tree in the corner. "So, you're not here to help Mrs. Finch finish decorating?"

I glanced over and saw an older lady—the owner, I assumed—standing on a rickety old stool, trying to hang a gold star that looked like it had seen better days. I snorted. "I'd probably break something."

"That would definitely add to the small-town charm," Amber quipped. "Speaking of charm, you coming to the White Pines party this weekend?"

I blinked at her, caught off guard. "Party?"

She leaned back in her chair, crossing her arms. "Yeah, big holiday bash for the therapy clients. We do it every year. Food, crafts, some caroling—it's a whole thing. You should come. You might accidentally have fun."

"Oh, I don't want to crash—"

Amber waved a hand, cutting me off. "Don't think of it as crashing. Think of it as diving headfirst into all the Christmas fun of Big River Valley. You're practically a local now, and this is what locals do."

I laughed, shaking my head. "I'll feel like I'm intruding."

"You won't be," she said simply, her tone leaving no room for argument. "The party's a good time, and the kids love it. Besides..." She tilted her head thoughtfully. "Actually, if you're not too busy this afternoon, we're decorating the therapy office. You could help out—it'd save me from trying to untangle a hundred miles of lights by myself."

I blinked at her, caught off guard. "Decorating?"

"Yeah." Amber shrugged, sipping her coffee. "Nothing fancy, just getting the place ready for the party. Stringing some lights, fluffing fake snow, that kind of thing. And just so you know, decorating is actually 'Christmas Party Beta Test.' Morgan bakes us cookies, and Kelli's donating extra decorations. And coffee... of course, coffee! It's usually fun—chaotic, but fun."

She smiled, as if daring me to say no.

"I don't think—"

"You should," she said, cutting me off again, her grin widening. "C'mon, what else do you have going on? Job hunting?"

My face flushed, and I stared down into my coffee, the sting of her words sharper than she probably meant. Amber's expression softened, and she added quickly, "Sorry. I didn't mean it like that. I just... You'd be doing me a favor, honestly."

"I don't even know where to start," I said, half-laughing, half-stalling.

"It's not complicated. Just follow me. And if you're lucky, you'll avoid the brooding cowboy. Trent's too busy hauling hay to come anywhere near a box of ornaments."

My face grew even warmer at the mention of Trent. Why would she say *that?* But Amber just grinned and finished her coffee.

I hesitated, then sighed. "All right," I said finally, surprising both of us. "I'll help."

"Good choice." Amber stood, tossing her empty cup in the bin. "See you up there, city girl."

"**L**AUREN, YOU COMING, OR what?"

Emily's voice floated in from the porch, muffled by the door I hadn't realized I'd closed behind me. I'd just pulled into the driveway at White Pines, my phone still clutched in my hand. Amber's dare to come help decorate for Christmas party had sounded like a great reprieve from all the stuff I'd been wrestling with. But now that I was here, my nerves were getting the better of me.

"Yeah, I'm coming!" I called back, shoving the phone into my pocket and stepping out of the car.

Emily was waiting at the door, her arms crossed and a smirk on her face. "You okay? You look like you're bracing for battle."

"Just distracted," I said, brushing past her.

"Distracted by a certain cowboy?" she teased, following me inside.

I shot her a glare, but she just laughed, linking her arm through mine and pulling me toward the kitchen. The smell of fresh-baked cookies hit me first, followed by the sight of Kate and Amber surrounded by trays of treats.

"Look who finally showed up," Emily announced, releasing me to grab a dish towel.

"About time," Kate said with a grin. "We were starting to think you bailed."

"Wouldn't miss it," I said, though my voice didn't sound as convincing as I'd hoped.

Kate slid a plate of cookies toward me. "Here, try one. They're not as good as Nora Langton's—don't tell Morgan I said that, because her cooking is kind of a sore subject. But they're decorated cute and bad for you, so that checks all the boxes."

I picked up a cookie, more to avoid the conversation than because I wanted it. The sweet, buttery taste melted on my tongue, and for a moment, I let myself forget about everything else.

"Okay, cookies are the fuel," Amber said, tying her dark hair up into a ponytail with an orange hair tie that clashed delightfully with her red flannel shirt. "Now it's time to get to work. Emily, did you find the ornament box?"

Emily groaned, pointing toward the living room where a plastic bin sat spilling tinsel onto the rug. "Found it, alright. I think it exploded on the way here."

Amber rolled her eyes and grabbed the bin. "Why is it always like this? Every year, it's like a glitter bomb went off."

"Tradition," Kate said with a wink, stuffing a cookie into her mouth before standing. "Let me help before Amber gets lost in her annual holiday meltdown."

Amber snorted. "I do *not* have meltdowns."

"You cried last year when we couldn't find the reindeer topper," Kate said, nudging her with an elbow.

"It's not Christmas without the reindeer!" Amber shot back, laughing despite herself.

I watched them with a growing sense of amusement. The easy camaraderie between them was infectious, even as Emily joined in, tossing a strand of garland over Kate's head like a lasso.

"Alright, city girl," Amber said, pulling me out of my thoughts. "You're on tree-fluffing duty." She pointed toward the corner, where a slightly sad-looking artificial tree leaned against the wall.

"Tree-fluffing?" I echoed, raising an eyebrow.

Kate grinned. "Oh yeah. It's an art form. You've gotta make it look alive again after it's been smashed in a box for eleven months."

I couldn't help but laugh. "Sounds like a dream job."

"Hey, we all pay our dues," Amber said, grabbing a handful of ornaments and heading toward the mantle.

I set to work, tugging at the wire branches and rearranging them until the tree looked less pathetic. Kate brought over a box of lights, untangling them with a speed that suggested years of practice.

"So," Kate said, glancing at me as she worked. "You've been spending a lot of time out at Ridgeview."

I shrugged, focusing on a particularly stubborn branch. "Just helping out with some marketing stuff."

Amber smirked from across the room. "Helping Trent, you mean?"

My hands froze on the tree, heat creeping up my neck. "I'm helping the whole ranch."

"Sure," Amber said, dragging the word out. "But if the cowboy *happens* to be there, that's just a bonus, right?"

Emily laughed, throwing a handful of fake snow in my direction. "Leave her alone, you guys. Trent's too busy brooding over feed prices to be charming right now."

Kate snickered. "True, but give it time. Those Langton boys don't stay grumpy for long."

I shook my head, smiling despite the teasing. "You're all impossible."

Amber tossed me a strand of garland. "Welcome to Big River Valley, Lauren. You're one of us now."

The rest of the morning passed in a blur of laughter and chaos. We draped lights and garlands over every available surface, arranged cookies and candy canes on the tables, and argued over where to hang the stockings.

By the time we were done, the room glowed with holiday cheer, and I had a faint ache in my sides from laughing so hard.

Amber surveyed the space with a satisfied nod. "Not bad, ladies. Not bad at all."

"It's perfect," Emily said, leaning against the couch and looking genuinely pleased.

I smiled, taking it all in—the cozy warmth of the room, the playful banter, the sense of belonging I hadn't realized I was missing.

"No. Not bad at all," I said softly, meaning it more than I expected.

Trent

THE TEXT WAS SENT before I could talk myself out of it.

Hey. You free for lunch?

The screen taunted me with its silence for a second too long. Then the dots appeared, stopped, appeared again, and finally resolved into her reply:

Depends on what it is.

I chuckled, already typing back. *Burger Shack okay?*

She replied with a thumbs-up emoji and a single word: *Always.*

Perfect. And easy! Good grief, Cassie used to have a mile-long list whenever I told her I'd pick something up for her. Lauren just said yes... almost like she trusted me.

I grabbed my keys, ready to head out, when my phone buzzed again.

Hold on. Emily says she's starving. Can you grab something for her and Kate?

I stared at the screen, feeling the first hint of doubt about this impromptu plan. I'd wanted to just hang out with Lauren, but... well, Emily and Kate were cool, too. I texted back: *Tell me what they want.*

My phone buzzed again.

Cheeseburger with extra sauce for Kate and a patty melt for Emily. Cokes for both.

I nodded and tapped out, *Got it.*

Another buzz.

Make that something for Cole, too. Kate just called him, and he's on his way back from Walker Ranch.

The buzzing didn't stop.

And Chase. He's heading up.

And Amber wants an order of chili fries.

I rubbed a hand over my face, muttering a curse. So much for lunch being just me and Lauren. I tossed the last toolbox into the bed of my truck and climbed into the driver's seat, still shaking my head at the barrage of texts. What had started as a great idea and an excuse to... I don't know, do *something* with a girl I liked was now a full-scale catering operation for half of Big River Valley.

I was reaching for the key when someone knocked on the window. Gage stood there, arms crossed and his breath fogging my glass.

I rolled the window down. "What do you want?"

"Where're you headed?" he asked, jerking his thumb toward the house. "Thought we were fixing that fence line."

"Change of plans," I said shortly, glancing at the overloaded bags of fence parts in the passenger seat. "Apparently, I'm the town burger delivery guy now."

Gage raised an eyebrow. "What're you talking about?"

I sighed. "I asked Lauren if she wanted lunch. Then Emily wanted lunch. Then Kate and Cole and Chase. Now, I'm hauling half of Burger Shack to White Pines."

Gage's grin widened. "You trying to impress her with your fry-fetching skills?"

"Get in or don't," I snapped, not in the mood for his teasing.

To my surprise, he opened the passenger door and climbed in. "Might as well. No way I'm missing this show."

I shot him a look, but he just chuckled, settling into the seat. "Relax, big brother. You're practically a hero. Saving the day, one burger at a time."

I started the truck with a muttered curse and pulled out of the driveway, the sight of Gage's smug grin making me question why I'd ever let him tag along.

BY THE TIME I pulled into the driveway at White Pines, my truck cab was practically a mobile Burger Shack. Gage hopped out of the passenger seat, balancing two drink carriers while I grabbed the overloaded bags of food.

Lauren stepped out onto the porch, her face a mix of guilt and amusement. "Sorry," she said, holding up her hands. "I tried to tell them not to hijack our lunch plans, but…"

Emily leaned around her, grinning unapologetically. "He didn't have plans. He had burgers. Big difference."

I shook my head, setting the bags on the counter. "Remind me why I put up with you people?"

Kate reached for one of the sodas. "Because we're adorable."

Emily grinned as she bit the end of a fry and chewed it right in front of me. "We just figured you wouldn't mind. You're such a good big brother!"

I shook my head. "You better be glad I like all of you. Where's everyone else?"

"They're on their way," Kate called from inside.

Gage chuckled, holding up the drinks. "Should've brought a cattle prod for this crowd."

Inside, the place smelled like cookies and pine, and the kitchen table was already crowded with decorations and snacks. I handed Lauren her drink and burger, lowering my voice. "Next time, don't tell anyone we're getting food."

She laughed, unwrapping her burger. "They told me it's my official 'Welcome to Big River Valley'."

Before I could respond, the door opened again, and Cole and Chase strolled in, shaking snow off their boots.

"This the burger joint?" Cole asked with a grin.

"Apparently," I muttered, shaking my head.

As the kitchen filled with laughter and conversation, I leaned back against the counter, watching Lauren as she effortlessly blended in with the chaos. It wasn't what I'd planned, but seeing her smile and just... fitting in like that... made the interruption feel a little easier to take.

Twenty-One

Lauren

T HE SMELL OF COFFEE drifted through the small apartment as I sat at the kitchen table, staring at my laptop. The Ridgeview campaign dashboard glowed in front of me, full of numbers and messages I didn't quite know what to do with. Normally, I loved this part—the analytics, the planning, the challenge of building something from nothing. But today? Today, it just felt... overwhelming.

The messages were the worst.

What's your shipping timeline for the Midwest?

Do you offer certifications for organic grass-fed beef?

How does your product compare to what I can get locally?

I had answers to some of the questions, but others? Trent hadn't mentioned certifications. Did they even have those? As for shipping timelines, that depended on the packer and the logistics partner—neither of which I could really control.

I rubbed my temples, resisting the urge to slam the laptop shut. Ridgeview's social media had exploded, the campaign generating more interest than I'd expected this early. But success came with questions, and I wasn't sure the ranch was ready for this kind of scrutiny.

I needed Trent.

No, I needed to figure this out myself.

Pushing back from the table, I grabbed my jacket and my mom's car keys. It wasn't the rental—I'd finally ditched the compact disaster for her much more reliable SUV. I needed coffee, and more importantly, I needed to get out of the apartment before I started screaming at a laptop that couldn't scream back.

THE BELL ABOVE THE door jingled as I stepped into Finch's Cafe, and the rich scent of roasted beans almost made me swoon. Just what I needed today—the cozy shop, all wooden tables, and twinkling string lights, had quickly become one of my favorite escapes from the chaos of Mom's apartment—and from my own spinning thoughts.

Behind the counter, that same red-haired girl, no older than seventeen, was steaming milk with the kind of focus that suggested she took her job seriously. Her nametag said "Lexi" but all I'd heard anyone call her was "Sweetheart." Typical cowboy town. She looked up when she heard the door, her freckled face lighting up. "Morning! Usual?"

"Yes, please." I fumbled for my wallet, glancing at the chalkboard menu even though I didn't need to. I always ordered the same thing, but it was impressive that she knew it. "You sure learned my order fast."

She grinned. "I have a good memory."

"Oh?" I got my card out and picked up a wrapped muffin that was sitting on the counter. "One of these, too. I guess a memory like that would come in handy. Bet you're a good student."

Lexi shook her head as she pressed the ground beans. "I *was*. I graduated early."

I nodded. I was wondering why she wasn't in school. She looked like she ought to be. "How did you manage that?"

She shrugged. "Homeschool. For the last two years, I was taking online college classes, and I had a zillion credits, so I didn't need to do any more."

"Hmm. And so now you're... just here?"

Lexi shrugged. "Grandma's a good boss."

"Gotcha."

She turned to the espresso machine, and I stepped aside to wait, scanning the shop out of habit. A few tables were occupied—an older couple sipping coffee and sharing a muffin, a man in a Carhartt jacket hunched over a newspaper, and two women sitting near the window, their heads bent close in conversation.

"...videos and whatnot," one of them was saying, her tone carrying easily over the gentle hum of the shop. "You seen them? They're all over that social media stuff."

"Yeah, saw one last night," her companion replied. "Looks good, I guess. But fancy pictures don't make beef cheaper."

I froze, my stomach twisting as I realized they were talking about Ridgeview. About me.

Lexi handed me my drink with a cheerful "Here you go!" and I forced a smile, murmuring my thanks. I headed to a table in the far corner, trying to ignore the sting of overhearing those words.

Sliding my laptop out of my bag, I opened it with shaky hands. The screen glowed to life, displaying Ridgeview's website, the project I'd poured so much of myself into these last few weeks. The social media profiles had been growing steadily, the feedback overwhelmingly positive—or so I'd thought.

I tried to focus, scrolling through comments and jotting down ideas for future posts. But the conversation at the front of the shop kept pulling my attention.

"It's just... too much," one of the women was saying now. "I mean, it's beef. Not a fashion brand."

The other laughed softly. "Exactly. All these bells and whistles might work in a city, but out here? People care about price, not packaging."

My cheeks burned, and I bit the inside of my cheek, trying to shove the words aside. It wasn't the first time I'd heard skepticism about the work I was doing, and it probably wouldn't be the last. But this felt... personal.

My drink sat untouched as I stared at the screen, the cursor blinking on an unfinished caption. What was I even doing? Trying to turn Ridgeview into something it wasn't? What if I was making everything worse?

A shadow fell across my table, and I looked up to see Lexi standing there with a tentative smile. "You okay?"

I blinked, startled by her question. "Oh, yeah. I'm fine. Just... distracted."

She glanced at my laptop, then back at me. "That's Ridgeview Ranch, right? I've seen the videos. They're really good. Grandma loves the one with the old horse."

"Marty," I said automatically, some of the tension in my chest easing.

"Yeah, him!" she said with a grin. "It makes everything seem... I don't know. Real, I guess. Like you actually care about the ranch and the animals."

Her words caught me off guard, and I found myself smiling despite everything. "Thanks. That means a lot."

She nodded, then returned to the counter, leaving me alone with my thoughts again. This time, the sting of the earlier conversation was dulled by her unexpected kindness.

Maybe I didn't need to convince everyone. Maybe it was enough to reach the people who got it—the ones who saw the heart behind the work.

I took a deep breath, my fingers hovering over the keyboard. The cursor blinked back at me, waiting, and this time I didn't hesitate.

Trent

THE LOW RUMBLE OF the diesel engine filled the cab as I pulled the truck into town, my fingers drumming on the wheel. I'd needed to grab some parts for the feed mixer, and I wasn't looking forward to it. The steady buzz of the past few weeks—the marketing, the orders, the deadlines—had started to feel more like a hornet's nest than progress.

I parked outside the hardware store and slid out of the truck, bracing against the bitter wind. Inside, old Mr. Harper was manning the counter, the same as he had since I was a kid. He looked up as the bell above the door jingled, his bushy eyebrows lifting in recognition.

"Trent Langton," he said, leaning on the counter with a knowing grin. "Funny coincidence. My wife was just talking about you. Heard you're trying something new with Ridgeview these days."

I nodded, keeping my face neutral as I grabbed a basket. "We're selling direct-to-consumer now. Lauren Carson... uh, Cole's sister-in-law... she's got the marketing up and running."

"Ah, the California gal," Harper said, his grin widening. "City girl's got you ditching the auction, huh? Bold move, I'll give you that. But bold don't always work out, y'know."

My grip tightened on the basket, and I forced myself to take a breath. Harper didn't mean anything by it—he was just the kind of guy who liked to poke at everyone. But today wasn't the day.

"We'll see," I said shortly, grabbing a box of bolts from the shelf.

"You're banking on city folks paying big for your beef? Hope they do, son. It'll fetch a good price per pound, if you can sell it. But I've been around long enough to know people around here don't like change. You'd better hope that girl's got more than pretty pictures backing her up."

I clenched my jaw, biting back the urge to snap. I wasn't about to explain myself to Harper, of all people.

I paid for the parts, exchanged a tight nod with him, and headed back to the truck, my shoulders stiff with tension.

T HE PHONE RANG JUST as I pulled into the ranch yard, and I grabbed it off the dash without checking the screen.

"Yeah?"

"Trent." Chase's voice was clipped, and I braced myself for whatever was coming. "We need to talk about this direct-to-consumer thing."

I sighed, resting my forehead against the steering wheel. "What about it?"

"What about it?" Chase repeated, his tone incredulous. "How about the fact that you've tied up all the ranch's resources on something that might not even work? I thought you guys were just fooling around, selling some on the side, but after I talked to Gage yesterday, I got a look at what you're actually doing. Were you planning to talk to me about this?"

"What do you mean, talk to you? You were one of the ones who dragged Lauren out to the ranch to talk to me about this in the first place!"

"Yeah, I figured you'd sell a load, make a few bucks on the side. You didn't bother telling me we were *all* in on this thing. Never, in two weeks, thought it would be worth picking up the phone?"

"That's two weeks of questions you haven't been askin'," I growled back.

"Well, I'm asking now. We've got bills piling up, feed and fuel costs through the roof, and you're gambling on social media to save us?"

"It's not lookin' like a gamble anymore. We've got orders coming in, a new shipping contract, and margins are good enough for a fair profit. The website's up and running, and Lauren's been—"

"Lauren," Chase cut in. "That's what this is about, isn't it? You let her waltz in here with her big-city ideas, and now we're putting everything on the line because she says it'll work?"

"That's not fair," I snapped, sitting up straight. "She's putting in the work, and we've already got results. The orders are there, Chase."

"For now," he shot back. "But what happens when the novelty wears off? What happens when the city folks move on to the next big thing, and we're left holding the bag?"

I didn't have an answer for that, and the silence on my end was enough for him to keep going.

"You're not thinking this through. You're letting her call the shots—a chick with *zero* experience in ranching. And it's not just your neck on the line—it's all of ours."

"Then what do you suggest?" I barked. "We just stick to the same old thing, keep grinding ourselves into the ground, and hope we make it through another year?"

"At least the same old thing's got a track record," he said.

"Yeah, a track record of barely keeping the lights on! Mom basically laid it out—if you'd've been there, you'd have got the same lecture. We try something big or we probably don't have much try left in us at all."

"Enough."

The single word from the other end of the line stopped me cold. I hadn't even realized how loud my voice had gotten until Gage stepped out of the barn, giving me a curious look as he wiped his hands on a rag.

Chase sighed, his voice softer now. "Look, I get it. You're trying to save the ranch, and I respect that. But you're flying blind here, Trent. Just... think about it, okay?"

I ended the call without answering, shoving the phone into my pocket as I climbed out of the truck.

T HE STING OF THE conversation stuck with me as I unloaded the parts and headed into the shop to start repairs. The tools felt heavier in my hands, the air colder against my skin.

Every bolt I tightened seemed to echo Chase's words. *Was* I letting Lauren call the shots? Was I risking everything for something that wouldn't last?

By the time I'd finished the repairs, my hands were aching, and my thumb was throbbing where I'd smashed it with the wrench. I leaned against the truck, letting out a long breath that fogged in the chilly air.

Across the yard, Liam was leading Hickory out of the barn for a ride. That was good... kid needed something that was all his. Chase was talking to Ethan by the tractor, his hand resting on the kid's shoulder as they discussed something I couldn't hear.

The sight should've grounded me, reminded me why I was doing all this. But instead, it just made the ache in my chest worse.

"Hey."

I turned to see Gage standing a few feet away, his hands in his pockets.

"You good?" he asked, his tone more curious than concerned.

I shrugged, not trusting myself to say much.

Gage tilted his head, studying me. "Chase giving you crap?"

"When isn't he?" I muttered, rubbing the back of my neck.

He snorted, crossing his arms. "You know he means well, right?"

"Yeah, I know."

"You gonna keep at it?" Gage asked, nodding toward the truck.

I glanced at the repairs, then back at him. "What other choice do we have?"

Gage grinned, clapping me on the shoulder. "That's the spirit."

But as he walked away, I couldn't help but wonder if it was enough.

Lauren

T HE BARN AT WHITE Pines glowed like something out of a Christmas postcard. Strings of white lights crisscrossed the beams over while lanterns hung from the stalls, casting a soft, warm glow that softened the edges of everything it touched. Tables lined the center aisle, draped in red and green checkered cloths and laden with cookies, hot cocoa, and crafts the therapy kids had made over the year. The mingling scents of hay, cinnamon, and something sweet wafted through the air, while snow fell steadily outside, blanketing the world i n white.

I stepped inside and froze, overwhelmed by the scene. The warmth, the light, the laughter—it all seeped into me like a hug I hadn't realized I needed.

"Lauren!" Amber's voice carried across the barn, snapping me out of my daze. She waved from near the cider station, a grin lighting up her slightly frazzled face. "Get over here and grab some cider before it's gone!"

"Coming," I called, tugging my scarf loose as I made my way toward her.

At the cider station, Doc Burns stood behind a table, pouring steaming mugs for a group of giggling kids. I'd bumped into him at the gas station the day before—he'd helped me with a frozen fuel door and told me who he was, so I guess I made a friend. He glanced up when he saw me, his weathered face breaking into a smile.

"Well, look who's still in town," he said, handing me a mug. "I figured you'd gone and run back to California by now."

I laughed, wrapping my hands around the mug. "Not yet. Still trying to figure out how to survive the snow."

Doc chuckled, his eyes twinkling. "You stick around long enough, it'll grow on you. Like a bad rash."

Before I could reply, a shout of laughter rang out behind me. I turned just in time to see a boy darting between tables, clutching a half-eaten cookie. This guy with a cane and a veteran's hat followed in hot pursuit, shaking a candy cane like a sword.

"You little rascal!" he bellowed, though his grin gave him away. "That's the last one, and it's mine!"

The boy ducked under a table, shrieking with laughter as the guy pretended to trip and fall against a chair.

Amber appeared at my side, shaking her head with a fond smile. "Every year, Walter pretends to be the Grinch, and every year, the kids eat it up."

I watched as the boy popped his head out from under the table, crumbs on his face and triumph in his eyes. "He seems like a good sport," I said, sipping my cider.

"Good sport doesn't even begin to cover it," Amber said. "Walter's been part of White Pines since day one. He's like family here."

The sound of boots on the barn floor made us both turn. Morgan strode toward us, her sandy hair pulled back into a practical ponytail, her sharp, kind eyes scanning the room before landing on me.

"Lauren," she said warmly, her hands in the pockets of her fleece-lined vest. "Glad you could make it. Amber mentioned you might swing by."

"It's incredible," I said, gesturing to the barn. "This whole place—it's like a Hallmark movie come to life."

Morgan laughed, crossing her arms as she looked around. "That's the goal. Christmas is a time for magic, and these kids deserve their fair share. Besides, it gives us all a chance to celebrate everything we've built together."

As if on cue, three therapy horses were led into the barn, their manes braided with garlands and bells. The kids squealed with delight, rushing to greet them with sticky hands and candy-striped ribbons.

Amber nudged me, grinning. "That's Biz over there. He's a crowd favorite and Morgan's heart horse. Even the parents love him, the big ham. Walter's always trying to take him home," she said with a laugh.

"He's gorgeous," I said, watching as one of the kids hugged the buckskin's neck. The horse lowered his head patiently, letting the little boy drape a garland over his mane.

"Watch out for Marty," a familiar voice drawled behind me.

I turned to find Trent leaning against a stall, his arms crossed, the brim of his hat tipped just enough to shadow his eyes.

"Marty's not here, is he?" I asked, a flicker of nerves tightening my chest.

"Nope. But if he were, he'd have escaped by now and polished off the egg nog and ginger snaps."

"Ignore him," Amber laughed. "Marty might be an Instagram sensation who makes every cowboy who ever mended a fence quake in his boots, but even he can't crash this party. Not without a costume, anyway."

I rolled my eyes but couldn't stop the smile tugging at my lips. Trent's presence, even when he was teasing me, somehow made the barn feel warmer.

Before I could come up with a witty reply, Morgan's voice carried across the barn. "All right, everyone! Gather round for the candle-lighting ceremony. We wanted to try something new this year."

The chatter quieted as people shuffled toward the center of the barn. A loose circle formed, with Morgan standing at its heart, holding a single lit candle. Kelli Walker was walking around, passing out more candles to everyone who didn't have one. Even the kids got one... so long as they had an adult helping them.

"Tonight, we celebrate not just the season, which is the greatest Gift of all, but the light we bring into each other's lives," she said. "If anyone can testify to the power of a single spark, it is those of us at White Pines—we who have seen the littlest dreams catch fire and become miracles. Every flame starts small, but together, they create something beautiful. So... this is my thank you to all of you this Christmas, for catching the flame and passing it on."

She lit the candle of the person next to her, and they, in turn, lit the next. The glow spread slowly, building and brightening until the whole barn shimmered with the soft, flickering radiance.

I held my breath, the lump in my throat growing with each new light. It wasn't just the beauty of it—it was the meaning. The quiet strength in the room, the connection between people who cared deeply about each other and this place.

A hand brushed lightly against mine, and I glanced over to find Trent standing beside me, his face illuminated by the candlelight. His expression was soft, thoughtful, and, for once, relaxed.

"You okay?" he asked, his voice low enough that only I could hear.

I nodded quickly, swallowing hard. "Yeah. It's just... a lot."

"Good kind of a lot?"

I met his eyes, unsure how to answer. I never was comfortable with all this... feeling. But the look he gave me—steady and unflinching—felt like he already knew the truth.

Before I could find the words, Morgan's voice rose gently above the quiet murmurs of the barn. "Before we blow out our candles, I thought we could sing together—one last moment to let the light and the music carry us through this season."

She nodded toward a young boy standing nearby, who hesitated before stepping forward with a shy smile. In his hands, he held a guitar, the body of it scarred and well-loved.

"Take it away, Jackson," Morgan said warmly.

The boy strummed a few uncertain chords, but as he began to play the opening notes of "Silent Night," the room fell into a reverent hush. Slowly, voices joined in—softly at first, then growing stronger as the melody filled the barn.

I sang along, my voice catching slightly as the lyrics swelled. "All is calm, all is bright..." The warm flicker of the candles seemed to dance with the music, casting golden light across the faces around me.

Next to me, Trent's deep voice joined the harmony. I glanced at him again, something tugging at my chest. He wasn't just singing the words; it was as if he felt them.

When "Silent Night" ended, Morgan glanced around, smiling as if she could feel the closeness in the room. "Let's do one more," she said. "What about 'O Come, All Ye Faithful'?"

Jackson struck up another tune, this time with more confidence, and the voices rose again. The familiar words wrapped around me like a blanket, pulling me further into the moment.

As the final chorus rang out, Trent leaned slightly toward me, his voice steady beside mine. It wasn't until the last note faded into the rafters that I realized I'd been holding my breath.

The barn stilled again, the warm quiet punctuated only by the soft rustle of coats and the occasional creak of the beams overhead. Morgan spoke softly, inviting everyone to extinguish their candles one by one, and the room slowly dimmed.

I felt Trent's hand brush mine again, and this time, I didn't pull away.

Morgan's voice broke the silence, wrapping up the ceremony with a few words of gratitude before the barn erupted back into life. Kids returned to their crafts, the horses jingled as they moved through the crowd, and the adults drifted toward the tables for cookies and cocoa.

Amber reappeared at my side, a knowing grin on her face. "So? What'd you think?"

I glanced around, taking in the laughter, the lights, and the sheer warmth of it all. "I think... I might be falling for this place."

Amber's grin widened. "Good. Because this place? It's falling for you, too."

I laughed softly, shaking my head as the sound of Walter's booming laugh and the kids' giggles filled the air. If this wasn't some kind of Christmas magic, I didn't know what was.

Twenty-Two

Trent

"**G**AGE! GRAB THE CHAINS, we're gonna need 'em!" I shouted, my breath visible in the frigid air as I leaned against the barn door, scanning the horizon. The snow had been relentless all morning, dumping a heavy, wet blanket over everything and turning the ranch into a maze of drifts.

Gage appeared from the workshop, shaking his head. "We just cleared that path yesterday. What's the point? It's gonna drift over again in a couple hours."

"The point," I said, gritting my teeth, "is that the truck's not getting out without it, and we've got orders to fill."

He sighed, tossing the chain into the back of the plow truck before slamming the tailgate shut. "This is why I told you we needed a bigger plow. But no, you said the old one would hold up fine."

I shot him a look, but he was already walking back toward the shop, muttering something about how I'd never listen to him.

The snow was coming down faster now, fat flakes that clung to my jacket and stung my face. I checked my phone for what felt like the hundredth time, hoping for a message from the packer that the roads were clear enough for their trucks to roll. Nothing. Just a screen full of static service bars and the time mocking me.

I climbed into the truck, cranking the heat and rubbing my hands together to thaw them out. The phone buzzed in my pocket just as I shifted into gear. The shipping coordinator.

"This is Langton," I answered.

"Trent, we've got a problem," the voice on the other end said.

"No kidding."

"We can't send our trucks until the county clears the roads. Everything's backed up. It's gonna be a couple of days at least."

"A couple of days?" I leaned my head back against the seat, staring at the ceiling. "We've got orders that need to be shipped now."

"I know," he said, sounding genuinely apologetic. "But it's out of our hands. I'll keep you updated."

The line went dead, leaving me gripping the phone like it was responsible for all this. I threw it onto the dash and slammed my hands against the steering wheel, the frustration bubbling over before I could stop it.

"Something else wrong?" Gage leaned into the window, his breath fogging up the glass.

"The shipper's trucks are delayed," I said, exhaling sharply. "They're saying it's gonna be a couple of days before they can move. That puts us behind all over again."

Gage whistled low. "A couple of days? What're you gonna tell the customers?"

I glared at him. "You think I have an answer for that right now?"

"Well, you better come up with one, or they're gonna want refunds faster than you can say Merry Christmas."

I threw the truck into park and climbed out, brushing past him. "Thanks for the insight, Gage. Real helpful."

His voice followed me as I stomped back toward the house. "Hey, I'm just saying—this whole thing was your baby, remember?"

I didn't need the reminder. The weight of this whole operation was already sitting heavy on my chest, and now, with Christmas a week away, it felt like everything was unraveling.

When I stepped inside, Mom was at the table, her laptop open and her reading glasses perched on the tip of her nose. She looked up as I shook the snow off my jacket, frowning at the tension that must've been written all over my face.

"What's happened now?" she asked.

"Storm's delayed the trucks," I said, collapsing into a chair. "We've got orders that need shipping, and nothing's moving until the county clears the roads."

Mom closed the laptop and set her glasses on top of it. "It's just a delay, Trent. It's not the end of the world."

"Feels like it," I muttered, scrubbing a hand down my face.

She reached across the table, resting a hand on mine. "You've come this far, Trent. Don't let a snowstorm undo all the good you've done."

I wanted to believe her, but the weight of everything—the orders, the finances, the expectations—felt insurmountable. I was in over my head, and no amount of reassurance was going to change that.

Lauren

"**E**MILY, STOP THROWING TINSEL at me!" I ducked as a handful of silver strands sailed past my head, landing in the middle of the wreath I was working on.

Emily grinned from across the kitchen island, where she was organizing boxes of decorations. "It's called adding sparkle, city girl. You're welcome."

"Pretty sure I've got enough sparkle," I muttered, trying to untangle the mess she'd just created.

Amber laughed from her spot by the window, where she was carefully wrapping garland around a banister. "You'll learn to just go with it. Resistance is futile when Emily's in full Christmas mode."

I shook my head as I turned back to the wreath. Despite the chaos, there was something oddly satisfying about the simple task of decorating Emily's little house. It was a welcome distraction from the email sitting unanswered in my inbox—the one from Rebecca that I hadn't had the guts to read yet.

"Hey, speaking of full Christmas mode," Kate said, stepping into the kitchen with a tray of cookies. "Anyone heard from Trent? Chase said he eats up the whole Christmas stuff. I figured he wouldn't want to miss the chance to help."

Amber raised an eyebrow. "Help? Or grumble about how much work this is?"

I laughed softly, but the mention of Trent sent a flicker of warmth through me. I hadn't seen him since our lunch earlier in the week, though we'd exchanged a few texts.

As if summoned by our conversation, my phone buzzed on the counter. I wiped my hands on a dish towel before picking it up, the sight of his name on the screen sending my heart into an annoyingly quick rhythm.

You free? Need to talk.

"Lauren's got that look," Emily teased, peering over my shoulder. "What's he saying?"

I swatted her away, typing back quickly. *Sure. Where are you?*

His response was immediate. *On my way to the barn. Meet me there?*

"I'll be back," I said, setting the wreath aside and grabbing my coat.

"Don't forget the sparkle!" Emily called after me, laughing as I slipped out the door.

T HE BARN WAS QUIET when I arrived, the faint smell of hay and horses mingling with the crisp bite of the snow-covered air. I spotted Trent by the tack room, leaning against the wall with his arms crossed and his hat tipped low.

"Hey," I said softly, stepping closer. "What's up?"

He looked up, his expression serious. "We've got a problem. The shipper can't move the shipments because of the storm. Orders are delayed and the packer's gonna run out of freezer space."

I frowned, leaning against the stall door beside him. "How long are we talking?"

"A couple of days at least," he said, his voice tight. "And Gage is already calling this a disaster. He's not wrong."

I bit my lip, thinking. "Okay, but it's not the end of the world. We just have to adjust."

He gave me a skeptical look. "Adjust how? People aren't gonna wait forever for their orders."

"Maybe not," I said slowly, an idea forming. "But they'll understand if we're honest about what's happening. Especially if we give them a reason to stick with us."

Trent arched an eyebrow. "Like what?"

"Like a discount on delayed orders," I said. "And a video explaining the situation. You've already got a loyal following online. This is the kind of moment where you show them what Ridgeview is really about—family, hard work, resilience."

He didn't look convinced, his jaw tightening as he stared at the floor.

"Trent," I said, stepping in front of him. "You've built something amazing here. People will understand if you're honest with them. You just have to trust them to stick around."

His eyes met mine, and for a moment, the weight of his doubt was almost tangible. But then he nodded, the tension in his shoulders easing slightly.

"All right," he said. "Let's do it."

"Good," I said, relief flooding through me. "Now, where's that camera? We've got a story to tell."

"I'M FREEZING," I SAID, rubbing my hands together as I stomped into the barn.

Trent chuckled from where he was crouched beside a bale of hay, fiddling with his phone. "You're the one who wanted to do this in the barn instead of the house."

"Because the barn feels authentic," I said, rolling my eyes. "I just didn't realize authentic came with frostbite."

"Should've brought gloves," he said without looking up, like he wasn't even fazed by the cold.

"I *have* gloves," I shot back. "But they don't help when I'm trying to work a touch screen."

He finally glanced up, his smirk infuriatingly charming. "City girl problems."

I groaned, but there was no real heat in it. The truth was, the banter felt good. It kept me distracted, kept me from spiraling into the endless loop of uncertainty that had been playing in my head since Rebecca's latest email landed.

I tucked my hands under my arms, glancing around the barn. The golden light from the hanging lanterns cast everything in a soft glow, and the smell of hay and leather was oddly comforting. It was the kind of place I'd never pictured myself in, but now that I was here, it felt...

It felt right.

"What's that look for?" Trent asked, standing and brushing the dust off his jeans.

"What look?" I asked, pulling myself out of my thoughts.

He crossed his arms, tilting his head. "You've got this faraway thing going on. Like you're dreaming about being anywhere but here."

I smiled faintly, shaking my head. "No. That's not it."

"Then what?" he asked, stepping closer.

I hesitated, the words tangling in my throat. How was I supposed to explain the chaos swirling inside me? The fact that I was starting to feel like I belonged here, in this small town with its quirks and its charm and its infuriatingly magnetic cowboy?

"I don't know," I admitted finally. "It's just... a lot."

Trent nodded slowly, his gaze steady, like he could see right through me. "It doesn't have to be."

I blinked, caught off guard by the softness in his voice. "What do you mean?"

He shrugged, the movement casual, but his eyes anything but. "Sometimes we make things harder than they need to be. Overthink 'em. Forget to just... be where we are."

Be where we are.

The words settled into me, quiet and unassuming but heavy with meaning.

I glanced down at my boots, scuffed and dusted with hay, and then back up at Trent. His hands were in his pockets now, his hat casting a shadow over his face, but I could still see the warmth in his eyes.

"Do you ever do that?" I asked. "Overthink?"

His lips twitched into a small, almost shy smile. "Not as much as I used to. Learned the hard way it doesn't get you anywhere."

"And what does?"

"Showing up," he said simply. "Being honest. Taking the next step, even if you're not sure where it's leading."

I let out a soft laugh. "That's... surprisingly insightful for a guy who just called me a city girl five minutes ago."

"Guess I contain multitudes," he said, the corner of his mouth tugging into a smirk.

Before I could respond, Trent stepped closer, his gaze locked on mine.

"Lauren," he said quietly, his voice steady but with an edge of something I couldn't quite name.

My breath caught, the air between us suddenly feeling charged. "Yeah?"

He reached out, brushing a stray curl from my face, his fingers warm against my chilled skin.

"I'm glad you're here," he said softly.

The words were simple, but they hit me like a freight train, unraveling something deep inside me.

I wasn't sure who moved first, but suddenly his lips were on mine, warm and firm and exactly what I didn't know I needed. My hands found their way to his chest, the solid weight of him grounding me in a way that nothing else had in weeks.

When we finally pulled back, his forehead rested against mine, his breath mingling with mine in the cold air.

"I probably need to let you get back to work," he murmured, his voice low and rough in a way that made my heart trip over itself. "We got a video to make."

I smiled, my hands still on his chest. "Work can wait."

And for the first time in a long time, I actually meant it.

Twenty-Three

Lauren

"**M**OM, WHERE'S THE SALT?" I called, peering into the cabinet over the stove.

"Should be right there," she replied from the dining room, where she was setting the table.

I shifted a few jars around and finally found the small container shoved to the back. Pulling it out, I set it on the counter next to the pot of soup simmering on the stove.

"You're sure you don't want grilled cheese with this?" I asked as she came into the kitchen.

She shook her head, smiling. "Soup's fine. Besides, you're already doing more than enough just being here."

I paused, the wooden spoon hovering over the pot. "What's that supposed to mean?"

Mom leaned against the counter, her arms crossed loosely. "It means it's been nice having you home. We haven't spent this much time together since... well, since you moved to California."

Her words hit me square in the chest, a mix of warmth and guilt tangling in my stomach. "It's not like I've been avoiding you."

"I know," she said, her tone gentle but pointed. "You've been busy, and I get that. But it doesn't mean I haven't missed you."

I stirred the soup, unable to meet her eyes. "I've missed you too."

The hum of my phone vibrating on the counter broke the moment. I glanced at the screen and felt my stomach twist. *Rebecca*. I still hadn't replied to her last email—the one that spent about a hundred words to say precisely nothing.

"Are you going to answer that?" Mom asked, her brow furrowed.

I hesitated. Was I any less fired than I had been the last time we talked? I swallowed, then grabbed the phone. "I'll be right back."

I stepped into the small hallway by the stairs, pressing the phone to my ear. "Hi, Rebecca."

"Lauren, glad I caught you," she said, her voice brisk but not unkind. "I wanted to follow up on our last conversation."

"Okay," I said warily, leaning against the wall.

"I spoke with the partners, and we've made some decisions about restructuring. Unfortunately, with the recent client losses, we're going to have to downsize further."

Her words settled over me like a cold fog. "What does that mean for me?"

There was a pause, and then she sighed. "We're offering you a position, but it would be a step down from where you were. You'd report to someone new, and the role would involve fewer responsibilities."

A demotion. She was offering me a demotion.

I swallowed hard, my throat tight. "Why?"

"You know why," Rebecca said gently. "The fallout from the incident with our client... it didn't help. But it's not just you, Lauren. The firm's in trouble, and we're having to make some tough calls."

I stared at the floor, the tiles blurring as tears threatened to spill. "I don't know if I can take that."

"I understand," she said. "And I want you to know, this isn't personal. You're talented, Lauren. I still think you should consider freelancing. Take some time to figure out what you really want. There's no rush to decide."

"No rush," I echoed hollowly.

"Take care, Lauren. We'll touch base after the holidays."

She hung up, leaving me standing there with the phone pressed to my ear and my thoughts spiraling.

"Lauren?"

I looked up to see Mom standing in the doorway, her face full of concern. "You look.... Honey, you look like you're about to cry. Was that about work?"

I nodded, swallowing hard. The weight in my chest made it hard to find my voice.

Her face softened, and she stepped closer, wrapping her arms around me in a hug that I hadn't realized I needed. "It's going to be okay," she said softly, her voice steady, like she was willing me to believe i t.

For a moment, I let myself sink into the comfort of her embrace, the familiar scent of her perfume grounding me. But then the words spilled out, unplanned and unstoppable. "I think I'm losing my job."

Mom pulled back just enough to look at me, her hands still on my shoulders. "What?"

I took a shaky breath, my gaze fixed on the floor. "They're restructuring, downsizing. They offered me a demotion, but... I don't even know if I can take it. And part of it's because of me—because of something *I* did. It's just... it's a mess."

Shock flickered across her face, but it was quickly replaced by understanding. "Oh, Lauren," she said, her tone full of sympathy. "Why didn't you tell me?"

"I didn't want you to know," I admitted, my voice shaking like a leaf. "I didn't want anyone to know... well, Emily weaseled it out of me, but I asked her not to tell you. I've worked so hard, and now it feels like it's all falling apart."

She guided me to a chair, sitting me down at the table before pulling a chair next to mine. "You've been carrying this by yourself all this time?"

I nodded, not trusting myself to speak.

Her expression softened, and she reached for my hand, holding it tightly. "You're strong, Lauren. I know you are. And you'll get through this, just like you've gotten through everything else. But you don't have to do it alone. Not here. Not with us."

The simple sincerity of her words made my stomach twist into a knot.

Mom gave my hand a squeeze. "Whatever happens, you're going to figure it out. And maybe," she added, her eyes twinkling just a little, "this is your chance to figure out what you really want, not just what you think you're supposed to want."

Her words stayed with me as she got up to stir the soup, the scent of butter and herbs filling the air. It wasn't the answer I needed, but it felt like a start—a glimmer of hope in the middle of everything falling apart.

T HE RHYTHMIC THUD OF boots on frozen dirt was the first sound I heard as I stepped out of the car. Across the yard, Trent was wrestling with a bale of haylage, his movements efficient but tense.

He paused when he saw me, one hand gripping the bale hook, his breath puffing in the air.

"Lauren?" His voice carried easily across the open space. "Didn't think you'd be out here today."

I raised a hand in greeting, my breath visible in the chill. "I needed to get out of the house."

Trent set the bale down with a grunt, dusting his gloves together as he closed the distance between us. "That's brave, considering this place is barely warmer than a glacier right now."

"Tell me about it," I muttered, pulling my coat tighter.

"You here for anything in particular, or just felt like visiting?" His tone was casual, but there was an undercurrent of curiosity. "I mean, should I go put a clean shirt on for your camera?"

"Mostly visiting," I admitted, shoving my hands deep into my coat pockets. "But if you've got work to do, I can stay out of the way."

He nodded toward the barn. "Come on. Might as well put you to work. We've got a haylage tube that split open, so I'm trying to get it fed up before it goes bad. I could use an extra pair of hands to get it loaded into the feeder."

Following him inside, I was struck again by how familiar the barn had become over the past few weeks. The scents of hay and earth mingled with the sharp tang of metal tools. It was all oddly comforting.

Trent grabbed another bale hook and handed it to me. "Think you can manage one of these without impaling yourself?"

I rolled my eyes but took the hook. "I'll try to keep the carnage to a minimum."

"Good." He smirked, his gaze lingering on me for a moment longer than necessary before turning back to the task at hand.

We wrestled with the haylage, pulling apart the half-frozen chunks and tossing them into the feeder. It wasn't glamorous work, but it gave me something to focus on—something besides the knot in my stomach that had been there since Rebecca's call.

"So, what's on your mind?" Trent asked.

I froze for half a second before forcing myself to keep moving. "What makes you think something's on my mind?"

"You've got that look." He tossed another chunk into the feeder. "The one you get when you're trying not to say something."

"Wow." I choked on a little laugh. "You know all my facial expressions already?"

He paused to look at me, and there was a little tick in his eyelid before he spoke. "Same look my mom gets."

"Oh." Well, that was... unflattering. Or maybe not. I couldn't even sort that out. I sighed, leaning on the pitchfork. "Trent... what are you looking for?"

He froze, his hand mid-air as he reached for another chunk of haylage. Slowly, he straightened, brushing off his gloves as he turned to face me. "What do you mean?"

"I mean, this life. The ranch. Everything. Is it just about keeping it going because it's what you're supposed to do?" I gestured around us. "Or is there something more you're working toward?"

He tilted his head, his eyes narrowing slightly as if he were trying to figure out where this was coming from. "Is this for some video script again? I've told you. This place isn't just work for me, Lauren. It's home. It's my family's legacy. I'm working toward keeping that alive. I want it to matter."

"I knew all that," I said, nodding. "But what about beyond that? You're not just Ridgeview Ranch. You're... *you*."

His mouth quirked into the faintest of smiles, though it didn't quite reach his eyes. "That's a little deep for a Thursday morning, don't you think?"

I laughed lightly, but my gaze stayed steady on his. "You asked me once why I left Big River Valley. Now I'm asking you—what is it you want?"

For a long moment, he didn't answer. His eyes flicked away, scanning the horizon like he might find the words out there. When he finally spoke, his voice was quieter than I expected. "I want this place to keep going. I want my brothers to have a shot at something solid to pass on to their kids. I want the boys..." He trailed off, shaking his head. "I want the boys to have the kind of chance we did. And yeah, I guess I wouldn't mind having someone to share it all with. Someday."

I hesitated, unsure if I wanted to push. But I needed to know. "What kind of someone?"

His jaw tightened slightly, and he glanced at me, his face looking like he had gears smoking inside his head. He threw another pitchfork full of haylage before pausing and staring at the ground. Then he got a strange little smile... one that didn't even look like a smile. "Not someone like you, if that's what you're asking."

The words hit harder than they should have, even though they were delivered without malice. I forced a laugh, hoping it didn't sound as hollow as it felt. "I... ahem. I wasn't asking about me."

There it was again—that little tick in his eyelid. "Good." He picked up the hay fork again, his movements sharper now. "Because you're scaring me with that pitchfork. You'd kill us both."

I chewed my lip, looking away, and tried to muster a laugh. It was a joke. Just not a funny one. "Yeah," I echoed in a hollow voice. "I'm a walking liability on a ranch."

Trent paused, and for a second, it looked like he was going to say... something to walk that back. Something nice. He rubbed the back of his neck in that funny way I'd noticed from the first—making his hat pitch forward and then having to fix it. I'd decided it was his way of stalling for a second. Thinking.

"Look, don't take it that way. I was just teasing. I mean... it's not like either of us were really thinking of it, were we? You've got your own life waiting for you. And... well, it's not here. You'd go stir crazy in this town."

I opened my mouth to argue, to say... something. But I didn't even know what. So instead, I dropped the hook and dusted off my gloves. "Guess I'll get out of your way, then."

He turned back toward me, his brow furrowing. "Lauren—"

"I'm fine." I forced a smile, even as my eyes burned. "You've got work to do, and I've got things to figure out. Thanks for the help earlier."

Without waiting for his response, I turned and walked back toward my car, keeping my steps steady even though my mind was anything but.

If Trent was right—if this was just a temporary thing, a fleeting chapter in both our lives—why did it feel so wrong to let it end this way?

Trent

THE BARN DOOR SLAMMED shut behind her, and the sound echoed like a rifle shot through the cold air. I stood there, frozen, the hay hook dangling uselessly in my hand.

What in tarnation had just happened?

Her words were like a vise around my ribcage, suffocating in their raw simplicity. She wasn't just asking about the ranch or the work. She was asking about us—about *me*.

And I'd pushed her away.

I dropped the hay fork onto the ground with a clang and dragged a hand down my face. "Idiot," I muttered under my breath, the word scraping like gravel in my throat.

But what was I supposed to say? "Sure, Lauren, let's forget about the fact that you're leaving and try to make this work anyway. Sounds great." Except it didn't. It sounded like setting myself up to get burned.

I grabbed the next forkload of haylage and heaved it onto the feeder, the muscles in my arms straining with the effort. The frustration rolling through me needed an outlet, and physical work was the only thing that had ever done the trick. But this time, even the repetitive motions weren't enough to drown out the storm in my head.

She didn't belong here. Not really. She'd miss the city, her career, her independence. She'd resent me for what she gave up, and eventually, it'd all come crashing down.

And yet, I couldn't shake the image of her standing there, looking at me like maybe she was asking for something more.

"Trent!" Gage's voice cut through the barn, pulling me back to reality. He appeared in the doorway, his boots kicking up dust as he approached. "We've got a problem with the south fence. The stupid cattle are rubbing up against it again, and it's about to give."

"Then fix it," I snapped, heaving another forkload.

He stopped short, his brows shooting up. "What's got you so worked up?"

"Nothing. Just go handle the fence."

"I'm not a mind reader, and I'm not your lackey," he said, crossing his arms. "If you want me to deal with something, you've got to give me more than that. Are we sinkin' new railroad ties or just drivin' some t-posts in to hold it 'till spring?"

I slammed the fork onto the ground so hard I bent the tines. "What more do you need? It's a fence, for crying out loud! You saw the problem first. Handle it! Or if you want someone to engineer a fence that'll last 'till your grandkids are in rocking chairs, go call Chase."

Gage stared at me for a moment, his jaw tightening. "You know, just because you're in a mood doesn't mean you get to take it out on me."

"I'm not in a mood," I shot back, even though we both knew it was a lie.

"Really? Because you're stomping around here like you got a burr under your saddle. What's your deal?"

I turned away, gripping the edge of the feeder so hard my knuckles turned white. "Nothing. Just... forget it."

Gage didn't move, and the silence stretched uncomfortably between us. Finally, he sighed. "Look, if this is about Lauren—"

"It's not," I interrupted, spinning around to face him. "And even if it was, it's none of your business."

He raised an eyebrow, clearly unimpressed. "You're kidding, right? You've been acting like a lovesick teenager ever since she showed up."

"I'm not—" The words caught in my throat, and I clenched my fists. "I'm not lovesick."

"Sure, you're not. That's why you've been moping around every time she's not here and snapping at everyone when she is."

I glared at him, the anger boiling under my skin, looking for a place to land. But deep down, I knew he wasn't wrong.

"She's leaving," I said finally. "There's no point in pretending this is anything more than... temporary."

Gage tilted his head, studying me like he was trying to figure out if I believed my own words. "Maybe. Or maybe you're just too scared to find out if it could be more."

I opened my mouth to argue, but nothing came out. Gage waited a beat, then shook his head and turned toward the door.

"Fence still needs fixing," he said over his shoulder. "And I got horses to shoe. Try not to take your existential crisis out on the hammer."

My hands flexed at my sides, the tension radiating through my shoulders. Maybe Gage was right. Maybe I was scared. But what good would it do to admit that now, when the one person I wanted to tell was already halfway out the door?

Twenty-Four

Trent

THE GATE GROANED AS I swung it shut, securing the cows in the south pasture. My gloves caught on the icy chain as I latched it, and I gave it a sharp tug to make sure it held. The morning had been one long checklist of chores, but no matter how many tasks I crossed off, my thoughts kept circling back to her.

Lauren had been here all morning, quiet and focused as she filmed. *Too* quiet. The usual warmth she carried—the way her laughter slipped in between her words, the spark in her eyes when she got an idea—was nowhere to be found. She'd smiled, sure, but it was polite, distant, the kind of smile that said she wasn't really here, not with me.

I leaned against the gate for a second, staring out over the pasture. How the heck was I supposed to focus on anything when all I could think about was how badly I'd screwed things up?

It was driving me crazy.

I latched the gate and turned toward the barn, catching a glimpse of her out by the fence line. She had her fancy still camera trained on the cows, the lens glinting in the pale winter sunlight. For a second, I thought about walking over, starting up some kind of conversation. But what would I even say?

Sorry I acted like a petty fool? Sorry I can't seem to figure out if I want to push you away or beg you to stay?

I shook my head and headed for the barn.

Inside, Gage was fiddling with one of the trough heaters, muttering under his breath. "Stupid thing's shorting out again. I swear, these cheap parts are gonna be the death of me."

"Let me guess," I said, grabbing a wrench from the workbench. "You've been fixing it all morning instead of doing the fencing that needs work?"

He glanced up, his expression sour. "You were supposed to fix the fence. If this thing freezes over, the cows'll be drinking ice cubes by noon."

"Fine," I muttered, crouching beside him. "Let's get it done."

We worked in silence for a while, the kind that usually didn't bother me. Today, though, it felt like every second dragged. My gaze kept drifting toward the barn door, wondering if she'd walk in.

Gage must've noticed because he finally huffed a laugh. "You've been twitchier than a green horse at a parade all morning. What's eating at you?"

"Nothing," I said too quickly, tightening a bolt with more force than necessary.

"Uh-huh." He leaned back on his heels, smirking. "This 'nothing' wouldn't happen to have curly hair and a camera, would it?"

I glared at him, but he just laughed, shaking his head. "Man, you're hopeless. Just talk to her already."

"It's not that simple," I snapped, standing and wiping my hands on a rag.

"No? Seems pretty simple to me." He stood too, crossing his arms. "You like her. She's here. Talk."

"It's not about whether I like her," I shot back. "It's about the fact that she has a life in California—a real job, real opportunities. She's not gonna stick around for this." I gestured broadly to the barn, the land, everything that felt impossibly small and inadequate in comparison to whatever she had waiting back west.

Gage's smirk faded, replaced by something quieter. "And what if she would? Stick around, I mean."

I stared at him, the words hitting like a punch I hadn't seen coming.

"She won't," I said finally.

"But if she did?" he pressed.

I didn't answer.

LATER, AFTER GAGE HAD wandered off and the trough heater was humming along, I found myself standing in the barn doorway, leaning against the frame as I watched Lauren pack up her gear.

She moved with her usual grace, securing lenses and batteries, zipping up cases, and slinging her bag over one shoulder. From a distance, she looked the same—confident, put-together. But I knew better.

I could see it in the way her shoulders sagged when she thought no one was looking, the way her smile didn't warm her face like it did before.

And I hated that I was part of the reason for that.

The problem was, I didn't know how to fix it.

The snow had started falling again, soft flakes drifting lazily through the air. Lauren glanced up, watching it for a moment before brushing a curl out of her face and heading toward her car.

I stayed where I was, gripping the edge of the doorframe as she walked away.

For the first time in a long while, I thought about Christmas—about all the years I'd spent making wishes I never believed in. Wishes for Dad to get better, for the ranch to thrive, for the kind of life that didn't feel like a constant uphill climb.

Now, for the first time, I wanted to make another wish.

I wished for her to stay.

But like every other wish, it felt impossible.

And maybe it was better not to wish at all.

Lauren

THE CAMERA SCREEN FLICKERED off as I powered it down, tucking it carefully into its case. My fingers moved automatically, double-checking the lens cap and securing the straps, but my mind was somewhere else entirely. Somewhere tangled in the mess of last night's almost-conversation with Trent.

I should have felt proud of the work I'd done today—getting shots of the herd against the snow-dusted hills, Gage bringing in hay bales, even Hickory nosing curiously at the camera. But all of it felt hollow.

The barn door creaked open, and I glanced up, startled. Trent walked in, his boots leaving muddy prints on the concrete floor. He stopped short when he saw me, his expression guarded.

"You're still here," he said, like the sight of me was unexpected.

"Just wrapping up," I replied, my tone brisk as I clipped the camera case shut. "I wanted to get some shots of the horses before the light changed."

He nodded, but didn't say anything else. The silence stretched, heavy and uncomfortable.

I slung the strap of my gear bag over my shoulder and moved toward the door, but Trent stepped to the side, blocking my path.

"Can we talk?"

I hesitated, not sure I had it in me to hear whatever he was about to say.

"I—" Whatever he was about to say was interrupted by the buzz of my phone in my coat pocket. I fished it out, relieved for the excuse, but my stomach sank when I saw the name on the screen.

Rebecca.

I glanced at Trent, then back at the phone. "I'm sorry, Trent, I have to take this," I said, stepping around him and out into the icy yard.

He didn't follow, but I felt his eyes on me as I walked away.

"Hi, Rebecca," I answered as I paced the side of the barn.

"Lauren, glad I caught you. We need to finalize things by the end of the week. Have you made a decision?"

My breath fogged in front of me as I turned, my boots crunching on the snow. "I'm still thinking about it."

"Lauren, I know this has been a tough adjustment," Rebecca said. "But the offer won't stay open forever. You need to ask yourself what's best for your career long-term. You still have connections with this company. Good ones."

I chewed my lip. Right, my career. The thing I'd built my life around. The thing I'd watched slip through my fingers, piece by piece.

"I'll let you know soon," I said, the tightness in my chest making it hard to get the words out.

"By tomorrow."

I tried to smile. "Right."

The call ended, and I stood there for a moment, staring at the barn wall like it might offer some kind of clarity.

"What was that?"

The voice startled me, and I turned to see Trent leaning casually against the barn door. His arms were crossed, but his posture wasn't confrontational. His gaze flicked from my face to the phone in my pocket.

"Sorry, what?" I asked, caught off guard.

"That call." He tipped his head toward my pocket. "Didn't sound like good news."

I hesitated, my grip tightening on the edge of my jacket. "It's just work stuff. Nothing I can't handle."

Trent's expression didn't change, but he stayed where he was, blocking my path. Not in an aggressive way—more like he wasn't quite ready to let me walk away.

"You sure?" he asked after a beat.

The quiet concern in his voice made something in me crack. I sighed, glancing past him toward the pasture. "Things aren't... perfect right now."

He stayed silent, giving me the space to continue.

"My boss," I admitted. "There's talk of downsizing. She's offering me a role, but it's a step down from where I was. I don't know if I want it."

Trent's brows furrowed, and he pushed off the door, taking a slow step closer. "That doesn't make sense. You're good at what you do—great, even. Why would they do that?"

I let out a dry laugh. "Why does anyone do anything? Budgets, politics, a mix of both. Doesn't really matter."

"It matters," he said firmly.

I glanced at him, surprised by the edge in his voice.

"You've built a name for yourself. They'd be crazy to let you go."

"Yeah, well, they might just be that crazy," I said, forcing a weak smile. Should I tell him that *I* was the reason for it all? That my mistake had not only ruined my own career, but probably hurt others, too?

He studied me for a long moment, his brow creased like he was trying to piece something together. Then he nodded, almost to himself. "You'll figure it out. You're the best one for the job."

The words weren't quite what I'd hoped for. I'd hoped he might suggest something... offer something. The same sort of something I'd been daydreaming about lately. But all he'd said was that I'd figure it out.

"Thanks," I said.

"Don't mention it." He stepped aside, giving me room to pass, but I hesitated.

There was more I wanted to say, but the words stuck in my throat. Instead, I brushed past him, heading for my car.

"Hey, Lauren," he called after me.

I stopped, glancing over my shoulder.

"You're the best at what you do," he said. "Don't let them make you think otherwise."

I nodded, the lump in my throat too big to speak around. Then I turned and walked away, wondering if I'd just missed the chance to say something important.

I STARED BLANKLY AT the open laptop on the kitchen table, the blinking cursor mocking me from the empty caption box on Ridgeview's social media page. The cozy, quiet apartment seemed thunderously loud in my ears—everything from the familiar hum of the radiator to the whir of the dishwasher breaking my focus.

The past few weeks had been a whirlwind of creativity and chaos, but tonight, my mind was a blank slate. The words wouldn't come, no matter how hard I tried to summon them.

"Everything okay, sweetheart?" Mom's voice drifted in from the kitchen, where she was finishing the dinner dishes.

I glanced at her, managing a weak smile. "Yeah. Just tired."

She dried her hands on a towel and walked over, her brows knitting as she studied me. "You've been tired a lot lately. Sure you're not running yourself ragged?"

"Pretty sure," I said, forcing a lightness into my tone that I didn't feel.

She didn't buy it. Mom always had a way of looking right past my words. "Is it the ranch? Or something else?"

I hesitated, my fingers brushing the edge of the laptop. Part of me wanted to spill everything—my changing ideas about my career, about Trent, about the aching uncertainty that had taken root in my chest—but the words stayed lodged in my throat.

"A lot on my mind," I said finally.

Her hand landed gently on my shoulder. "You know you don't have to do everything on your own, right?"

The sentiment was kind, but it only made the weight on my chest heavier. Because for as much as I didn't want to do everything alone, I didn't see another option.

"I know," I murmured.

Mom gave my shoulder a squeeze and then retreated to her chair by the window, where she picked up her knitting. When did she start knitting? Must have been when Emily left—gave her something to do with her hands. By the look of the little quilt or whatever it was taking shape, she wasn't that great at it... yet.

Yet... Because nobody nailed a new thing on their first try every time. They screwed up sometimes. But they got better if they stuck with it.

I swallowed and turned my attention back to my laptop. The cursor blinked at me, daring me to find the right words. I glanced at the folder full of fresh photos I had pulled up in a secondary window—shots of Marty prancing in the snow, the Langton family smiling at the camera, kids from White Pines beaming as they held their handmade crafts. Each image was a perfect snapshot of this town's story, but none of them felt like the whole truth.

Because the truth was complicated.

It wasn't just a ranch with quirky characters and picture-perfect moments. It was long days and uncertain nights, broken fences and tough choices, frustration, and heartache. It was a place full of life and struggle, joy and grit—all the things I wasn't sure I had the strength for. And somehow, Trent did.

The thought made my eyes blur, and before I could stop myself, I shut the laptop and shoved it aside.

The sudden scrape of the chair startled Mom, who looked up from her knitting. "You sure you're okay?"

"Yeah," I said, standing. "I just need some air."

I grabbed my coat and slipped out the door before she could ask any more questions.

The cold hit me like a slap as I stepped onto the snowy sidewalk. The sky was a muted gray, the kind of color that made it hard to tell where dusk ended, and night began.

I walked without a destination, and no idea why I felt better out here than inside. The streetlights cast a warm glow over the sleepy town, and a few scattered holiday decorations twinkled in the shop windows.

Everywhere I looked, Big River Valley exhaled a kind of contented quiet, the kind that made me feel like an outsider no matter how long I stayed. It wasn't just the small-town charm, the shopkeepers who knew your name, or the sense of belonging that seemed to weave itself into every corner. It was the weight of knowing this wasn't my world—not really.

I crossed the street toward the small park near the town square. The gazebo in the center was wrapped in twinkling lights, a giant wreath hanging from one side. A snowman stood lopsided in the middle of the lawn, its carrot nose pointing slightly off-center.

I leaned against the wooden railing, watching as a few kids ran through the snow, their laughter cutting through the stillness. The sound tugged at something deep in my chest—something that felt achingly close to hope and impossibly far from it at the same time.

What was I doing here?

The question hung in the air, unanswered.

I thought of my mom's words earlier—about putting things back together the way I wanted. But what did I *want?*

I wanted a job I didn't feel like I was losing my soul for. I wanted a life that felt bigger than meetings and client pitches and climbing a corporate ladder that never ended.

I wanted…

I swallowed hard, my breath fogging in the air.

I wanted friends who would miss me if I wasn't around. I hadn't even heard from Stacy in almost two weeks, and nobody else had reached out at all.

I wanted to be seen when I needed help. Not laughed at, not belittled. I had been the one everyone was trying to take down from the top rung of the ladder—the one whose failure meant success for someone else.

I wanted someone to hug me and fetch me cocoa when I'd had a rough day. And I wanted someone in my life for whom I could return the favor—someone who depended on me for *me*, not for what I could bring to the table professionally.

I wanted to belong.

A gust of wind sent the snow skittering across the pavement, and I pulled my coat tighter around me. Somewhere in the back of my mind, I knew I needed to go back to the apartment and face whatever came next. But for now, I stayed in the cold, letting the quiet of the valley settle into my bones.

Twenty-Five

Lauren

T HE CLINK OF MUGS and hum of conversation filled Mrs. Finch's coffee shop, the warmth from the old radiator doing its best to combat the December chill creeping through the door every time it opened. I shuffled forward in line, trying to avoid the eyes of a couple seated near the window. They weren't exactly subtle about the way they glanced in my direction, whispering behind their hands.

My stomach knotted. I'd heard whispers like that before. They didn't have to say it aloud for me to know they were talking about Ridgeview and the online buzz the ranch was starting to generate.

It should have felt good—validation that the work was making an impact. Instead, it felt like a spotlight I hadn't asked for, shining on every flaw I'd been working so hard to cover.

"Lauren?"

I turned to find Amber standing near the sugar station, her auburn curls pulled into a loose ponytail and a curious look on her face. "Hey," I said, managing a smile.

"Grabbing a caffeine fix?" she asked, her tone light as she sipped her coffee.

"Something like that," I replied, stepping out of line. Lexi had already seen me and nodded that she was getting my usual ready.

Amber gestured to a small table near the corner. "Care to join me? Unless you're in a rush."

I hesitated, the idea of sitting with her a welcome distraction from the nerves buzzing in my chest. "Sure."

We settled into the chairs, and for a moment, neither of us spoke. Amber stirred her coffee absently, her eyes scanning my face. "You okay? You seem... off."

I let out a soft laugh, shaking my head. "That obvious, huh?"

"Not to everyone. But I work with kids and horses every day—I've gotten pretty good at reading people."

I stared into my cup, the words bubbling to the surface before I could stop them. "I might not have a job to go back to in California."

Amber blinked, her mug hovering midair. "What?"

"Rebecca, my boss, called the other day. They lost a major client. Apparently, the deal was already on shaky ground, but my screwup was the final straw." I swallowed hard, feeling my throat tighten. "She offered me a demotion—said I could come back if I wanted to, but I'd have to work under someone else. Basically, I'd be starting over."

Amber set her mug down, leaning forward. "You screwed up? What happened?"

I hesitated, the shame of it still fresh. "Oh, gosh. I posted something online—something personal—embarrassing—and it went live on the business account."

Amber winced. "Ouch."

"Yeah. Ouch," I echoed, staring into my coffee. "Rebecca tried to soften the blow, but... I know the truth. She said I should consider freelancing or reevaluating my goals, but what kind of client is going to trust me after that?"

"Hey. We all screw up. But Lauren, what you've done for Ridgeview? It's incredible. Anyone who's paying attention can see that."

I managed a small smile. "Thanks. But Ridgeview isn't exactly a Fortune 500 company. It's not the same."

Amber arched a brow. "You think those people staring at you when you walked in are whispering about Fortune 500 companies? They're talking about you. About the videos you've made, the way you've brought Ridgeview to life for people who don't know the first thing about ranching. That's not nothing."

Her words landed heavier than I expected, the weight of them settling somewhere between pride and uncertainty. "It's just... hard to know what's next."

Amber nodded. "Sure. But sometimes, the next step isn't about knowing. It's about deciding."

The door jingled, and we both glanced up as a group of teenagers spilled inside, their laughter and snow-dusted jackets bringing a burst of energy with them.

Amber grinned. "Looks like the lunch rush is picking up. But hey—if you ever need to talk, you know where to find me."

"Thanks, Amber."

Trent

T HE MORNING SUN HUNG low in the sky, still too weak to cast any shadows over Ridgeview's frozen fields. I leaned against the barn door, staring at the notebook in my hands. The numbers were there in black and white, plain as day.

We were making progress. Small, barely noticeable progress, but progress nonetheless.

"Chase!" I called, my voice echoing across the yard.

Chase stepped out of the workshop, wiping grease from his hands. "What's up?"

I waved the notebook at him. "You gotta see this."

He jogged over, eyebrows raised as he took the notebook. "This the latest numbers?"

"Yeah. Look at the orders coming in. We're still not hitting auction prices, but it's climbing. If it keeps on like this, we'll be in the black by the end of next month."

Chase scanned the page, his brow furrowing. "Huh. Not bad. Still feels risky, though."

I crossed my arms. "Everything about ranching is risky. This isn't any different."

He nodded, but his lips pressed into a thin line. "I'm not saying it's not working, Trent. Just... maybe we're relying on the wrong advice."

That hit like a kick in the gut. "What's that supposed to mean?"

Chase hesitated, flipping the notebook closed and handing it back to me. "I ran into Myra Parsons at the feed store yesterday."

I groaned. "Myra? What's she got to do with anything?"

Chase hesitated, shoving his hands into the pockets of his jacket. "She was at the coffee shop the other day. Said she overheard Lauren talking about some big disaster she caused at her company."

I rolled my eyes. "And you're taking Myra Parsons at her word?"

Chase raised an eyebrow. "I didn't say I was. But she seemed pretty sure of herself."

"Yeah, because when has Myra ever *not* been sure of herself?" I shot back, my voice dripping with sarcasm.

Chase snorted. "Fair. But come on, Trent, it's not like she's making up that Lauren's from California and had a career there. We both know she did."

I folded my arms, not willing to give an inch. "And we both know Myra. She had a thing for me when we were in high school—"

"And me after you graduated," Chase cut in, grinning. "Don't forget that."

"Exactly," I said, ignoring his jab. "She spent half her life acting like we were supposed to sweep her off her feet. Just because she was the Dairy Princess at the county fair doesn't mean she's a reliable source of information."

"Maybe not," Chase admitted, the grin fading from his face. "But that doesn't mean she's wrong."

The words sank in like a stone, heavier than I wanted to admit.

Myra Parsons was the type who thrived on gossip and drama, always ready with a story or a not-so-subtle dig at someone who'd slighted her. And since neither Chase nor I had ever given her the time of day romantically, we'd both been on the receiving end of her theatrics more than once.

"She's jealous," I said flatly. "She's always been jealous."

"Probably," Chase said with a shrug. "But does that mean she didn't overhear something real? She's not making it up that Lauren's been talking about Ridgeview a lot. And you can ask Amber from White Pines—she was the one Lauren was talking to when she said she hosed her career. You sure she's not using us—using you—to keep her hand in the game while she figures out her next move?"

I narrowed my eyes. "Even if she is—and I'm not agreeing with you—where's the harm? Hasn't she helped us?"

Chase stuck his thumbs in his belt loops. "Maybe. Or maybe she's been blowing smoke and rainbows up your nose. I'm just saying... keep your guard up."

I clenched my jaw, the frustration bubbling under my skin. Myra wasn't trustworthy, and I knew that. But what if this time, she wasn't spinning a story just to get a reaction?

What if Lauren really was "helping us" for her own reasons, and I was just a convenient part of her plan?

The thought made me sick, twisting in my gut like barbed wire. I didn't want to believe it.

I *couldn't* believe it.

"Look, Trent, I know you don't want to think the worst of her. I like her, t0o—and heck, she's Cole's sister-in-law, so that makes her family already, and nobody's doubting her talents. Maybe you're right to trust her. But just... make sure you know where she stands before you get in too deep."

I nodded reluctantly, though the tightness in my chest refused to ease. I wanted to defend Lauren, to tell Chase he was wrong. But the doubts crept in, uninvited and relentless.

Who took a whole month off of work to come back to the town they hadn't visited in years? Work problems? Was that why she'd come back when she did? Why she'd poured herself into this project?

I thought about the late nights she spent editing videos, the way she lit up when she talked about Ridgeview's potential. But I also thought about the way she avoided certain questions, the tension in her shoulders when her phone buzzed with a call from California.

"Maybe I'm just saying it wrong," Chase added, his voice softer now. "It's working, yeah. But is she in it for you, or is this just her way of fixing something she broke?"

I shook my head, trying to focus on the notebook in my hands. But the numbers blurred, and all I could see was Lauren's face, her bright smile, the way she'd made me believe in this crazy plan.

Chase clapped me on the shoulder. "Don't let it get to you, man. Just... keep your eyes open, all right?"

I nodded, but the pit in my stomach told me it wasn't that simple.

THE STEADY THRUM OF my truck's engine quieted as I parked outside the main barn. Cole's truck was already here, parked crooked like he was in a hurry. I sighed, grabbing my gloves off the dash and stepping out into the sharp December air.

The sight of Lauren and Emily climbing out of Cole's cab hit me like a punch to the chest. Emily was talking animatedly, waving her hands as Lauren nodded along, but Lauren's eyes drifted toward me, uncertain.

I quickly looked away, muttering a curse under my breath. *Keep it professional, Langton. Keep it distant.*

Cole rounded the truck, giving me a grin. "Hey, man. Chase told me y'all could use an extra set of hands with the barn roof."

"Yeah, the snow's not melting off, and I'm worried about the weight buckling it," I replied. "I was about to climb up there with a snow shovel."

Emily looped her arm through Lauren's, pulling her toward the house. "We're helping Mom with cookies! Lauren said she might take pictures for the Ridgeview page—wouldn't that be adorable?"

I froze mid-step, the words grating like nails on a chalkboard. Pictures of cookies for the ranch's page? That's what she was thinking about?

Lauren looked at me hesitantly, like she could feel the heat building in my glare.

"That sounds... cute," I said, unable to keep the sarcasm out of my tone. "Real adorable. I'm sure the followers will love it."

Emily tilted her head, frowning. "What's with the tone, Trent?"

"Nothing," I muttered, turning toward the barn. "Just seems like maybe cookies aren't exactly gonna save the ranch."

I caught Chase's quick glance at me from where he stood near the workshop, his expression unreadable but definitely not neutral. He knew what I was thinking.

Lauren blinked, her face a mixture of confusion and hurt. "I didn't think cookies were supposed to save anything."

Emily's frown deepened. "Okay, what's going on here? Did something happen?"

"Nope," I said sharply, pulling open the barn door. "Nothing at all. Go enjoy your baking."

Cole cleared his throat. "Emily, why don't you show Lauren the cookie recipes while we get started on this roof? Shouldn't take us more than an hour."

Emily shot me a glare, but she turned, tugging Lauren along toward the house. Lauren hesitated, glancing back at me one last time before disappearing inside.

Once they were gone, Cole shoved his hands into his jacket pockets, his easygoing demeanor gone. "What the heck was that?"

"Nothing," I snapped, grabbing a ladder and slamming it against the barn wall.

"No, no, pretty sure that was something."

"I said it was nothing," I barked, climbing the ladder without another word.

But as I shoveled mounds of snow off the groaning metal roof, Lauren's face lingered in my mind—the confusion, the hurt. And worst of all, the flicker of hope I'd seen there before I'd crushed it.

I wasn't sure what made me angrier—that I'd been the one to do it or that I still cared.

Twenty-Six

Lauren

E MILY KNOCKED ON THE doorframe of the Langton's barn office, her grin wide as she leaned in. "You're hiding out in here now? I don't see any cowboys around."

I glanced up from my laptop, startled. "I'm working."

She raised an eyebrow. "Really? Because it looks more like you're stress-scrolling through email and pretending you're not thinking about Trent."

I sighed, sitting back in the chair and folding my arms. "Not everything is about Trent."

"Sure, sure," she said, waving me off. "Anyway, I'm here to grab you. Mom's making dinner, and I don't want you driving that deathtrap rental on these roads."

"I was fine getting here," I protested.

"Barely. I heard about your near-death experience last week. I'm not risking it." She leaned her shoulder against the doorframe. "Besides, I saw Gage when I drove up, and he said Trent's out fixing fences for the rest of the day. Can't make any more cowboy videos, unless you want to hike out and hunt him down on foot."

She was needling me, on purpose but I let it slide. I'd been editing a post about Ridgeview's holiday traditions, piecing together clips of the boys stringing lights on the barn and Trent leading Marty back into the paddock after yet another escape.

"Fine," I relented, pulling my coat from the back of the chair. "Let me just shut this down."

I T WAS LIKE AN arctic blizzard the second I stepped outside, and I tucked my hands deep into my pockets. Trent was really out *working* in this? If I'd ever doubted his work ethic, that was done away with now.

Emily strolled beside me, unbothered by the cold, her scarf fluttering in the breeze. "So," she started, her tone casual, "how's it going?"

"What do you mean?" I asked, keeping my gaze on the ground.

"You know what I mean." She nudged my arm. "Things between you and Trent."

I stopped walking and turned to face her. "Emily, it's not like that. We're... friends."

She snorted. "Yeah, okay. Friends who make goo-goo eyes at each other when they think no one's looking."

Heat rose to my cheeks, and I started walking again, faster this time. "You're imagining things."

"Am I?"

I stopped. "Emily, I know what you're hoping. Part of me would even like the same thing, but it... it's just not possible. Trent..." I swallowed and blinked against the wind that whipped a sudden tear into my eyes. I'm sure it was the wind.

"Yes?" she asked.

I drew a shuddering breath. "Trent doesn't want someone like me."

Emily's eyes widened. "What, are you kidding? He'd be an idiot to pass you up! Look at you! You're... well, you got all the looks of the family. You're dizzyingly smart, accomplished, you've made something of yourself, you're fun to be with, and—"

"— and I wouldn't be able to ride my way out of a paper bag," I finished. "I mean... think about it, Em! Me, on a ranch? Have you ever heard anything so dumb?"

Emily blinked. "Laur... do you think you have to wrestle calves and buck hay to fit into Trent Langton's life? You don't. He wouldn't ask you to be someone else."

I stuffed my hands deeper inside my pockets. "That's right, he wouldn't. And I wouldn't ask him to try to fit a square peg into a round hole just because we had some laughs. We're friends, and that's how it has to stay. Not fair to him for me to expect anything more."

She opened her mouth—probably to argue some more—but before she could say more, my phone buzzed in my pocket. What a relief!

I pulled it out and saw Rebecca's name flashing on the screen. "Oh. Sorry, Em, it's work. Let me go back inside to take this."

She nodded, swallowing hard. "Yeah. I'll be waiting in the car."

I DUCKED INSIDE THE small office, closing the door behind me before answering the call.

"Hi, Rebecca," I said.

"Hello, Lauren. I wanted to touch base before the holiday. Have you made a decision yet?"

The ache in my chest returned. "I've been thinking about it."

"Well, we need to finalize some things on our end," she said, her tone clipped. "This opportunity isn't going to wait forever."

"I understand," I said, my fingers tightening around the phone.

"Good. Because, frankly, Lauren, the longer you wait, the harder it will be for us to justify keeping the offer open. You're talented, but you know how competitive this industry is."

Her words stung, but I bit my lip and stayed quiet.

"I'll need your answer by the end of the day. And, Lauren? Don't overthink it. Just make the smart choice."

The line went dead, leaving me standing in the middle of the tiny office, staring at the screen like it held answers I couldn't see.

Emily had the car warmer than Hades when I opened the door and got in. Her hand was on the gear shift, but she dropped it when she saw my face. "You good?"

"Yeah," I said, forcing a smile. "Just work stuff."

Emily studied me for a moment, her brow furrowing. "You sure? You don't look okay."

I sighed, tucking the phone into my pocket. "I'm fine. Let's go."

Just make the smart choice Rebecca had said.

I wasn't sure I even knew what that was anymore.

Trent

T HE SQUEAK OF THE gate hinges should've been a soothing rhythm, but every push felt like it ground my nerves tighter. The pasture fence was almost finished, the last row of barbed wire glinting in the weak December sunlight, but the satisfaction I usually got from a job well done wasn't coming today.

I hammered in another staple, gritting my teeth when the metal edge nicked my glove. The storm had set us back days, and even though we were finally catching up on orders, there was still too much left to do

.

"Hey," Chase's voice called from behind me. "Got a minute?"

I didn't stop hammering. "Not really."

"Too bad," he said, leaning against the gate. "Because I've got news."

I straightened, rolling my shoulders as I turned to face him. "What kind of news?"

"The kind you're going to want to hear." He handed me a piece of paper, his face serious.

I wiped I wiped my hands on my jeans and took the paper from him, squinting at the small print. My eyes scanned the numbers, slowly piecing together what I was looking at.

"This from the packer?" I asked, still reading.

Chase nodded. "Yeah. They sent an updated invoice. They're ahead of schedule on processing the last batch and have capacity to take on another load before the end of the year."

That should've been good news. No, it *was* good news. But instead of relief, I felt that gnawing pressure in my chest. "Another load? We're barely keeping up with the shipping on the first one."

"Maybe," Chase said, his words methodical, in that way he got when he was working through a problem. "But the numbers are looking solid. Orders are picking up, Trent. If we can push through the next few weeks, this might actually work."

I stared at the paper again, the words blurring for a second. " *Might*," I repeated. "You said it yourself. That's a heck of a gamble."

"And like *you* said, what isn't, these days?"

I let out a short laugh, but it didn't have much humor in it. "Fair point."

Chase leaned on the gate, watching me like he was sizing up a wild animal. "Speaking of gambles... you want to tell me what's going on with you and Lauren?"

The question hit like a stray kick from a cow, sharp and unexpected. "Nothing," I said, too quickly. "What makes you think anything's going on?"

"You mean besides the fact that you've been brooding like a storm cloud for days?" Chase asked, his eyebrows lifting. "Or that you practically bit Emily's head off when she asked if Lauren was still here?"

I looked away, focusing on the twisted wire at my feet. "It's nothing. She's leaving soon. End of story."

Chase didn't answer right away, and the silence stretched just long enough to make me uncomfortable. Finally, he sighed. "You know, for a guy who's usually got his head screwed on straight, you're being pretty dense about this."

I shot him a look. "What's that supposed to mean?"

"It means," he said, crossing his arms, "that maybe you should stop assuming you know what she wants and actually ask her."

The words landed heavier than I wanted to admit, and I shoved them aside with a shake of my head. "She's got a whole life waiting for her in California. This was never going to be permanent."

Chase shrugged. "Maybe not. But it seems like she's done a lot for this place. More than just social media and videos. You think she'd put that kind of effort into something she didn't care about?"

I opened my mouth to argue, but nothing came out.

"Exactly," Chase said, pushing off the gate. "Just think about it, Trent. You've already got enough on your plate without sabotaging yourself."

With that, he turned and walked back toward the barn, leaving me alone with the fence, the invoice, and the uncomfortable truth that maybe—just maybe—he was right.

I hammered another staple into the post, the sharp ring of metal on wood cutting through the quiet. If Lauren cared as much as Chase seemed to think she did, why hadn't she said anything?

Why hadn't I?

The thought stayed with me long after I'd finished the fence and headed back to the barn. I was rolling up the last coil of wire when I heard a familiar sound: the steady clop of hooves.

I looked up just in time to see Marty trotting through the open gate, his ears flicking forward like he was daring me to stop him.

"You've got to be kidding me," I muttered, dropping the wire and grabbing a lead rope. Marty didn't run, of course. That would've been too much effort. Instead, he sauntered toward the yard, his tail swishing like he owned the place.

As I followed him, rope in hand, the ridiculousness of it all hit me. Here I was, chasing a horse with more personality than sense, running a ranch on fumes and prayers, and wasting time trying to ignore feelings I couldn't seem to shake.

Maybe I was dense.

But if Lauren was still here tomorrow, maybe it wasn't too late to do something about it.

Twenty-Seven

Lauren

DECEMBER 23RD. THE DATE felt like a drumbeat in my head as I zipped my suitcase, the sound of the zipper loud in the quiet room. My phone sat on the nightstand, the screen still lit with the last message from Rebecca.

Looking forward to having you back. First meeting is December 26th at 9 a.m. sharp. Let me know if you need anything before then.

The words felt clinical, like a placeholder for the apology I'd never get. I'd agreed to come back, knowing full well it wasn't the job I'd left. It wasn't even close.

But it was still a job.

"Lauren?" Mom's voice drifted from the living room, soft but with an edge of hesitation.

I took a steadying breath and grabbed the handle of my suitcase.

She was waiting by the couch, a mug of tea in her hands. The apartment smelled faintly of cinnamon, the candle on the coffee table flickering gently in the dim light.

"You sure you don't want to wait until after Christmas?"

I shook my head, forcing a smile I didn't feel. "I'm so sorry to miss it, Mom. Flights are impossible on Christmas Eve, and even worse on Christmas Day. It's better this way."

I figured she'd cry. Or just turn away and all I would hear would be a quiet sniff. I deserved a bit of guilt, after all—how long had it been since I'd been back? I promised to spend Christmas with her, and now, I was bailing. She could've laid it on thick. Instead, she set her mug down and opened her arms.

"Come here, kiddo."

I didn't hesitate. I folded into her embrace, the scent of her perfume instantly taking me back to simpler times—when a hug from her could fix anything.

"I'm so proud of you," she whispered, her hand rubbing small circles on my back. "I miss you, but I'm so... *so* proud of you."

Tears pricked my eyes, and I blinked hard, determined not to let them fall. "Thanks, Mom."

We stayed like that for a long moment before a knock at the door broke the silence.

Emily was there, bundled in her coat, her cheeks pink from the cold. "Ready?" she asked, her voice overly bright.

"Yeah," I said, even though I wasn't.

She stepped inside, glancing at my suitcase. "This feels weird. Like... wrong weird."

"Tell me about it," I muttered, grabbing my coat.

Mom handed me a scarf, her hands lingering for a second longer than necessary. "You text me when you get to the airport. And when you land. I mean it."

"I will," I promised.

Emily gave her a quick hug, then looped her arm through mine as we headed out into the cold.

Emily kept stealing glances at me as we walked down the stairs, but I stared at my feet.

Finally, she broke the silence. "So... you're really doing this?"

"I don't have a choice, Em. It's not like I can just stay here and... and what? Pretend I don't need a paycheck?"

"You don't have to pretend anything. But maybe you should think about what makes you happy. Not just... what's practical."

I didn't answer. I didn't know how to. I just turned to my little sister with the kind of smile that is too full for more words. "Bye, sweetie. You and that cute cowboy of yours take care of each other, you hear?"

She wasn't as good at hiding her feelings as Mom. Emily had to wipe some sudden tears off her cheeks, and she leaped up to wrap her arms around my neck. "Miss you, sis!"

I gagged and patted her back. "Em... you're choking me!"

She laughed and hopped back to the pavement. "Try not to get fired again. Or... well, get fired. I wouldn't mind, actually."

I laughed and looked up at the window above the street. Mom was waving, and I was pretty sure her eyes already looked puffy. And I almost couldn't climb into that rental car.

Finally, however, I did. Buckled my seat belt and prayed the car that had caused me nothing but headaches for weeks would actually start. Emily leaned against the window, her expression somewhere between frustrated and sad. I rolled it down for one more goodbye.

"Don't wait so long to visit next time," she said, her voice tight.

I nodded, swallowing hard. "I won't."

She reached in and squeezed my hand. "And if you change your mind—about anything—just call, okay? We're here."

The tears I'd been holding back threatened to spill over, but I blinked quickly, forcing a weak smile. "Thanks, Em."

As I pulled out of the lot and onto the snowy road, my ears were drumming with my pulse and I could hardly make my foot press the gas pedal.

Christmas lights flickered from the storefronts in town, their cheer a sharp contrast to the hollow ache inside me.

I was leaving Big River Valley. Again. And this time, I wasn't sure if I'd ever come back.

Trent

The shop was too quiet.

Normally, I appreciated the stillness after a morning of chaos, but today it felt oppressive. I leaned against the workbench, staring at the open toolbox in front of me, every wrench and socket neatly lined up like it mattered. Like *this* mattered.

A faint sound of laughter drifted in from the barn, the boys messing around as they finished up chores. Ethan had finally figured out how to handle Hickory, and Liam had been in rare form all morning, cracking jokes that even had Gage laughing.

And Lauren was gone.

I was too late.

I hadn't seen her leave, but Emily mentioned something about her taking that job and flying out before Christmas. It didn't make sense, her leaving now. Not when everything was starting to come together.

Not when I finally let myself believe she might stay if I'd only ask.

I raked a hand through my hair, scowling at nothing. What was I even thinking? Lauren was never going to stay. She had a life waiting for her in California, a job she needed to get back to.

I just wasn't part of it.

The sound of someone's voice outside snapped me out of my thoughts. Chase appeared in the doorway, his coat unzipped and dusted with snow.

"You gonna stand there all day, or you actually gonna get something done?"

I shot him a look but didn't bother answering.

He walked in, stuffing his gloves in his coat pockets. "Gage said the boys finished the south fence. All by themselves! Ethan's getting pretty handy with those pliers."

"That's good," I muttered, reaching for a random wrench and pretending to check the tightness of a bolt on the workbench vice.

Chase studied me for a moment, then leaned against the doorframe. "So, Lauren's gone, huh?"

The wrench slipped from my hand, clattering onto the bench. "What's it to you?"

"Nothing. Just seems like you've been walking around like someone stole your dog all day."

I glared at him. "You done?"

"Not yet," he said, crossing his arms. "I mean, you want to mope around because the girl left, fine. But maybe instead of sulking, you could try, I don't know, talking to her?"

I barked out a laugh, shaking my head. "You don't get it, Chase. She's gone. That's it. She's got a whole life in California. Why would she stay here?"

He shrugged. "Maybe for the same reason you want her to."

His words hit like a punch to the gut, but I didn't let it show. "She doesn't want this life. She made that pretty clear."

"Did she?" he asked, his voice quieter now. "Or is that just what you keep telling yourself so it hurts less?"

I froze, my hands tightening into fists at my sides.

Chase held my gaze for a long moment, then sighed, pushing off the doorframe. "You're the one who taught me not to give up on something I want. Maybe you should take your own advice."

He turned and walked out, leaving me alone with the words I didn't want to hear.

I sank onto the stool at the workbench, Chase's voice echoing in my head.

Maybe for the same reason you want her to.

But what if he was wrong? What if Lauren *didn't* want this life? What if she didn't want me?

I stared at the empty doorway, the ache in my chest growing heavier with every second.

And then, like a fool, I reached for my phone.

Lauren

T HE ROADS WERE WORSE than I expected.

Snow had started falling again as I left Big River Valley, the kind of thick, heavy flakes that stuck to the windshield no matter how high I cranked the wipers. The rental car, useless as ever, rattled against the uneven highway, its tires barely holding traction on the icy pavement.

The voice of reason in my head told me I should've left earlier—or waited until tomorrow when the plows had more time to clear the roads. But I couldn't. Not with Rebecca's deadline looming over me like a storm cloud.

Not with Trent's words still echoing in my head.

You'll figure it out.

I gripped the wheel tighter, the memory cutting deeper than it should've. He hadn't said it cruelly—he wasn't like that. But it felt like a dismissal, like he didn't want me to consider any other option.

Like he didn't want *me.*

I blinked hard, shaking the thought away as the car started to fishtail.

"Come on, come on," I muttered, easing off the gas and trying to steady the wheel. The tires skidded, the back end swerving out, and my heart leaped into my throat.

The car spun sideways, sliding off the road with a cascade of snow and gravel crashing against the quarter panels.

When the world finally stopped spinning, I sat frozen, my hands white-knuckled on the wheel, my breath coming in sharp gasps. The car had landed nose-first into a shallow ditch, tilted just enough that the tires spun uselessly when I pressed the gas.

"Perfect," I muttered, slumping back in the seat.

I reached for my phone, hoping against hope that there'd be service this far out. There was only one person I could think to call—a cowboy who had every right not to answer.

A single bar flickered at the top of the screen, and I let out a relieved breath as I tapped Trent's name.

The call rang twice before his voice came through, sharp and familiar. "Lauren?"

"I, uh... I slid off the road," I said, wincing at how pathetic I sounded.

There was a pause, then, "Where are you?"

"About ten miles south of town, maybe less. Just past the old Sinclair station."

"I'm on my way. Stay put."

Stay put. Right. The line went dead before I could respond, leaving me staring at the phone in my hand.

THE RUMBLE OF TRENT'S truck was the most beautiful sound I'd ever heard.

His headlights cut through the swirling snow as he pulled up behind the rental car. He climbed out, his coat already dusted with snowflakes, and strode toward me like he was on a mission.

"Are you okay?" Trent asked, yanking open the driver's side door.

"Yeah," I said quickly, though my voice was shaking more than I wanted it to. I shoved at the seatbelt, which felt like it was trying to strangle me. "Just rattled."

His eyes narrowed like he didn't quite believe me. "You sure?"

I nodded, finally freeing myself and fumbling for the door. "The car's stuck, though. I tried, but—"

"Don't worry about it," he said, cutting me off as he stepped back. "I'll get it out."

I climbed out of the car, hugging my arms to my chest as the cold wind smacked me in the face. Trent circled the car, muttering something about "rental junk" and "the worst tires he'd ever seen."

The wind whipped through my hair—*my real hair.* The long, messy, unruly blonde curls I hadn't bothered to smooth down this morning in my rush to leave. I caught Trent giving me a quick, curious glance, and I cringed inwardly, shoving my hands deeper into my coat pockets and pretending not to notice. I looked like a ragamuffin.

He paused mid-mutter, his gaze lingering just a second too long. "You're sure you're okay?"

"Yes," I said, but then I saw him squint slightly, as though trying to figure something out.

"What?" I asked, defensive already.

He tilted his head. "Your hair."

Heat shot straight to my face. "Yeah. What about it?"

He raised a brow, a faint smirk playing at the corner of his mouth. "It's different."

"I didn't flat iron it today," I said quickly, waving him off. "I got up early to drive all the way to Boise, and it's not like I had time to—"

"It's fine," he cut in, like I was overreacting. Then his voice softened. "You could wear it however you wanted, Lauren. I'm not in love with your hair."

The words hit me sideways, and my heart did something weird in my chest.

I stammered, completely unsure what to say. "Well... good."

But Trent didn't let me linger in the awkwardness. He turned back toward the car, grabbing a chain from the back of his truck and muttering again, though this time it sounded suspiciously like, *"Looks like you totaled it anyway."*

"What?"

He shot me an amused glance. "The rental. There's no way that bumper's supposed to look like that."

I glanced back at the car and groaned. The poor compact looked even worse than I'd realized, the rear bumper askew and the tires spinning uselessly every time I touched the gas.

"Good riddance," Trent said dryly. "I told you that car wasn't meant for mountain roads."

"Thanks for the pep talk. It's a rental. I didn't exactly pick it for its rugged capabilities."

He hooked the chain onto the car with a practiced hand, ignoring me. "You know," he said casually, "there's no way you're making it to the airport on time."

I stared at him. "Excuse me?"

He straightened, wiping his gloved hands on his jeans, looking for all the world like he was enjoying this. "The snow's too deep, the roads are worse, and even if you get this thing moving, you'll never make it to Boise in time for your flight."

My jaw tightened. "And I suppose you have a better idea?"

Trent shrugged one shoulder, his smirk softening into something gentler. "Depends. I could drive you, but it's a long shot." He tilted his head, meeting my gaze. "Or... you could just stay."

There it was.

I opened my mouth to respond, but nothing came out. *Stay?* He made it sound so simple, like the answer was obvious. But it wasn't obvious—not to me.

He must've seen the hesitation on my face, because he chuckled softly and turned toward his truck. "Think about it while I get the chains, okay. I'll get the car out of the ditch, but you're not going anywhere until it's sorted."

And as I watched him climb back into the cab, I couldn't help the little twist in my chest—the part of me that wondered if maybe, just maybe, he wanted me to stay for more than just the snow.

Twenty-Eight

Trent

MARTY WAS AT IT again.

I found him standing in the middle of the yard, pawing at the snow like he was trying to dig for buried treasure. His breath puffed in rhythmic clouds, and his ears twitched toward every creak and shuffle of the ranch.

"C'mon, you troublemaker," I muttered, grabbing a lead rope from the fence post and trudging through the snow.

He snorted when he saw me coming, tossing his head like he had better places to be.

"Yeah, I don't care," I told him, slipping the rope over his neck. "You're not running loose today."

Marty let out a huff of air but followed me back toward the barn. I couldn't even muster my usual irritation with him. My head was too full of other things—mostly Lauren.

I shoulda left it alone. Shoulda just enjoyed the moment—her hand in mine as we drove back to the ranch, with her luggage in the back seat like she belonged with me now. But no, I had to poke the bear and ask her about the town gossip. Ask *why...* what she was really doing with all those videos. Were we just a test case? Something for her portfolio for when she went job hunting again?

It was a stupid question, and I knew it. I shoulda been able to see the answer before I ever asked it, but I asked it, anyway, and the hurt in her eyes, I'll never forget to my dying day.

"I was never using you Trent."

I'd replayed that moment a hundred times, wondering if... no, I wasn't wondering. I *knew* it. I'd doubted the one who believed in me. And at the worst possible moment, too.

She hadn't denied her job situation, but the anger of the accusation... well, let's just say I spoiled any chances of talking to her more about the things I really wanted to ask.

And I didn't get to drive her to the ranch, after all, but back to her mom's place so she didn't have to see my face.

I hadn't been able to take a single breath since, when I didn't feel a hole somewhere under my lungs where my heart was supposed to be.

It had been a day and a half since I pulled her car out of the ditch, and the ranch felt emptier without her. She was still in town. Hadn't left yet—I know because Cole was my spy. But I wasn't quite brave enough to text her after I'd basically called her out—that conversation had *not* gone the way I planned.

Every time I walked past the barn where she'd been filming or saw one of the boys staring at the social media page she'd built, the ache got worse.

"Maybe you're the lucky one, Marty," I muttered as we reached the barn. "At least you don't overthink things."

I led him into his stall and leaned against the door for a moment, letting the quiet settle over me.

That's when I heard a car pulling into the yard.

I froze, my heart thudding hard against my ribs. Marty tilted his head, ears swiveling toward the noise, as if he knew exactly who it was.

I stepped outside, squinting against the glare of the winter sun, and sure enough, there she was. Lauren, climbing out of Emily's pickup, her arms wrapped around herself against the cold.

She saw me and hesitated, her breath fogging in the air as she stood there like she wasn't sure she should've come.

I didn't wait for her to change her mind. I started toward her like a starving man lunges for the dinner table.

She squared her shoulders and met me halfway. "I need to talk to you."

I closed the distance between us. "About what?"

"Everything." She let out a shaky breath, meeting my eyes. "I need to apologize."

"Look, I was the stupid one. You've got nothing to—"

"Yes, I do. I should have told you the truth sooner. About my job, about... everything. The way I left it, you were right to question my motives." She glanced down, then back up. "I thought if I didn't say it out loud, it wouldn't feel real. That I wouldn't sound like such a failure."

The rawness in her voice cracked something open inside me. "Failure? How could you think that?"

"Because I didn't want *you* to think I was a failure. I wanted..." She swallowed. "I guess I wanted to prove to you that even if I don't know a... a heifer from a steer... I still have something to offer."

I grinned. "You totally Googled that before you came here."

Her smile widened and she inched closer to me. "I did. Yes, I did. Did I say it right?"

I shrugged. "Close enough. So... I couldn't help but notice you're still in town. Doesn't your new job start tomorrow?"

"Yeah. But in case you didn't notice, Cowboy, today is Christmas."

I let her saunter a little closer and pretended to act confused. "What is that, like a holiday or something?"

Lauren nodded, and a few seconds later, her hands were threading themselves around my neck. "Worst day of the year for travel."

"Says who? I bet it's the best, because nobody wants to be away from home."

She wove her arms a little tighter, and I could feel her breath warming my cheek. "Bingo. Neither did I."

Well, that... *that* was sure an interesting thing to hear. "And just where is 'home' to you, Lauren? Not California anymore?"

Lauren sighed and loosened her arms—much to my disappointment. "It never was 'home' like that. I don't think anything has really felt like 'home.' Not until I came here."

"What, your mom? Your sister?"

She raised a brow, as if chiding me without a single word. "I don't know what's waiting for me back in California besides an empty apartment that costs too much, a few 'friends' who have already stopped texting me because their attention spans are really that short, and a boss who just fired me for missing my flight."

I frowned playfully. "Tough choice."

"But if I stay *here*..." She hesitated, her gaze locking on mine. "If I stay, it has to be because *you* want me to. Not because I'm out of options."

I stared at her, my throat tight, the words I wanted to say lodged somewhere between my heart and my pride.

"Trent, Marty's still loose. I thought you caught him just a few minutes a... Oh! Hi Lauren."

Lauren and I both turned to see Mom standing on the porch, her arms crossed and a knowing smile on her face. And sure enough, that stupid old horse was already out of his stall and trying to break into the chicken coop to get at their corn.

"Marty's fine," I said quickly, stepping back. "Go back inside, Mom. *Please*."

She grinned but didn't argue, disappearing into the house with a little wave.

When I turned back to Lauren, she was watching me with eyes dark with feeling. "I need to know, Trent," she said softly. "What do *you* want?"

That was easy. "You," I blurted all in a rush. "I want *you*. For Christmas, for everything... Forever."

She caught her breath with a sharp gasp, her eyes wide, and for a moment, I thought I'd said too much. But then she leaned a little closer and slid her hands down from my chest to capture mine.

"You could've said that sooner," she whispered.

"Yeah," I admitted, catching her hand and bringing it to my lips. "I'm an idiot."

Her laugh was soft, warm, and it melted the last bit of ice between us.

Lauren

"**H**EY, COME OUTSIDE WITH me for a second," Trent said, appearing in the doorway of the living room. The soft glow of Christmas lights reflected off the snow on his boots.

I looked up from where I sat on the couch next to Emily, my hands still curled around a mug of cocoa. The day had been perfect—family, laughter, the smell of cinnamon and pine drifting through every corner of the house. My mom, Emily, and I had spent half the morning cooking with Nora while the Langton boys playfully bickered about who would eat the most mashed potatoes.

Now, the fire crackled in the woodstove, and the warmth of being surrounded by this family made me feel like I belonged in a way I hadn't in years.

"Outside?" I echoed, narrowing my eyes at him. "What for?"

Trent tilted his head toward the front door. "I think I just saw someone messing with the barn door."

"Marty?" I asked, already rolling my eyes as I set my mug down on the coffee table.

"Probably," he said casually. "I bet he smells the peppermint from that huge batch of cocoa. He's a sucker for peppermint."

With a groan, I got to my feet. "That horse has it out for me, I swear."

Emily laughed from the couch. "Better you than me."

Trent held the door open for me, and I stepped out onto the porch, inhaling sharply as the winter air hit my face. It was beautiful outside. The snow had stopped falling, leaving a fresh blanket of white that sparkled beneath the starlight. The porch was lined with Christmas lights, their soft glow turning everything warm and magical.

"You're gonna freeze if you don't grab your coat," I said, glancing at Trent, who had barely buttoned up his flannel.

"I'll survive," he said, his voice softer now.

Something in his tone made me pause, but before I could say anything, I caught sight of Marty.

Sure enough, he was standing at the edge of the porch, his black coat dark against the snow, his ears flicking forward as he stared straight at me like he knew I was coming. But there was something around his neck.

"What the—" I blinked, stepping closer as Marty turned his head slightly. A wreath of fresh pine boughs hung around his neck, dotted with tiny red berries and gold ribbons. And tied to the very center, dangling on a silk ribbon, was a ring.

I froze, my heart hammering in my chest as my breath clouded in the frigid air.

"Trent..."

He was behind me now, and when I turned, I found him standing there, his hat in his hands, snow dusting his hair like little frosted diamonds. His eyes met mine, steady and serious, but there was a spark of warmth there that made my soul leap.

"Marty was just helping me out tonight," he said. "Figured he owed us after everything this year."

I let out a shaky laugh, one hand flying to my mouth as my heart thudded painfully in my chest.

Then Trent dropped to one knee.

I couldn't move. Couldn't breathe. This cowboy was serious!

"Lauren," he began, his voice rough with emotion, "I spent a lot of years working this ranch, wishing for things to get better—for Ridgeview to hold on, for my family to be okay. But I never really wished for anything for myself."

He paused, his gaze never leaving mine. "Then you showed up with your cameras, your big ideas, and your way of seeing things nobody else could. And for the first time, I wanted something just for me."

The tears that had been threatening finally spilled over, warm against my freezing cheeks, as I stared down at him, speechless.

"This Christmas," he said softly, "my wish is that you'll take my grandmother's ring and wear it forever."

I blinked hard, trying to focus through the haze of tears. Behind us, I could hear the door creak open, and I turned just enough to see our families—his brothers, my mom, Emily and Cole—all crowded in the doorway, watching silently.

Well, they tried to be silent. Nora was laughing and sobbing at the same time, her shoulders shaking as she clapped a hand over her mouth, and Cole wrapped an arm around her shoulders. My mom wasn't in a much better state—she was gushing happy tears and squeezing Emily's hand.

I looked back at Trent, my breath hitching. This man—this life—was everything I hadn't known I wanted. And standing here, surrounded by the people I'd come to love, I felt whole for the first time in as long as I could remember. Like... I belonged here.

With *him*.

I stepped closer, my voice shaking, but I managed to say the only word that mattered.

"Yes."

Trent smiled—a real, radiant smile that I didn't think I'd ever seen before—and reached up to take the ring from the ribbon. Gently, he slipped it onto my finger, his hands warm and strong even in the cold.

As soon as it was in place, he rose to his feet and pulled me into his arms, holding me tight against his chest. I buried my face in his flannel, breathing him in, my tears dampening the fabric as I whispered, "You're my wish, too."

His arms tightened around me, and for a long moment, we just stood there, wrapped in each other as the snow sparkled on the porch around us and the stars stretched wide above us.

When I finally pulled back, he grinned down at me, brushing his thumb over my cheek. "You know Marty's gonna expect extra treats for this, right?"

I laughed, my voice breaking a little with happiness. "He deserves them."

Our families cheered from the porch, and I turned to see them clapping, Emily wiping at her eyes, my mom beaming with pride.

I looked back at Trent, my heart full to bursting.

Home.

I was home.

From our hearts to yours

T HANK YOU FOR SPENDING a little time with the family at
Ridgeview Ranch.

I hope you've enjoyed getting to know everyone. I'd love it if you
would share this family with your friends so they can experience life
on the ranch with these swoony cowboys and sassy cowgirls. As with
all my books, I have enabled lending to make it easier to share. If
you leave a review for *A Christmas Wish for the Cowboy* on Amazon,
Goodreads, Book Bub or your own blog, I would love to read it! Email
me the link at **TheCowgirlWrites@TessThornton.com**

Would you like to read Blake Walker's romance? Dive into Blake
and Meryl's story, and stay up to date on upcoming releases and sales
by joining my newsletter: https://mailchi.mp/11ce46b43f43/join-t
he-family

And now, keep reading for a sneak preview of Gage and Amber's
story!

Epilogue

Gage

L UKE'S LOOP SHOT OUT like it was on rails, snagging the black steer's horns so clean it was like the ropes had been drawn tight by some invisible force. I grunted, pushing Banner forward with a nudge of my heels, and swung my loop, timing my throw with the steer's back legs.

One... two...

The rope sailed out and snatched both hocks just as Banner slid to a stop. Dust flew up in a fine cloud, coating my lips and making my lungs burn. I let out a satisfied breath, dallying up and feeling the sweet tension of a clean catch humming through the rope in my hands.

"Seven-three!" Luke called, his grin stretched wide as he looked back from his horse, Jester. "Still got it, old man."

"Old man?" I snorted, loosening my dally and letting the steer trot off. "If I'm old, what does that make you? Retirement age?"

Luke laughed, loud and easy. "I've got a house, three kids, and a back that reminds me I'm thirty-one every time I get out of bed. I'm halfway there." He tipped his hat back, the sun catching on his sweat-dampened hairline. "But you? You've got plenty of tread left on those boots, my friend. Best heel side I've roped with all week."

"That's because you've only roped with me," I shot back, wiping a dusty sleeve across my forehead. "Slim pickin's doesn't count as a compliment."

Luke grinned and tossed his loop to Jester's saddle horn. "Yeah, yeah. Take the win where you can."

He was all easy charm these days, the sharp competitive edge we'd shared back in the day mellowed by a wife, a gaggle of kids, and a little more life under his belt. Didn't mean he couldn't still rope circles around most guys at the jackpots, though.

Including me.

I swung Banner around to the back of the pen as the next steer was run in, Jester jogging right alongside us. It felt good to rope again, the kind of good that settled under my skin and got my blood pumping in a way that not much else did these days.

Not that I had a whole lot of time for it anymore. Between holding the ranch together and running enough cattle to keep us above water, fun was a luxury I couldn't afford most of the time. But with things finally starting to look up around the place, I'd let myself give in to Luke's pestering about entering the jackpot this coming weekend. A little roping. A little breathing. I deserved that much, didn't I?

"You're quiet today," Luke said after a beat, pulling his horse to a stop at the edge of the pen. His eyes narrowed in that way they always did when he was trying to pry something out of me. "What's on your mind?"

"Nothing."

Luke snorted. "Yeah, right. You've had that look on your face since you got here. The one where you're thinking too much and telling me too little."

I swiped my hat off and ran a hand through my hair. "It's nothing."

Luke just stared at me, waiting. If there was one thing the man had mastered over the years, it was patience. He didn't push. He didn't prod. He just let the silence do the work for him. Luke Walker, of all people—the yammeringest cowboy I ever knew, and now he was silent as a hilltop sage. Must've been his wife rubbing off on him.

I sighed, shaking my head. "It's just..." I shrugged. "Feels like everything's changing all at once, you know?"

Luke leaned forward on his saddle horn. "That so?"

"Cole's married. Chase and Trent are planning their weddings. Even *your* brothers have wives and kids now." I shoved my hat back on and gave him a hard look. "What happened? Last I checked, we were all trying to beat the other guy's time, and now half the people I know are handing over rings and arguing about table settings."

Luke chuckled. "It happens quick."

"Yeah, no kidding." I stared out at the pasture, where the steer had trotted off to join the others. "I'm not mad about it or anything. It's just... weird."

"You feel left behind?"

I snorted. "No. I'm not crying into my drink at night about it, if that's what you're asking."

Luke grinned. "Didn't figure you for the pining type."

"I'm not," I said quickly. "I just..." I trailed off, fumbling for the right words. "I don't know. I guess I didn't expect everyone else to settle down so fast. Feels like I blinked, and everything changed."

Luke nodded, like he understood exactly what I was saying. "You'll get used to it. And hey, maybe it's not so bad being the last man standing. You don't have to share your time or your remote."

"Yeah, that's what I'm missing. Control of the TV."

He laughed again, but his expression turned thoughtful as he watched me. "I will say this, though: don't count yourself out, Gage. Life has a funny way of sneaking up on you when you least expect it."

I scoffed. "Yeah, sure."

Luke didn't push it, and I was grateful for that. He just nodded to the steer pen and said, "We running another one, or you need to go back to making money and bossing people around?"

I grinned despite myself. "One more. I need the practice if I'm going to keep up with you this weekend."

Luke tugged his hat lower with a cocky smirk. "You're not gonna keep up with me, but I appreciate the effort."

I flipped him a salute as I pushed Banner into a lope, the rhythm of hooves pounding against dirt settling something in me I hadn't even realized was out of place. Maybe Luke was right. Life was changing all around me, faster than I'd expected. But for now, there was still this—this quiet steadiness, this feeling of doing something right, if only for a little while.

For now, it was enough.

***

Amber

"That's it, Jesse. You're doing great." My voice stayed soft and even—my professional voice, even though I could feel my phone buzzing for the third time in less than ten minutes in my back pocket.

Jesse, a lanky teenager with shaggy brown hair and bright green sneakers, didn't look up. His focus stayed fixed on Jasper's mane as he reached down, tentative and careful, brushing his fingers through the horse's soft forelock.

"This is the best he's done all week," Kate murmured, walking alongside Jasper with the lead rope in her hands. Her voice was low, for my ears only, but I caught the note of pride.

"Yeah, it is." I smiled as Jesse sat straighter in the saddle, his shoulders easing like he was finally finding the rhythm we'd been working on for weeks. "How does that feel, Jesse?"

He shrugged, his expression shy, but I didn't miss the tiny smile tugging at the corner of his mouth. "It's okay, I guess."

"That's better than 'not great,'" I teased gently. "Let's try for a little more movement. Kate, let's pick up the pace—nice and slow, though."

Kate gave me a quick nod, and I fell into step beside Jasper as he moved into a steady walk. Jesse adjusted his balance, his hands twitching nervously toward the saddle horn before he caught himself.

"Good job, Jesse. Trust yourself," I said. "And trust Jasper. He's got you."

The phone buzzed again. I clenched my jaw and ignored it. Gina. I didn't even have to check. It wasn't like my sister to stop at one missed call.

Jasper flicked an ear toward the sound, but Jesse didn't seem to notice. His shoulders were still relaxed, his hands finding a natural rhythm with Jasper's movement. I exhaled slowly. For Jesse, this was a win, and I wasn't going to let anything disrupt that.

When the session finally wrapped up, I helped Jesse dismount while Kate praised him for the progress he'd made. The pride on Jesse's face—small but real—made the buzzing phone worth ignoring. Moments like this were why I did what I did. They reminded me why the therapy center mattered, why it was worth every ounce of stress.

As Kate led Jasper back toward the barn, I finally pulled my phone out of my pocket, my frustration flaring as I saw the missed calls lined up like soldiers. Three calls. *Three.* And a new voicemail.

I stepped around the corner of the barn and pressed play, bracing myself.

"Amber, it's Gina. Again. Look, I don't know why you're not answering, but I'm at the center now, and they're ready for me to sign the lease papers. Mom and Dad are going to love it here, I promise—it's clean, the staff is friendly, and the community is active. It's perfect for them. But I can't do this without you because of the power of attorney thing. Just call me back, okay? This is important, Amber."

I groaned and rubbed a hand over my eyes. *She's signing the lease?* Gina wasn't just pushing for assisted living anymore; she was halfway to making it a done deal.

"Everything okay?"

I turned to find Kate coming around the corner, Jasper's bridle looped over her arm and her expression curious but cautious.

I tried to smile, though I could feel how thin it was. "It's fine. Family stuff. Can you finish up here? I need to take this call."

Kate gave me a quick nod. "Go. I've got it."

I shot her a grateful look as I ducked back around the barn, my phone already dialing Gina's number. It rang twice before she picked up.

"Finally," Gina said. "Amber, I—"

"What do you mean you're signing the lease?" I cut in, my voice sharper than I intended.

Gina sighed, the exasperated kind that made me feel like *I* was the unreasonable one. "I'm not *signing* it yet. I just said they're ready for me to. It's a formality. I need you to say yes."

"Well, I'm saying no," I shot back. "You don't even know if this is what they want."

"Oh, come on, Amber," Gina said, her tone inching toward condescending. "You know Mom and Dad. They're not going to *ask* for this, but we both know they need it. This place is perfect for them. They'll have meals cooked for them, cleaning taken care of, round-the-clock care—"

"And do *they* know you're there trying to get them an apartment?"

There was a beat of silence. "Not yet."

"Gina." My voice dropped.

"They wouldn't come look," she said defensively. "And you know them, Amber. They'll fight it tooth and nail if it's not already a done deal. They don't want to be a burden, but once they see how nice this place is, they'll come around."

"They're *not* a burden." My voice was low and tight, but it trembled with the kind of anger I didn't have the energy to hide. "And you don't get to decide this for them. We need to talk to them first—"

"And let them say no?" Gina snapped. "What's your plan, Amber? To keep them in that big old house forever? Let Dad fall down the stairs when no one's looking? Mom can barely get around, and you know it. This place is safer. It's better for them."

My chest squeezed. I turned my back to the barn, staring out at the mountains that rose up in the distance. *Mom will die if she can't see the mountains.* I'd said it once without thinking, but now the thought lodged itself in my chest, painful and unmoving.

"I'll come home this weekend," I said finally. "We can sit down with Mom and Dad and actually *talk* about this. You don't need to make it a done deal before they've even had a chance to weigh in."

"Amber—"

"No." I cut her off. "I can't talk about this right now. I'm at work, Gina. *Working.* I can't do this over the phone."

Gina sighed again, but her voice softened, just a little. "Fine. Come home this weekend. But you know I'm right."

I hung up before I said something I'd regret. My phone buzzed again with a text—Gina, sending me a picture of the retirement center's cheerful lobby, complete with potted plants and smiling seniors playing cards at a round table. I shut off my screen and shoved the phone back into my pocket.

I walked back toward the barn, my legs suddenly heavier than they'd been all day. Kate met me halfway, Jasper's coat gleaming from a fresh brush-down.

"Everything okay?" she asked again, her brow furrowed as she studied me.

I forced a smile. "Yeah. Just... my sister. Thanks for finishing up."

Kate nodded slowly, like she knew better than to press me for details. "Anytime."

As I watched her lead Jasper back toward the paddock, my shoulders slumped. I'd promised Gina I'd come home, but even as I said it, doubt crept in like a shadow. *What if she's right? What if I'm just being selfish? Sentimental?*

Maybe I was holding on too tight to the past. Maybe my parents *would* be better off somewhere with round-the-clock care and friendly faces. But the thought of them leaving everything—their home, the mountains, the life they'd built—made me feel like I was watching something precious slip through my fingers.

I leaned against the barn wall, staring out at the mountains I knew my mom loved as much as I did.

"They'd hate it," I whispered to no one but myself.

And yet, for the first time, I wondered if I was fighting for them... or for me.

***

Reserve your copy of Gage and Amber's story today!

A Winter Surprise for the Cowboy

Blake Walker has built a legacy in his family and his ranch. His five boys are starting to find love and build their own lives, and he's beginning to wonder what adventures are left for him.

Meryl Justice has raised everyone's kids but her own, and now she's looking forward to retirement from the job she's had for thirty years. She loves her home and her farm animals, but is that all there is?

Find out when these two hearts set out to discover if wintertime might not just be the best time of all to fall in love!

Click HERE to get your story.

More from Tess Thornton

The Walker Ranch Series

A Home for the Cowboy

Cody and Morgan's Story

A Second Chance for the Cowboy

Marshall and Kelli's Story

A Winter Surprise for the Cowboy

*Blake and Meryl's Story

An Angel for the Cowboy

Dusty and Jess's Story

Taming the Cowboy

Luke and Audrey's Story

A Heart for the Cowboy

Evan and Meg's Story

*_A Winter Surprise for the Cowboy_ is a Free Novella available only to newsletter subscribers

The Ridgeview Brothers Ranch Series